Miss Katie's Rosewood

Books by Michael Phillips

Is Jesus Coming Back As Soon As We Think?
Destiny Junction • *Kings Crossroads*
Make Me Like Jesus • *God, A Good Father*
Jesus, An Obedient Son
Best Friends for Life (with Judy Phillips)
George MacDonald: Scotland's Beloved Storyteller
Rift in Time • *Hidden in Time*
Legend of the Celtic Stone • *An Ancient Strife*
Your Life in Christ (George MacDonald)
The Truth in Jesus (George MacDonald)

American Dreams

Dream of Freedom • *Dream of Life*
Dream of Love

The Secret of the Rose

The Eleventh Hour • *A Rose Remembered*
Escape to Freedom • *Dawn of Liberty*

The Secrets of Heathersleigh Hall

Wild Grows the Heather in Devon
Wayward Winds
Heathersleigh Homecoming
A New Dawn Over Devon

Shenandoah Sisters

Angels Watching Over Me
A Day to Pick Your Own Cotton
The Color of Your Skin Ain't the Color of Your Heart
Together Is All We Need

Carolina Cousins

A Perilous Proposal • *The Soldier's Lady*
Never Too Late • *Miss Katie's Rosewood*

07B

Miss Katie's Rosewood

A NOVEL

MICHAEL
PHILLIPS

BETHANY HOUSE PUBLISHERS

Minneapolis, Minnesota

Cover design by The DesignWorks Group
Cover photography by Steve Gardner, PixelWorks Studio

Published by Bethany House Publishers
11400 Hampshire Avenue South
Bloomington, Minnesota 55438

Bethany House Publishers is a division of
Baker Publishing Group, Grand Rapids, Michigan.

Printed in the United States of America

Paperback:	ISBN-13:	978-0-7642-0044-1	ISBN-10:	0-7642-0044-5
Hardcover:	ISBN-13:	978-0-7642-0397-8	ISBN-10:	0-7642-0397-5
Large Print:	ISBN-13:	978-0-7642-0398-5	ISBN-10:	0-7642-0398-3

Library of Congress Cataloging-in-Publication Data

Phillips, Michael R., 1946-
Miss Katie's Rosewood / Michael Phillips.
p. cm. — (Carolina cousins ; bk. 4)
ISBN 978-0-7642-0397-8 (hardcover : alk. paper) — ISBN 978-0-7642-0044-1 (pbk.) — ISBN 978-0-7642-0398-5 (large-print pbk.)
1. Reconstruction (U.S. history, 1865–1877)—Fiction. 2. Women plantation owners—Fiction. 3. Plantation life—Fiction. 4. Kidnapping—Fiction. 5. Racism—Fiction. 6. Race relations—Fiction. I. Title.

PS3566.H492M57 2007
813'.54—dc22 2007011982

To courageous, bold-thinking Christians . . .

—and our many loyal readers through the years who have written to express their appreciation for the ways in which my books, and those of George MacDonald, have helped them think and pray more expansively about the nature and character of God and His work.

In a world where perceived "doctrinal correctness" exerts an almost pervasively overpowering influence in the church, not all Christians appreciate bold and honest challenges in faith. Most are content to dwell in the comfort zones of safe theological harbors where every question has a predetermined response, passed down through the years by the accepted "traditions of the elders." For those finding themselves in such an environment who choose to launch out into deeper scriptural waters, the spiritual journey can be a lonely one. Though there are a few exceptions, to whom the body of Christ owes a great debt, the courage to examine status-quo doctrines more carefully than is customary is neither honored nor encouraged by many pastors, priests, leaders, teachers, publishers, or evangelists. Those who attempt to explore such deeper waters usually find themselves swimming upstream against a tidal deluge of proof-text theology (with little fresh *thought* included) massed against them. Yet they are driven on in their quest. They hunger to probe the far-reaching themes of Scripture and thus to know the Father-heart of God more intimately.

It has been to encourage *you*—and you know who you are—in that quest that I write. Your responses have confirmed that it is an adventure—a difficult one—that we have shared, and continue to share, together. And we must all take heart to continue! Because in no other way than by probing the Scriptures prayerfully and expansively can we learn to know God the Father as Jesus did.

To know God *aright*, not by doctrine but by the high

Logos truth of His nature as revealed by His Word, and then to obey Him in *Not my will* Christlikeness, is the one true goal of spirituality. This book and the journey herein depicted is dedicated to you who have made that right knowing, and the prayerful desire for Christlike obedience that of necessity proceeds out of it, the deep cry of your heart and the focus of your life's pilgrimage. From the bottom of my heart I thank you for your encouragement and support in my quest. And I encourage and honor you in your own!

Contents

Prologue

We'd been through a lot together, Katie and me. First we were strangers. Then we began thinking of ourselves as sisters trying to survive together. Then we found out that we were actually cousins.

But mostly we were friends. And that made all the difference in the world.

And now these two friends, Kathleen Clairborne and me, Mary Ann Daniels—Katie and Mayme as we called each other—were just about grown-up young women. It was hard to imagine, but I was twenty and when you get to be that age you look at things a little differently than you do when you're fourteen or fifteen. That's how old Katie and I were in the spring of 1865 when we met just after the war ended. Now it was 1870. The South had changed and things were dangerous.

As I said, I was twenty and Katie was nineteen. We loved our North Carolina home, the plantation called Rosewood in Shenandoah County, but my father and our uncles (Templeton Daniels was my father, Ward Daniels was my uncle, and they were both Katie's uncles) had been encouraging us to think about our future. Their sister, our aunt Nelda, had visited Rosewood a while earlier and had invited us north for a visit. She had written a few times since too, telling us about a girls' school for young women in Philadelphia where we could get more of an education than either of us had ever dreamed possible.

It wasn't that my papa or Uncle Ward were anxious to see us leave Rosewood. If they could have had their way, they would keep us there permanently. But they wanted what was best for us, even if it meant leaving for a while to attend school in the North. They recognized that things were changing for women as much as for Negroes. They wanted to give us every opportunity to do as much with our lives as possible.

The idea of being separated wasn't one any of us liked. But Katie and I gradually realized that maybe my papa and Uncle Ward and Aunt Nelda were right, and that we needed to see what schooling might offer two girls like us who weren't really girls anymore. If we didn't take advantage of schooling pretty soon, it could be too late. That's not the kind of thing you can do after you start a family.

My beau, Jeremiah Patterson, was in the North, and not so very far from our Aunt Nelda's in Philadelphia. That gave me another reason for looking forward to the trip. I hadn't seen him in over six months, since just after his daddy Henry's marriage to Josepha, our cook and friend. And Robert Paxton, Katie's young man friend, had just moved to Hanover, Pennsylvania, also not so very far away from Philadelphia.

So we decided to take the train north to visit Aunt Nelda for three or four weeks, to visit the school in Philadelphia and see if we liked it there. And also hopefully to arrange a visit with Jeremiah and Rob.

We planned to go north in May.

Even without Jeremiah's help, the six of us at

Rosewood (my papa and Uncle Ward, Henry and Josepha, along with Katie and me) had got the fields ready and the year's cotton crop planted. We'd even managed to get ten more acres planted than the previous year. So it would be a good time for us to be away. The weather would be good, the cotton would keep growing, and we'd be back in plenty of time for the harvest. And we needed a good harvest too, because a few debts had piled up over the past year or two.

At least that's how we had it planned.

But one thing about plans . . . you never know when something's going to come along and upset them.

Midnight Warning

1

A LONE RIDER GALLOPED THROUGH THE NIGHT.

Luckily there was enough of a moon for his horse to see its way along the deserted dirt road. He could not slow down or it would be too late. Many lives, and his own future, could depend on his getting there in time.

He had his own sleeplessness to thank that he had gotten wind of the plot at all. Otherwise he might have slept through the whole thing.

Something had awakened him shortly after midnight—fate, an inner premonition, maybe the voice of God telling him to wake up and sound the warning. Whatever it was, suddenly he was awake in his bed, with blackness and silence around him.

He rolled over, groped for his nightstand, struck a match, lit a candle, then looked at his watch where it lay at his bedside.

Twelve twenty-three.

He sighed and lay back down. This was no time for sane men to be awake. Yet some inner sense told him that he ought to get up and have a look around. He crawled out of bed, pulled on his trousers and boots, picked up the candle lamp, and went downstairs.

What he was afraid of, he wasn't sure. There had been some petty thievery in town. Deke Steeves and a few of his cronies were always up to no good. But what could they steal from *his* place?

Unless . . .

His mind clouded with dark forebodings.

The warnings that had been given him were threatening enough. Were they perhaps not going to wait to see if he complied? He had been sure they would do nothing unless he crossed them. Even then, he had doubted they would try anything serious. Their own livelihoods were too dependent on him.

But had he misjudged their intentions?

His heart beat rapidly. Thinking something was afoot against him, he hurried into the night to inspect the mill and warehouse.

A hurried walk throughout the premises, however, revealed nothing. The whole town was quiet except for the occasional bark of a dog. He tried to tell himself that he was letting his imagination run away with him. Everything was fine.

He turned and made his way back toward his house.

Suddenly a noise disturbed the quiet of night . . . booted feet clumped along the street half a block away.

Quickly he blew out his candle and crept back against the wall of the warehouse.

Whoever it was, they were coming this way. It sounded like there were two of them. He waited in the shadows.

". . . said they'd meet us at one . . ." whispered one of the men as they drew closer.

The listener recognized the voice instantly. He knew practically everybody in town, but he hadn't known *he* was involved. This thing was more widespread than he had imagined.

Cautiously he slipped out to follow them, straining to

listen to the subdued conversation ahead of him.

". . . why tonight?"

"They been given enough warnings . . . time for action . . ."

From somewhere a third man joined them. Under his arm he carried something white.

". . . the horses?"

"McSimmons is bringing enough from his place. Didn't want to wake up the whole town."

". . . meet on the north end of town."

". . . Sam said . . ."

". . . same thing I heard . . . through fooling around . . ."

". . . blood spilled tonight . . . before morning . . ."

". . . that plantation house . . . smoldering cinders . . ."

The listener had heard enough. He hurriedly retraced his steps to his own place. He knew well enough what plantation house they were talking about. Whether he could get there in time to save it and prevent bloodshed, he didn't know.

But he had to try.

Five minutes later, after hastily gathering a few papers from his office, he was saddling his own horse in the darkness. He would leave town by the southern road, then circle back around, hoping the others wouldn't hear him.

On he rode in the night.

By his reckoning he had left town somewhere around twelve-forty. That gave him at least twenty minutes on them, though organizing a group of fifteen or twenty would take some time. A few would probably be late. The six-mile ride would take them longer. They would have more reason for stealth than haste. He would probably gain a forty-minute lead on them, maybe an hour at best.

How to wake up his friends without getting his head blown off was a question he had not thought about until he neared his destination.

As he considered it, he realized there was no need for delicacy or quiet. The situation was desperate. Every second counted. He needed to get them out of their beds and gone as quickly as possible. He might as well go in with gun blazing!

He reached the plantation and slowed. There wasn't a sound or a light anywhere.

Well, he thought, *I've come this far . . . there's no turning back now.*

He rode into the yard between the house and barn, then pulled out his rifle and fired two quick shots into the air.

As the echoes died away, amid the howls of a couple dogs and a few whinnies and bellows from the barn, lanterns were lit and yells of alarm sounded throughout the house.

"Inside there," he called up toward the second-floor windows where the reflection of a few lights had appeared. "Hey, wake up . . . it's Watson! Templeton . . . Ward . . . I've got to talk to you!"

A window slid open. Ward Daniels' face appeared along with the barrel of a rifle.

"Who's there?" he called down.

"Daniels . . . it's Herb Watson!" shouted their visitor. "Get down here, both of you—I've got to talk to you. Now! Be quick about it. They're coming . . . they're coming tonight!"

Ward pulled his head back inside and shut the window. A minute later both brothers appeared on the front porch, Templeton coming from the barn and carrying a lantern, Ward with his rifle still in hand.

"What's it all about, Herb?" asked Templeton. "You'll have everyone in a tizzy, shooting off guns in the middle of the night."

"Yeah, that might have been a mistake," said Watson. "I hope they're far enough away and didn't hear it. But I had to get you out of your beds—there's no time to lose . . . they're coming. They're on the way. We've got to act fast. You've got to get out of here, all of you."

"You think it's that serious?" asked Ward.

"I overheard a few of them as they were going to join Sam and Bill and the others. They're determined to kill someone tonight, and burn this place to the ground. They said that blood would be spilled and your house in cinders before morning. They said that Sam had ordered it—that he was through fooling around with warnings."

The two brothers glanced at each other. They could tell from the urgency in his tone that their friend had never been more serious in his life.

"What about what we talked about before?" asked Templeton. "Now there's no time. We can't just run out—where will that leave you? They'll just burn the place anyway."

"I've been thinking about it riding out here," said Watson. "If you're willing, we could arrange it now. As long as we all sign, it will be legal. I brought some preliminary papers. You'll have to trust me that you'll get what's coming to you. We'll have to arrange for that later, after I've got your harvest in."

Templeton thought a minute, then sighed.

"We trust you, Herb," he said. "I don't suppose we have much choice. But even if we did, we'd trust you. You've proved yourself a good friend and a man of honor. Besides that, you may just have saved our lives and put yours in danger coming here like this. So maybe you're right . . . maybe the time has finally come."

"It has, believe me."

"I don't like the idea of leaving you to face them alone. We'd have a better chance if we all—"

"Look, Templeton—if they see any of you, *none* of us will have a chance. The only way there will be any chance of saving Rosewood is if you are all gone when they get here. Don't even think of trying to fight. There are too many of them.

They would surround us and have the barn and house in flames in five minutes."

"We could hide out in the woods."

"That's the first thing they'll think of. They'll search the place before they're going to believe me. Come on, make up your minds—they're on the way, I tell you!"

Templeton looked again at his brother. As he did, two young men walked quickly toward them from the direction of what had once been the slave cabins. One was black, the other white. The latter had a Colt 45 in his hand. They had heard the shots, assumed danger, and had come running.

"It's all right, boys, it's Mr. Watson."

"Jeremiah—good to see you," said Watson, extending his hand to the young black man.

"Mister Watson," said Jeremiah as they shook hands.

"Trouble is on the way, boys," said Templeton. "We've got to get everybody up and dressed. Ward, you take Herb inside and the two of you start drawing something up. You'll know what to say, Herb. I'll go upstairs and get the girls. Jeremiah, you two get your father and Josepha up here. We'll all meet in the house in five minutes. Tell Josepha we need coffee—lots of it . . . and strong. Let's go!"

Even as they spoke, on the outskirts of Greens Crossing, eighteen men were mounting their horses and pulling white capes made from bedsheets over their heads and shoulders. Each rider carried a torch made of rags soaked in kerosene, though they would wait to light them until they were closer.

Every man also had a gun. On this particular night, no one had been invited along who wasn't prepared to use it.

TRAGEDY

2

AS THE YOUNG WHITE MAN WITH PISTOL IN HAND hurried through the night with his black companion, though he was a newcomer to this place, he knew as well as any of them that the danger approaching was real. He had been in enough tense situations to recognize the urgency and fear in the man Watson's voice, even though he had never seen him before in his life.

He had faced danger before. He knew that sometimes danger brought tragic endings. He also knew that out of tragedy unexpected life could blossom. He had experienced such life, yet the path toward it had been a road marked with suffering, pain, and personal grief.

The very fact that he now carried a gun in his hand was one of the unexpected results of that road of suffering, as well as that unexpected blossoming of life. A gun was the last thing he had expected to become the tool of his chosen profession. For him, his gun was an instrument of peace, to be used if possible for the preservation rather than the taking of life.

He hoped on this night that he would not have to use it. But if he did, he would be ready to do so to protect this family he had grown to love.

The road that had led him here had been one he could not have foreseen, would never have chosen, but one for which he had grown quietly thankful. As they ran toward the new house in the darkness, for some reason his sister came to mind and how he and she used to run and play and chase each other long after night had fallen.

With the image of her face, memories of the past flooded in upon him. . . .

"Jane . . . Robert . . ." called his mother from the porch. "It's dark outside. It's time to come in."

But the twin brother and sister ran on. Jane, older by twenty minutes and the acknowledged leader, raced after her brother along the wide city street where their home was located next to the church. Children will turn any place into a world of play, whether country farm or town, whether house of wealth or squalor. And for these two youngsters, twins and best friends, the crowded city, with its rows of houses, church basement next door, and attic of their own house, was a world of endless delight and adventure.

"Jane, Robert!" their mother called again.

Gradually the chase ended, with Jane the victor as usual. The two ran laughing and perspiring with the jubilation of childhood back to the bright warmth of the parsonage.

How quickly the years went by.

Though the two were the same age, by the time they were thirteen, Jane seemed fifteen and Robert eleven. Both were approaching the outer reaches of adulthood. Their oldest sister, Rachel, was already a young woman, being courted by an army officer. In their youthful way, Robert and Jane knew that conflict was engulfing the nation. But they were still too young to realize the implications, or the political ramifications, when their father took to his pulpit in 1860 and preached the sermon that was destined to change their lives four years later.

That Maryland was *almost* in the North, and the northernmost Southern state, mattered nothing. It was still a slave state and pro-slavery sentiment was strong. Response had not been altogether favorable among his congregation when their minister took his stand with but a handful of Southern evangelical ministers to denounce the institution of slavery in the strongest of terms. A move had been initiated in the week following the fateful sermon to oust the pastor from his position. But it had not gained much momentum, for he was generally highly thought of, respected, and loved even by those who disagreed with him.

At thirteen, Robert was old enough to admire his father for his courage. Several days later when the hubbub within the congregation was reaching its height, he announced his intention to follow his father's footsteps into the ministry.

Little did either Robert or Jane, or anyone in the family—older sister Rachel or father or mother—know anything about the man who had been sitting in one of the pews listening with the fire of hatred in his eyes at what he heard. He left the church that day and they forgot all about him.

But it was that day's sermon that would change both the lives of the minister's son and the angry listener.

For young Robert, his commitment to the ministry was not just an idle whim. He took to reading his Bible, and within two years he was studying seriously, reading theological books, and following with great interest the careers of the most notable evangelists of the day. At sixteen he preached his first sermon, filling in for his father one Sunday when he was away. The entire congregation was impressed, even a little awed by the maturity that was clearly developing in the young man's outlook and perspective.

But other things were growing within him as well. His rapid spiritual and intellectual progress provided fertile soil for the unseen growth of youthful pride and ambition—seeds that lay dormant within all but which often sprout most vigorously in the most gifted. He did not merely want to be a minister, his dream was to become a *great* minister. His aspirations mounted as his knowledge of evangelical doctrine increased. He had no deep personal awareness of his own sin and fallen nature. And although his belief was real enough, it had not been tested against the realities of life, and as yet possessed little of the humility that is forged in failure and self-doubt. Things came easily, he was admired by all, and thus pride spread its subtle tentacles throughout his character.

As for the obscure listener who had slipped in and out of the church almost but not altogether unnoticed, his hatred deepened, as hatred that is not rooted out and destroyed always will. It grew to such passion during his years as a Confederate soldier that he spoke openly of killing Abraham Lincoln one day for freeing the nation's slaves. He never forgot the pastor's sermon he had heard years earlier. In his mind it was always linked to the Emancipation Proclamation, almost as if Lincoln himself had been sitting in the same pew that day listening to the minister's words and had based his later decision upon them. Deep in his heart, the vengeance he vowed on behalf of the South and the Confederacy, if opportunity ever presented itself, remained equally directed toward the president and the minister. Both were part of the same evil cause. Vengeance must be exacted against them.

Opportunity did present itself in the year 1864 when he found himself back in Baltimore. The war had begun to turn against the Confederacy. Some master stroke was needed to arouse the South with new passion for its cause. What more fitting public display than the assassination of a leading Southern minister who was a traitor to the Confederacy? It would make his assassin a hero, and reignite the war effort.

One Sunday morning, halfway through the morning worship service, the doors of Baltimore's Congregational Assembly suddenly burst open with a crash and bang.

The minister glanced over the heads of his congregation at the interruption. His voice stopped. Heads throughout the building turned. But there was no time to think what to do. A man wearing Confederate grey, long dirty blond hair flying wildly, ran halfway down the center aisle shouting curses and threats and waving a pistol in the air.

"He's got a gun!" someone shouted.

A shot rang out toward the front. One of the stained-glass windows shattered and glass fell to the floor.

Screams erupted throughout the church. Pandemonium broke loose. The minister dove behind the pulpit while the congregation fell to the floor, seeking cover beneath their pews. More shots exploded wildly in every direction, their echoes mixed with piercing screams from the women in a frenzy of terror.

"Death to all traitors!" shouted the mad intruder. "Long live the Confederacy!" Then he turned, blasted another random volley of explosive gunfire, and fled as quickly as he had come.

As the terrified echoes died away, the men and women of the church slowly crept out of hiding. One of the men ran outside and hurried for the police. The sound of weeping could be heard at the front of the church.

Slowly everyone stood and looked around to see if anyone was hurt. Murmurs spread about as some moved to the aisles. A cluster formed in front. Gradually people moved toward it.

Sudden gasps and exclamations of shock broke the subdued quiet.

"Oh no . . . God . . . no!"

Sobs of stunned grief spread as the rest hurried forward and beheld the horror.

The minister's wife sat, face white, eyes glazed over, her daughter in her arms. The girl's entire chest was red with blood from a stray bullet straight through her heart. They all knew from a single glance that she was dead.

Without pausing to think what he was doing, the girl's seventeen-year-old twin and aspiring preacher sprinted from the church, fighting stinging tears that blurred his vision. As he emerged into the street, he was just in time to see the murderer disappear at the end of the long street and turn to the left.

At the sight, a sensation arose within him foreign to what he had ever felt in his life. A huge wave of fury, indignation, and wrath filled his being. He did not at the moment identify it as *hatred*. He simply felt its passion and acted as it urged him—to get the man and make him pay for what he had done.

Without hesitation, he ran inside the house and up the stairs to his father's bedroom. Seconds later he was descending the staircase, his grandfather's Colt 45 in his hand and the box of bullets that had come with it stuffed in his pocket, his vow of the pastorate temporarily forgotten. The gun was only a family heirloom. He didn't know if it had ever been fired. But it was the only weapon in the house.

Hastily he saddled a horse and galloped along the street in pursuit.

PURSUIT
3

AT SEVENTEEN ROBERT KNEW HE HAD REACHED THE age when most young men throughout the South were in the army and fighting in the war. He must reach a decision soon, whether to join up or enter the seminary as had long been his intent. But what was the *right* thing—that he didn't know. He did not know it yet, but this day would be pivotal in that decision.

Because of his own personal quandary, the progress of the war had been much on the mind of the minister's son. He read the newspaper accounts and kept track of troop movements. He had been well aware of the march of Confederate troops under General Early that had been coming this way in hopes of threatening Washington from the north. He knew that a regiment had set up camp a few miles west of the city only days earlier. How long they were scheduled to be here, he did not know. They were waiting for the remainder of General Early's command, as well as instructions from General Lee.

As he galloped away from the church in pursuit, blinking back tears and trying to shake from his brain the image of his dead sister's face, he was driven on by a seething fury within him. Yet, he did not know what he expected. He had gone after the man almost without realizing what he was doing, hoping desperately that *something* would come of it. At the moment the adrenalin of stunned shock drove him with instinct more than rationality or reason.

He bent his horse's head around to the left where he had seen the gunman disappear. The street was empty. Gradually he slowed. Reason, to the extent it was capable, slowly returned to his feverish brain.

The man had probably had a horse waiting. He was obviously gone. But this street led west out of town. That's where the troops were garrisoned. Where else could he be but there? Where better to hide than among five thousand men all dressed exactly alike?

He dug his heels in and galloped ahead. Maybe it would be like looking for a needle in a haystack. But he had one advantage. He had seen the man's face and would recognize him in an instant. No matter how many years went by, he would never forget it. The image of that face had been seared into his brain forever.

Forty minutes later he rode into the Confederate encampment. He slowed and surveyed the scene before him. His heart sank. Never had the needle and haystack analogy seemed more appropriate. He had hoped to see *something* or *someone* along the way that might betray the man's whereabouts. But there had been nothing. For all he knew the man wasn't even part of this regiment. He could have left the city in the opposite direction. He might not be a soldier at all. The uniform could have been a ruse. He could have disappeared in any of ten thousand places.

Yet the likelihood seemed greatest that he was here. But how to find him?—Walk around, listen, watch . . . hope he overheard something, or happened to catch sight of him?

It was a long shot . . . but what else was there to try?

He rode forward, dismounted, tied his horse to a tree, and began to walk casually between the tents and campfires. No one paid much attention to him, glancing his way as he passed but saying nothing. They were used to civilians coming to gawk when they were near cities. What was one more teenage boy wanting to see soldiers up close? That he looked younger than his seventeen years contributed to the ease of his anonymity. The soldiers, some of them younger than he was, were obviously weary of this war and anxious to go home.

The passion of his anger slowly subsided. He never saw it for what it was, thinking it only the terrible emotion of the moment. It settled into a fierce quiet resolve to find the killer and bring him to justice if it took the rest of his life. The seed of hatred had sprouted and quickly sent down its roots. But it shrank back into invisibility again, and he had no idea what was growing in his heart.

He walked aimlessly for several hours, listening to conversations as he went, trying to detect anything that might provide a clue, hardly aware what a drain it was to block from his mind the horror of why he was here. He had had nothing to eat or drink since morning, but the emotional fatigue was far deeper.

At last, however, mental and physical exhaustion setting in, and no longer able to keep the morning's events at bay, the fact of his sister's death returned upon him with overwhelming force. He found a place a little away from anyone and slumped down beside a tree and broke into sobs.

That's where an officer found him several minutes later as he walked by on his way to the horse corrals. He looked down and stopped.

"You all right, son?" he asked. "Anything I can do for you?"

"No . . . no, thank you, sir," he replied, struggling to regain his composure.

"You a soldier?"

"No, sir . . . just out from the city for a look around."

"Personal trouble?"

"Yes, sir."

The officer's eyes went to the gun in his hand.

"In a place like this," he said, "I'd keep that out of sight if I were you. People might get the wrong idea. They might think you mean to use it."

"Yes, sir."

"It's also the kind of gun that somebody might take a fancy to, if you get my meaning."

"Yes, sir."

The officer continued to look him over for another second or two, then walked on.

He got up, wiped his eyes, returned to his horse, and rode home.

In the midst of their terrible grief, no one from the church or in the crowd that came and went all day at the parsonage realized the minister's son was not among them for most of the afternoon. Several policemen came, as well as the doctor. The minister had been wounded in the shoulder and was taken to the hospital. Another lady had a flesh wound in the arm and was treated on the spot.

But the great tragedy was the senseless killing of an innocent young girl for no reason that anyone could comprehend. All day the pressing question was asked in a hundred different ways: *Why?*

Upon interrogation of church members, gradually the face of the soldier began to remind a few of the witnesses of a young man who had attended Congregational Assembly several times three or four years earlier. As they began to piece their recollections together, the name Damon Teague surfaced.

It was something to start with, said the man in charge. They would look into it and see if he could be tracked down through military sources. In the meantime, he added, it would be helpful if they were to search their church records to see if any evidence could be found of when Teague attended Congregational Assembly. It would offer no proof of anything, but might be one more missing piece in the puzzle.

The girl's body was taken to the undertakers. The mother was put to bed, still in shock. A number of windows in the church had been shattered. Some of the men spent the afternoon boarding them up. Thoughts of the women all turned to food and the grief-stricken family. There was no shortage of volunteers to make sure the minister's family was well provided for.

When Robert finally returned, few realized that they had not seen him since the incident.

WATCH 4

THE FOLLOWING MORNING, AFTER MAKING SURE HIS mother and older sister were in the care of several church ladies, and after a visit to his father in the hospital, Robert returned to the Confederate camp. He had not yet told his father what was in his mind to do. He would have to tell him eventually, but just not yet. His father needed to heal too.

His wits and emotions were a little more in control after some sleep. It had been a tearful night, but he had managed to get a few hours' rest when exhaustion overpowered his grief. By the time he awoke, his determination to find his sister's killer was slowly settling into a plan to search the camp methodically. When he visited the camp again, he took the officer's advice and kept his grandfather's Colt concealed in the large pocket of an oversized coat.

A pall of devastation hung over the parsonage all week. Parishioners came and went, doing what they could to comfort and offer support and help with daily needs. The minister returned home the next day, arm in a sling and still under the doctor's close observation. His wife remained in bed, though she was now talking and eating, ministered to by older daughter Rachel, an aunt, and more church women than it was comfortable to have around.

Within two days the police were able to confirm that a Sergeant Damon Teague was indeed registered with the Confederate Army. Initial leads placed him in Mississippi. Robert was convinced that he was closer than that, and remained determined to locate him. Not wanting to worry his father about his activities, he confided his plan with the policeman in charge, a detective named Heyes. The policeman didn't seem to think much of it.

"Look, young man, I know you mean well," he said. "But you're just a kid and you're still in an emotional state. You just lost your sister and we all feel bad for you. But you've got to let us do our job and not interfere with your wild schemes and theories."

"But I'm sure he's there, Mr. Heyes."

"*Sure* . . . how?"

"I don't know . . . a hunch."

The policeman could not help smiling.

"Believe me," he said, "hunches are overrated in this business. It's persistent detective work that always pays off in the end. If the guy's a soldier, we'll track him down through channels. He'll turn up."

"Why couldn't we just go to the regimental commander and ask if Damon Teague is in his unit?"

"Because we might spook him and he'd make a break for it."

"Then we could go after him, Mr. Heyes."

The policeman laughed. "This isn't the Wild West, son. We don't do things with posses and lynch mobs. That's the stuff of dime novels. We do our police work slowly and carefully until all the pieces fit into place."

"But, sir," insisted the minister's son, "surely if he is in this regiment here, we could find out."

"And we will find out. But the army protects its own. If we start asking questions, the commander will go to him and ask him if he was involved. He'd deny it, then the army would back him up and we'd never get to him. They would protect him behind a wall of military secrecy. I've dealt with the army before. If your man's there, the only way to root him out is by going through proper channels and not upset the apple cart too soon."

But Robert was not to be deterred. He continued to haunt the camp, now taking with him a large notepad and sketching pencils. He was enough of an amateur artist to make it convincing that he was using the camp as a setting for a series of drawings about soldiering life. As he wandered about the camp, with sketch pad, easel, and pencils, gradually the soldiers began to recognize him and talk to him, some even offering to pose while he drew them. He became known as "the artist"—none suspecting his identity or real motives.

Six days after the shooting, the funeral was held. His mother recovered. His father's sling was removed. Gradually the family began to return to a normalcy that would never truly be normal again. No family who has lost one of its precious ones, from whatever cause, can ever be completely whole again in this life, until that place in the next where all is healed, rejoined, and where all that has been lost is restored.

"What are you up to, young man?" asked the same officer he had seen before. "Are you the artist I've been hearing about, doing some sketches of the men?"

It was three or four days after the funeral and Robert was spending several hours a day at the army camp.

"I see . . . uh, that you're feeling better than that first day I saw you last week."

"Yes, sir," said Robert, forcing a smile.

"And you're not carrying that gun around anymore. You had me a little worried."

Robert added a few strokes to the paper in front of him but did not reply.

"Mind if I have a look?" asked the officer.

"No . . . go ahead," answered Robert.

The officer walked over and stood behind him.

"Hmm . . . not bad," he said.

"How much longer are you going to be here, sir, if you don't mind my asking?" said Robert.

"You're not a Union spy, are you, son?" said the officer with a smile.

"No, sir," replied Robert, also smiling.

"To tell you the truth, we don't know. We're waiting for orders from General Lee and General Early. My guess is another week or two at the most."

Robert watched the man go. When he was out of sight, the boy picked up his things and moved on. Without drawing attention to himself, and under the cover provided by his sketch pad and easel, he was trying to systematically make his way through the camp in such a way as to be able to look over every tent and every group of soldiers within each tent. The fact that they came and went freely and drilled and had other duties throughout the day made it difficult. He knew there was no guarantee of success and that in the end he had to get lucky. But he had often heard his father say from the pulpit that luck was the opposite side of the coin of hard work. So maybe if he put in the hard work, he would eventually be rewarded with being in the right place at the right time. His father said that's how life worked—the harder you worked the more "luck" came your way.

In the middle of his sketch pad, on a page never on top nor seen by any of the soldiers who came and went looking at his work, was a sketch of the layout of the camp. It showed every tent, every temporary barricade, all the corrals and equipment and mess wagons. On it he kept track of his own thoughts and observations. He referred to it many times a day and marked out his own movements accordingly.

As he went about he watched . . . and listened . . . and waited.

By the Stream Bank
5

MIDWAY THROUGH HIS FIFTH DAY PRETENDING TO be an artist, young Robert's patience at last paid off.

He was a little ways away from the camp, sketching a man trying to train a horse—which wasn't easy since they kept moving—when suddenly behind him he heard the words,

"All I've got to say is, long live Corporeal Jacob's beef stew!"

Then followed the sound of two or three men laughing.

"You're right, Sergeant," said another. "The last unit I was with had an old boy as cook who must have been seventy and didn't know the difference between a chicken leg and a mutton chop."

"You think that's bad . . . down in Mississippi we had a fellow who put the leftover oatmeal in the bottom of the coffeepot—said it added character!"

But the listener hardly heard any of this. The words *long live* had gone off in his ears like a gong. They had an eerily familiar ring. It was not only the words . . . he was sure he also recognized the voice!

Quivering, he hurriedly glanced behind him. But he was only in time to see the backs of three men as they walked into a tent forty or fifty feet away. He had not been able to get a look at any of their faces.

He crept toward the tent as the three men disappeared inside. But little was visible through the open flap.

He couldn't afford to look too conspicuous or call attention to himself. He backed away, returned to his easel, flipped up the pages to his drawing of the camp, and marked the tent.

Too agitated to make a convincing appearance of trying to concentrate on his work, he picked up his things and started wandering about, thinking what to do next.

He glanced back every few seconds, keeping the tent in view from a distance.

Several minutes later one of the three soldiers reemerged. He wore a hat, the shadow from the small bill in the late afternoon's sun partially obscuring his face.

He had a feeling it was the man he had heard with his *long live the stew* comment. But he couldn't tell.

Maybe it was the hat that was throwing him. He had not thought about it until this moment. But as he recalled that day in the church, at the first sounds of commotion as the man had stormed in, he had turned around in the pew where he sat with the rest of his family . . . yes, the memory was suddenly clear—the man who had run in *hadn't* been wearing an army hat. His hair was waving about as he ran.

No wonder he hadn't been able to spot him yet. It was impossible to separate the face he had seen from the long hair.

Nothing eventful happened the rest of the day. It was late. Dusk had already begun to fall. He went home eagerly anticipating the next morning and already trying to scheme a way to get close enough to see the man's face clearly, hopefully *without* his hat.

He arrived early, hoping to catch the men in the process of washing and getting dressed in the informality of early morning.

He wandered about, eyeing the man's tent in the distance.

He hoped that no one would notice that he seemed to be doing more staring than drawing. But he was so near the end of his search, he couldn't stop now.

The smell of coffee and bacon was in the air. Several men in his vicinity headed toward the nearby stream in their undershirts. Unfortunately they were all wearing their hats. He followed from a safe distance. The men reached the stream. Others slowly joined them. Some drank, some doused their faces and heads, others took off their hats and shirts and doused their entire heads and shoulders and torsos and made a mini-bath of the occasion.

As he stood watching, while most of the men's backs were turned, a voice spoke beside him.

"Not much of a scene for a painting, I wouldn't think."

Robert turned to see the same officer he had run into several times before.

He laughed, though a little uneasily. The man had startled him.

"No, sir!" he said. "But it's all part of camp life, I suppose."

"It hardly seems it would interest a civilian."

"I, uh . . . thought I would try to capture some daily life like this. I've just been thinking of a few ideas to see what might be best to work with."

"Ah, right . . . I see. But your pad is still under your arm."

"I only got here a minute ago. I hadn't decided what kind of scene to do."

The captain eyed him a moment longer, a hint of suspicion apparently brewing under the surface whether this young so-called artist was telling him everything. But he did not pursue it and continued to stand at his side watching the men wash.

The man was certainly inquisitive!

One of the men along the row at the stream bank took off

his hat, bent low, and completely dunked his head into the chilly water, then rose up with a wild exclamation of delight. Shaking his wet hair, he reached for the towel at his waist. Then he walked up away from the stream, eyes wide and sparkling from the exhilaration of his cold dunking.

An audible gasp escaped the lips of the minister's son.

It was him!

"What's that?" asked the man at his side.

"Oh . . . oh, nothing," replied Robert. "I just thought . . . it's nothing."

His brain was spinning. He had to act fast. The man was returning to his tent.

"Excuse me," he said to the officer.

He walked quickly after the man who had arrested his attention, trying to calm down so his voice wouldn't tremble and give him away.

"Sergeant Teague," he said from behind, hurrying to catch up.

The man paused and turned, obviously surprised when he saw who had spoken.

"That's right," he said.

"I heard that you used to be stationed in Mississippi," Robert said. "I've never been there. What's it like? Is it just like this?"

"Any camp is just like another," the sergeant answered. "Hotter and wetter is all."

"How long have you been here?"

"Not long. I was at Vicksburg. That was a nasty one. But I managed to get my share of Yanks. That all you want to know?"

"Uh, yeah . . . I suppose so."

Teague hesitated. His eyes narrowed and he gazed intently into the young man's face as if revolving something around in his mind. Then he shook his head and returned to his tent.

Robert watched him until he was inside, confirming once more the tent location on his camp drawing. In the distance the inquisitive captain was watching him. Robert hurried back to his horse and rode out of camp back toward the city.

APPREHENSION
6

HE RODE STRAIGHT TO THE BALTIMORE POLICE headquarters and asked for Detective Heyes.

"Mr. Heyes," he said excitedly, "I've found him. I found Damon Teague. It's him. I recognized him from the shooting."

"What do you want me to do?" asked Heyes skeptically.

"Well . . . go arrest him, what else?"

"Have you ever heard of proof . . . innocent until proven guilty?"

"Sure. But can't you arrest him on suspicion? He's got to be arrested if he's going to be brought to trial. You've got to do something before they break camp."

"What would be the basis of an arrest?"

"A witness—me!"

The detective eyed him and his thoughts were plain enough to read on his face, that he didn't think much of the so-called witness's credibility.

"And when time for a trial comes," Robert added, "I can guarantee you, there will be a dozen or more eyewitnesses who will agree with me. I saw him, Mr. Heyes. I was there. I tell you, Damon Teague is at the camp outside of town right now. He's a sergeant in the Confederate Army and is the same man who visited our church four years ago, and he is the man who shot my sister. If you don't do something about it, I will."

The detective saw that the young man was not going to be dissuaded.

"All right," Heyes finally agreed. "I'll talk to my superiors."

"When?"

"When I can."

Unconvinced, the minister's son hurried from the room in obvious frustration.

Heyes watched him go, then realized he could have a mess on his hands if the kid ran into the camp and started shouting accusations. He'd better follow him and make sure there was no trouble.

But by the time Detective Heyes and several of his men reached the camp, the ruckus they had hoped to avoid had already begun.

When the minister's son next walked into the Confederate camp, he was carrying no sketch pad or pencils, though he still wore the large overcoat that had also been his trademark during the past week.

His stride was purposeful for a seventeen-year-old. A gleam of determination shone in his eye. Two weeks ago his heart had been set on entering the ministry. But for nearly all of the previous sleepless night he had been asking himself if he was prepared to kill, to take another human life. The consequences to his own life and future were not ones he could think clearly about right now. He only knew what he had to do—bring his sister's killer to justice . . . one way or another. Who could tell what the man might do in the future if not brought to justice? What if he killed again? Robert had not analyzed his own motives deeply enough to distinguish between vengeance and justice in his own heart. That was a quandary whose resolution would have to wait. At this moment he was acting on impulse, emotion, grief, and perhaps more human vindictiveness toward the sinner rather than righteous indignation toward the sin than he would have been capable of recognizing. He was also little aware of the danger to himself.

The captain saw him walking through the camp and knew immediately from the expression on his face that something had changed.

"Hey there, son . . . just a minute," he called after him. "I want to talk to you. I have a few questions."

But Robert continued on. The captain followed, quickening his pace. He was just in time to see the boy walk straight into the tent of one of his sergeants and several of his men.

"Sergeant Teague," said Robert.

The man glanced up from his bunk. The heads of two or three others in the tent also turned toward the intruder.

"Get up!" demanded Robert.

"What?" said the sergeant in annoyance.

"I said get up."

Damon Teague was not the kind of man who took kindly to being ordered about by a boy half his age. His annoyance instantly turned to anger.

"Look, kid, I don't know who you are, but unless you—"

The boy reached into his pocket.

Teague stopped in midsentence. Suddenly he found himself staring into the barrel of a Colt 45.

"Get up," repeated the boy. "You're under arrest."

"For what?" Teague shot back. His temporary shock at the sight of the gun subsided as quickly as it had silenced him. He was not one easily intimidated, though he warily kept his eye on the boy's finger. "Get out of here!" he said.

"I said you're under arrest," said Robert again. "For murder. Now get up!"

Teague glanced around at the other men, then broke out in laughter.

Just then the captain hurried in. In the dim light it took him a few seconds to make sense of the situation.

"What's going on here?" he demanded.

"I am making a citizen's arrest of Sergeant Damon Teague for murder," said Robert.

Again Teague laughed. All the while Robert kept the gun pointed straight at his chest.

"The kid's crazy, Captain," said Teague. "Can't you get rid of him? He's a lunatic. He barged in here waving that gun and making ridiculous accusations."

"Don't make a move, Captain," said Robert. "Or any of the rest of you. This man is a murderer."

"What's it all about, Teague?" asked the captain.

"I tell you the kid's a lunatic. I don't know what he's talking about."

"You're going to have to come with me, son," said the captain, taking a step forward and laying a hand on Robert's arm.

Suddenly a shot echoed through the small tent. Teague cried out in momentary alarm as dirt flew up beneath his cot. The two corporals watching from their bunks leapt up and ran outside.

"I'm serious, Captain," said Robert, again pointing the gun up at Teague. "I am taking this man with me."

He stepped forward, reached down, and grabbed Teague's arm and yanked him to his feet. His strength took Teague by surprise. He found himself in a vise grip and on his feet before he could resist, with the barrel of the 45 jammed into his ribs. Robert pulled him toward the door of the tent.

Not anxious to lose one of his men, and now convinced that Teague's accuser was indeed crazy, the captain cautiously stepped aside. Outside, men were running to the scene from all directions, several with weapons in hand.

Detective Heyes and his men, who had arrived moments

earlier and had also heard the shot, saw the movement and hurried toward it.

A standoff had just begun to develop. They saw the minister's son emerging from a tent with a Colt 45 in the side of a soldier, with eight or ten rifles trained on him from the man's fellows.

They ran up as the captain walked out of the tent. He saw them and approached.

"Is this boy with you men?" he asked.

"I know him," replied Heyes, "but he's not one of our men."

"He's making wild accusations and talking about a citizen's arrest of my sergeant here."

Heyes could not help smiling. The kid had guts, he'd give him that much!

"This is the man I was telling you about, Detective," said Robert. "Now that you're here you can arrest him."

The captain looked at Heyes again. Heyes glanced about at the growing crowd of soldiers.

"Look, Captain," said the detective, "this is a tense situation. None of us want anyone to get hurt. Why don't you call your men off and we'll talk about it."

"Then, what's it all about?"

"We've got a pending homicide in the city. We'd like to ask your man here some questions regarding it—that is, if you have no objections. If he's innocent, he'll be returned to you with an official apology. If it turns out there's evidence, then he'll get a fair trial."

"Why do you think he's involved?"

"The boy here was a witness."

"And you're going to take his word for it above my sergeant's? Look at him, he's just a kid."

"That may be. But that is no reason to take your sergeant's word above his. That's why we want to question your man and get his story. That's how the law works. Believe me, I'm inclined to think this kid is as crazy as you do. But I can't ignore what he says. He was a witness to the shooting. I've got no choice but to investigate. These two are telling different stories and we've got to get to the bottom of it. We all want the same thing."

The captain thought a moment, then nodded.

"All right, men," he said to those who had gathered about, "stand down. Go back to your tents."

He turned to Teague. "Go ahead and go with him, Sergeant," he said. "We don't want a run-in with the civilian authorities."

"What—you're going to let me get railroaded by this kid!"

"Don't worry—we'll have you out and back here by tonight."

Heyes stepped forward, eyed Robert coldly for having instigated such a ruckus, then took charge of Teague himself.

Reflections
7

WITH DAMON TEAGUE IN JAIL, ROBERT'S LIFE gradually began to flow again into its previous channels. But nothing would ever be the same again. The two preceding weeks, and what would result from them, would forever change him and mark out a destiny he never could have foreseen.

Teague's increasing belligerence on the way into the city caused Heyes and his men to regard him as a more serious threat than they had at first. By the time they reached police headquarters, he was nearly out of control, yelling and swearing wildly, vowing to kill the minister's son and everyone else within earshot. Heyes put extra guards on him and ordered him locked up. What he had intended as a mere routine interrogation had turned ugly. If he was not quite yet prepared to take the boy's side, neither was he going to send the man back to camp without looking into the thing further.

He sent word back to the man's captain that, owing to new developments, on which he did not elaborate, Sergeant Teague would *not* be returned to camp by nightfall but would be held pending a thorough investigation. Then he sent for the deacon who had been acting as his liaison with the church and the minister.

While they were waiting, Robert asked if he could see the prisoner. Heyes thought a moment, then nodded.

He led Robert toward the block of cells.

"I'll station a guard right outside the door," said Heyes. "Yell if he tries anything. He's pretty worked up.—And you had better let me have that Colt of yours before you go in."

Robert gave him the gun and followed the guard down the dark hall. Teague glanced up as the door opened. He had calmed down in the thirty minutes he had been sitting there.

"So . . . you're the one they call the artist, eh, kid?" he said. "Guess you had us all fooled with that sketch pad of yours. What were you, a police informer all along?"

"No, just someone who wanted you brought to justice," replied Robert.

"What was it to you?"

"I had my own personal stake in it."

"What stake? Who are you anyway? What's your name, kid?"

"Robert . . . Robert Paxton. Reverend Paxton is my father."

Teague laughed bitterly. "What do you know—a preacher's kid carrying a gun and getting the drop on me."

He sighed and shook his head. "I can't believe it . . . caught by a preacher's kid! I should have taken care of you when I had the chance."

He kept shaking his head in disbelief, then began to grow angry again.

"But why, kid?" he said. "Why couldn't you just leave it alone?"

"Because I watched you kill an innocent girl!" Robert shot back angrily.

"What are you talking about? I've never killed a girl in my life."

"What were you trying to do in that church, then?"

"I was after the minister. I think I got him too. I hope his soul rots in hell."

"What do you have against him?"

"He's a nigger lover and a traitor."

"How dare you say such a thing! You're the traitor . . . against everything this country stands for!"

Teague jumped up from his bunk, his fist clenched, and took two quick steps forward. But then he seemed to think better of another assault and backed away.

"It's because of people like him that this country is in this mess," he said. "Did I kill him?"

"No, but you killed his daughter, and you're going to pay."

The news sobered the prisoner. But gradually a smile spread over Teague's lips. "Maybe that's even better," he said. "He can suffer for the rest of his life for his treachery."

"That was my twin sister you killed. She was my best friend. When you shot her, you killed a part of me too. That's why I came after you. That's why I couldn't leave it alone."

Robert turned to go, then hesitated. "Did you ever stop to think," he said, "that it's *you* who's going to rot in hell, you son of a—?"

He stopped himself, shocked at what had been on his lips.

He turned again and left the cell, wondering where such an outburst had come from.

By the time the deacon arrived at police headquarters, Robert was on his way home. Heyes asked the church leader if he would bring two or three reliable members of the congregation, in addition to himself, who would be willing to look at the prisoner and see if he was the man who had shot up their church and killed their minister's daughter.

They came the following morning. All four identified Teague with absolute certainty. Teague's volley of hateful accusations and threats confirmed the likelihood of their testimony, and his final, *I should have shot you all!* was not lost on Heyes nor any of the rest of those listening. It did, however, unnerve the church people with concern that, if he should ever get out, he might come after them.

By the end of the second day, Heyes was ready to admit that young Robert Paxton was not the crazy kid he had taken him for.

In the weeks that followed, Robert was viewed as almost a celebrity by the people of the church and as a hero in the Baltimore papers. In the midst of the devastation of the tragedy, his heroic actions helped everyone begin the long process of getting on with life. If the terrible question of *why* remained unanswered from an eternal perspective, at least temporal justice could be carried out.

All involved began putting it behind them. All, that is, except Robert Paxton. His struggle with conscience was only beginning. He was too young and too confused by it all to be put on such a pedestal of acclaim by the boys of the church. Even Detective Heyes was singing his praises. As word spread about what had happened, that a dangerous murderer had been arrested by a seventeen-year-old minister's son, requests for newspaper interviews became regular.

In his own mind, however, Robert was far from at peace.

He did not question *what* he had done. But he now began to question *why* he had done it. Were his motives as honorable as his actions were being lauded? His very celebrity status forced him to look inward and realize that revenge and anger had driven him, not virtue or heroism. There was also the matter of his outburst in Teague's cell to contend with. From what cesspool inside him had *that* come! To talk to a man of God's creation about his soul rotting in hell . . . what a horrible thing to say! He was God's witness to the man! Yet what had come out of his mouth but hateful venom?

A gloom slowly settled upon him. He began questioning his very faith itself. How real was it anyway? He had not prayed once since the moment of the shooting. He had acted with the base instinct of fleshly anger. He had not once thought of Damon Teague as a man, but only as a villain, an enemy, something less than human.

The incident placed a mirror in front of his soul. He saw things that disgusted him. How noble was vengeance as a motive for action? Why had such malice unexpectedly risen within him? When the moment of crisis had come, had *faith* carried him through, or the desire for revenge? He knew the answer well enough.

During his brief visit to Teague's cell, what had been the intrinsic difference between them? None. Two men had faced each other, feeling the same things, reacting in the same ways. Each despised the other. He was no different than Teague! If that was true . . . what did his faith really *mean*?

Where had such a vindictive spirit come from?

He had been preparing for a life in the ministry. Now he began to wonder if a core of evil had existed in the depths of his heart all along. How well did he really know himself? He thought himself so mature. Everyone in the church looked up to him as wise in spiritual matters beyond his years—a prodigy. Suddenly the past few years began to look like a sham. He had just been pretending at religiosity!

A great spiritual battle had begun, a battle to know himself, to know what he was made of, to know whether he had a personal faith that meant anything or not.

Meanwhile, the wheels of justice confirmed that in the matter of Damon Teague, he had been right all along.

An unsolved murder in Mississippi coincided with his transfer to General Early's regiment. Another killing in Chattanooga had taken place during the week he had been there.

When Heyes came to see Robert and his father at the parsonage two weeks after the arrest, the news, though answering many questions, was bittersweet.

"The man has been on his own personal vendetta for several years," Heyes said. "It looks like I owe you an apology," he said, turning to Robert, "for not taking you more seriously. Now that he's behind bars and we know a little more, it looks like he may be linked to up to half a dozen killings. New evidence is coming in every day. I don't think we're going to have any trouble getting a conviction."

"What will happen to him, Detective?" asked the minister.

"He will stand trial," Heyes replied. "The way it looks now, with what's piling up against him, even from some of his fellow soldiers, he will probably hang."

The word stung Robert's heart. Even if the man was guilty, he could not help feeling responsible.

When Heyes left, Robert went out for a long walk filled with self-recrimination and despair. A deep sense of his own hypocrisy and sin began to haunt him. He taught Sunday school classes in his father's church about how to be born again, about leading the unsaved to the Lord. He was looked up to by most in the church as a paragon of virtue and sure to be a minister of widespread influence one day.

But they did not know what ugliness festered inside him.

Sure, he thought, in the world's eyes he was a "good" young man. He had never killed, never stolen, never uttered a harsh word to father or mother, never done anything counted by the world as sinful. Yet now the Lord's words probed his conscience with a finger of illuminating fire—*But I say unto you, that whosoever is angry with his brother shall be in danger of hell.* And John's shocking words—*Whosoever hateth his brother is a murderer.*

According to the Bible, hate and murder were one. They grew from the same root cause. The stunning conclusion was that Teague was no more a sinner than he was himself. They were *equally* sinners.

The worst of it was . . . he had believed the idea of himself as good and pure and virtuous. He too had considered himself a model young Christian man preparing for a life of service to God. But what was his seeming goodness but the self-righteousness of Isaiah's filthy rags! He was nothing but a self-righteous hypocrite on the inside, a whitewashed tomb full of the dead bones of his own conceit.

He had hated Damon Teague. He had not just hated what he had done . . . he had hated *him*. According to John, he too was a murderer!

He knew he could not hide behind the old adage about hating the sin but loving the sinner—he had hated the sinner too.

Because of him, the man was going to face trial and probably the gallows. All the while everyone was treating *him* like a hero.

He was no hero. What he had done was despicable. He wasn't some knight in armor fighting for justice—he was an angry brother seeking revenge. Lashing out at the man, telling him he was going to rot in hell! The memory of his own words stung him with remorse and guilt. But worse than the words themselves was what they said about his own heart!

At last he went to his father and told him that he needed to go away, that he needed time to think.

"What is it, Robert?" asked his father. "Is it about Jane?"

"Indirectly, I suppose," he replied. "This has been hard on me, Dad. More my involvement with Teague than Jane's death. I'm full of doubts right now. I need some time to sort things out. I'm confused about it all."

"Jane's death has tested us all," said Reverend Paxton.

Robert nodded. It was testing him in deeper ways than his father had any idea.

"Why don't you go visit your aunt Ruth in Ohio?" suggested his father. "It's peaceful there, away from the war. I'm sure she would love to have you."

"That's a good idea, Dad. Some time in the country sounds good. I'll write to her today."

In the Country
8

ROBERT LEFT BY TRAIN FOR CLEVELAND TEN DAYS later.

He spent two months on his aunt's farm south of the city. He worked hard, took long walks, and in solitude and prayer began slowly to rebuild his spiritual foundations.

Now he built them, however, on the solid foundation of metal tested in the fiery crucible of trial, doubt, and suffering where all God's true men and women are made strong.

But he did not simply resume his system of belief in the former mold after his sojourn in the country. Instead he discovered new foundations for life based on a deeper sense of God's being. All his previous study had been concerned with doctrines *about* God and His work. Now he sought to understand God *himself,* what He was like, how He thought about His creatures, and what the Fatherhood toward which Jesus continually pointed must suggest about God's work among men. He now sought to discover the character of God's being.

For the first time in his life he worked through his entire belief system from the ground up—not because of what he had been taught, not because of what he had heard his father preach, not because of what evangelical theology said was the correct interpretation of its prized doctrines . . . but because of what, after further prayerful reading of Scripture, he was discovering for *himself*. It was a long, slow process whose foundations had to be newly anchored in the bedrock of his brain and heart and spirit as he became convinced of what the Bible was saying to him, stone by stone, precept upon precept.

As he walked one day among the fields planted in green-ripening wheat, the silence of the land grew upon him. In the midst of that quiet arose the words *God is good*.

They were words whose general sense he had known from earliest memory. There was nothing strange in them. He had heard them, or words that expressed the same general idea, from very infancy, in childhood, in boyhood. But now in the season of his dawning manhood but still questioning youth, it flashed upon him, almost as if for the first time, that God truly was *good*.

It was a revelation as powerful as it was simple.

Suddenly he wondered what the "goodness" of God was. What was God really *like*? What was His personality? What would it be like to actually sit down and talk with Him?

These were enormous questions of powerful impact. He realized that in all his years he could never remember hearing any evangelical pastor or preacher or teacher or evangelist, or even his own father, speak of God the Father *personally*, as one you could talk to, laugh with, cry with, to whom you could take your questions and doubts. He could not remember Him once being spoken of with the characteristics of a *person*.

Jesus he felt he knew. Jesus was close. With Jesus one could achieve intimacy. But God the Father seemed distant, obscure, far-off. Surely it was not meant to be so.

He fell to his knees in the warm soil, a great hope suddenly born within him, and cried, "God, show me your goodness!"

No more words came to his lips. He rose and continued on.

In the days that followed, the earth all about him and everything in it began to live again. The odors of the growing grasses and the dirt itself beneath his feet rising to his nostrils, the drone of insects flying above the lush growing fields, the cries of crows and songs of sparrows and finches, all entered his senses like a mysterious dance of nature that had truths to speak about their Creator, if only he could lay hold of them. The wind kissed him on the face as he went. The blue of the sky over his head and the white clouds suspended there crowned the earth with a moving and changeable glory which swelled his heart yet found no expression in words. All the world began to minister to him anew, as one who had been through his season of doubt and despair and had now embarked on the road of recovery, healing, and new life.

He continued to haunt the fields, the woodland, the banks of several streams that meandered through the peaceful farmland on their way to the great Ohio, sometimes with a book, often with his pocket New Testament, and occasionally with only his thoughts and prayers to keep him company. Sometimes he walked, sometimes he sat for hours watching the simplest of nature's displays, or listening to the water burbling beside him, or the wind rustling through the treetops overhead. And ever the prayer he had prayed was before him: *Show me your goodness.*

As he probed beyond the boundaries of his former belief system, he slowly explored new regions within the Divine Character which his heart and Scripture told him must exist. But as he did he could not prevent the theology of the respected names of evangelicalism—names he had revered, men he had sought to emulate, whose teachings he had diligently studied, rushing back upon him, threatening to snuff out the light of joyful revelation he now felt growing within him. His mind flooded with imaginary reprisals warning him against attributing *too* much goodness to God. Holiness, omnipotence, justice, wrath, hatred of sin, righteous vengeance . . . none of these, said the theology of his upbringing, must be compromised an inch. The preaching he had so long been familiar with seemed invariably to emphasize the wrath of God over the love of God, even though the Bible was clear that above all things . . . God *is* love.

The contradictory voices within him were confusing. Ideas he had once taken for granted now rang with dissonance as he read the Gospels. The God of theology began to repel him. What he was reading in Scripture, what Jesus himself said about His Father in heaven, did not square with what he had heard from the pulpit over the years.

He didn't know if he *wanted* to believe such things anymore.

Surely the Father of Jesus could not be as they said!

He himself was the final evidence against the dour and judgmental theology that he had once embraced. What had it produced within him but a self-righteous spirit beneath which lurked, not God's love for the lost, but hatred and vengefulness?

God's love must be higher. And that *love* he determined to find . . . or perish.

It would be impossible to follow every avenue his thoughts and prayers took during the two months on his aunt's farm—the new spiritual vistas, the dead ends, the questions, the hopes, the new insights, the fading of doctrines, the doubts, the fears brought by new ideas, yet the wonder of beginning to behold a smile rather than a scowl on the face of the Father of Jesus Christ.

In the end, his revelations could be summarized by an expanded perspective on what the goodness of God must mean.

The first and most important truth, the very truth of the universe, it seemed to him, had to be simply this: That if a being called God exists, He must be good, nothing but good.

Building upon that, he became convinced that this goodness must be complete, infinite, uncompromising even in the face of sin, and must be a goodness that defines His character above all of His other attributes except love, and indeed is one with His love.

Furthermore, this goodness must seek the best for all its creatures, and must go on seeking that good and best through all eternity.

And finally, the conviction grew upon him that to come to Jesus must mean, not being protected from God's wrath and anger, but coming to God the Father as He meant us to come to Him, just as Jesus did, by recognizing and trusting His infinite goodness and love.

With the foundation of these insights, his spiritual journey had only begun. But his season in the wilderness of dejection now drew to an end. A light now shone on the path ahead to illuminate whatever doubts and questions still lay ahead—the light of God's goodness.

He continued to walk, continued to read Scripture, continued to ponder and brood and contemplate and pray.

Answers did not come easily. The old theology was deeply rooted, and the elder traditions difficult to let go of.

A pivotal day came.

He sat down on a low stone wall over a stream. From somewhere faint words rose up to meet the thousand questions in his brain: *I am Damon Teague's Father.*

He glanced about, almost wondering if he had heard an audible voice. But he knew the words had come from within his own spirit.

"Did you just speak to me, Lord?" he asked silently.

I am Damon Teague's Father, came the simple words again, but with growing force.

There could be no mistake—God was trying to tell him something.

I am Damon Teague's Father, said the inner Voice a third time.

"How can that be, Lord?" said Robert, half to himself and half to God. "Teague is a murderer and reprobate. God cannot be . . . *his* Father."

Yet the power of the words could not be dislodged from his brain. To his other prayers he now added perhaps the most profound of all:

God, reveal to me the fullness of who you truly are.

It was the prayer above all prayers, save the prayer of obedience and Christlikeness, that God is waiting for all men and women to pray, that He might abundantly answer it.

With the prayer, and with the increasing sense that infinite love and goodness lay at the heart of a *unified* Godhead, came also an opposite yet related revelation—a keen and stinging consciousness of his own sin.

It was a slow revelation, for Robert was still young, just seventeen. Awareness of sin is not easily born in the youthful heart that tends to think much of itself. But it had begun, and all beginnings, if followed, are pathways to growth, maturity, and wisdom. He had seen within himself that which disgusted him. He had thus begun to see himself truly and so enter upon a new level of personal faith.

Recognizing his own sin anew, he asked God to forgive him for his meanspirited and un-Christlike attitudes. At long last he began to pray for Damon Teague, and for the strength and humility to truly forgive him. Where hatred had sprouted unbidden in his soul, he asked God now to plant love.

Robert returned home two weeks before the trial was scheduled to begin. He would have remained away if possible, but he knew it was his duty to be present. He could not shirk the responsibility of his own involvement.

The day of the trial came.

By the fall of 1864 General Early's troops had moved

south against Washington and had been defeated by General Sheridan's Union Army as Confederate fortunes continued to decline.

The case had been widely publicized and the courtroom was full. A dozen witnesses were brought forward. Teague was defiant, unrepentant, full of venom and hatred. When Robert took the witness stand, he could not look him in the eye. Much had been resolved within him. But he still could not openly face the man his own accusation had brought here.

The jury took less than an hour to reach the verdict: *Guilty*.

The judge banged his gavel several times to silence the temporary uproar, then announced his own decision in the matter of the sentence.

"I sentence you, Damon Teague, to hang by the neck until dead."

Tears stung Robert's eyes.

He stumbled out of the courtroom and outside, amid jubilation of the spectators both inside and outside.

He walked hurriedly along the street, broke into a run as he heard voices calling his name, finally turning into a deserted alley. He continued to run through it, turned again, and finally collapsed on the back stairs of an abandoned brick warehouse.

He sat down and wept. The trial had been just. The sentence was just. The wages of sin was death. But the wages of *all* sin. In Robert's ears, the sentence was pronounced, not against Damon Teague, but against *him*.

What about me? he thought. *I am a sinner. I deserve the same! I—Robert Paxton—am guilty too.*

The pounding of the gavel brought all his doubts from before Ohio back to the surface.

"Oh, God," he cried, "forgive me of my *own* sin! That poor man! May I never judge anyone again by a different standard than I judge myself, or by a different standard than you judge all men. Forgive him for what he has done . . . and forgive me!"

And with that simple prayer for forgiveness, truth began to grow in Robert's soul—truth that soon turned to hope. Yes, he was a sinner along with Damon Teague. But such a thing as *forgiveness* also existed. Sin and death were not the end for either of them.

It was in God's heart of goodness to forgive! He sent His own Son to earth to open the door into that forgiveness by His own willing and sacrificial death.

As he sat, tears still pouring from his eyes, a simple revelation stole into Robert's heart—simple, yet a revelation upon which turns the destiny of eternity: As he and Damon Teague were *both* sinners, so too they had both *been* forgiven.

"God, oh, God," he prayed, "thank you that you love me and forgive me in spite of the sin I have seen within myself. I want to be your son, your obedient son. Help me to learn to call you Father just as Jesus did, and to know you as He knew you."

The Cell
9

When the visitor appeared at the Baltimore jail to see the condemned prisoner, it took the guard on duty by surprise. Teague had not had a single visitor since the trial.

"You be careful in there," he said. "He's a violent one—you call if he tries to start something."

"I will," said the visitor.

The guard led him in, and unlocked the door.

Teague glanced up. His visitor walked into the cell and stood waiting. Teague remained seated on the edge of his bunk, elbows on his knees, dirty fingers clasped together, stringy hair falling around his shoulders.

"Come to gloat, did you?" he said cynically.

"No, I did not come to gloat," said Robert quietly.

"What, then? You got what you wanted. Why don't you just get out of here!"

Robert stood silent.

Even now at this eleventh hour of earthly opportunity, the condemned man still had defiance written in every line of his face. But a great change had taken place within Robert Paxton. For the first time since the arrest he was able to look straight into Teague's eyes without the remorse of his own personal guilt.

And now he did look into those eyes.

In the passage of but seconds, eternity itself opened into his spirit. For those brief moments he saw into the depths of Damon Teague—murderer and unrepentant sinner—and seemed to see his soul with a fragmentary glimpse of what God himself saw.

The words he'd heard returned to him with tenfold force: *I am Damon Teague's Father.*

Robert's heart nearly burst with sudden intense love and compassion for the man who had killed his sister.

He truly *loved* him!

He could not condemn this man. He could no longer hate him.

And he knew in that moment how much God loved him too.

Thoughts and flashes of light like momentary bursts from heaven tumbled in a cascade of insights into his brain, plunging him straight into God's heart. Suddenly everything began to fit into place.

Of course God was his Father!

If he, weak sinner that he knew himself to be, could find mercy to forgive in *his* heart, how much *more* mercy must exist in God's infinite heart? Was it possible that he could be more merciful than God?

The answer was obvious—no.

God must be *more* merciful and forgiving than any man or woman could even imagine!

For the first time he grasped what God had been trying to tell him that day beside the stream, and more recently in the alley where he had prayed for forgiveness. There could be no artificial theological divisions within humanity. *All* humanity is God's. He is calling His wayward prodigal children home, to the home of His heart, where all will one day call Him Father.

It was such a simple yet powerful truth. How could it have taken him so long to see it? God's desire was not to punish but to heal, not to condemn but to restore, not to banish but to reconcile, not to torment but to burn clean.

Only a few seconds had passed. But they were seconds that would change Robert's outlook forever. For he did not merely see into the soul of Damon Teague, he had been given a glimpse into the Father heart of God himself. His prayer to be shown who God truly was had been gloriously answered—God was an infinitely forgiving and merciful Father!

Teague was still looking at him with a fierce expression of hatred.

"Get out of here!" he repeated angrily. "I didn't ask for you to come."

It was all Robert could do to contain what was bursting within him. His heart overflowed with an intense almost physical joy to realize that he had at last truly forgiven the man. A great burden had been lifted in the liberation of forgiveness!

He tried to smile.

"I'm sorry to cause you annoyance, Mr. Teague," he said, a slight quiver in his voice the only betrayal of the emotions stirring inside him. "I only thought that maybe you would like to talk to someone . . . that you might want to make things right with God."

"With God!" Teague spat back. "What would He want to have to do with me? Or me to do with Him for that matter?"

"Don't you care that He loves you?"

"Loves me . . . bah, that's nonsense! It's little enough He's ever done for me."

"It's hardly nonsense, Mr. Teague—His love is the truth that holds the world together."

"How has He ever loved me?"

"It's much that He has *tried* to do for you," said Robert. His tone was completely unlike that of his previous exchange with Teague. Rather than lashing out in anger, his was now the voice of compassion, probing that which needed to be exposed to the light of truth.

"What are you talking about!" said Teague irritably. "Who prevented Him doing it?"

"You did, Mr. Teague. Look at what you've made of your life. Whose doing is it but your own?"

"Who asked you to come preach to me!"

"I thought you might want—"

"I want nothing from you! You're the reason I'm stuck in this hole!"

"You don't think it has more to do with what *you've* done?" asked Robert, his voice soft, almost tender.

"What I've done is none of your business!"

"Have you forgotten whom you murdered? If it's not my business, I don't know whose it is. God might also consider it *His* business."

"Don't preach to me about God, I tell you!" Teague cried.

"You are going to have to face your sin sooner or later," said Robert. "Considering the alternatives, it seems that it might be best to face it now."

Teague leapt up, took two quick strides toward him, and shoved Robert back against the opposite wall with tremendous force.

"If you say one more word about God," he shouted with menace, nearly spitting in Robert's face, "I will kill you too . . . I'll kill you with my bare hands. I've done it before. I've got nothing to lose. You'll be lying on this floor with a broken neck before the guard can even get his key in the lock."

Robert held his gaze a moment. "You can try to intimidate me all you want," he said. "You can push me, you can try to frighten me. But I don't want to add anything more to your conscience which you will have to atone for one day. So I will comply with your wish and leave you. I have but one more thing to say to you, Mr. Teague. Whether you can understand it, I don't know, but I must tell you regardless. I forgive you. It has not been an easy thing to do, but I can honestly now say that I bear no ill-will toward you and wish you only the best."

Teague laughed sarcastically. "The *best*?" he said. "Sure, kid!"

"I will continue to pray for you," Robert went on undeterred. "You cannot stop me doing that—in hopes that you will one day discover the love God has for you. His love *is* truth, Mr. Teague."

Behind them the hurried step of the guard, who had heard the ruckus, came running along the corridor. Quickly he opened the cell door.

"I will not force myself upon you again, Mr. Teague," said Robert. "But I am at your service should you change your mind."

A minute later, with a breaking heart and blinking back tears, he emerged back out into the light of the sunny Baltimore street.

Oh, God, he said silently, *break through into that man's heart with hunger for you!*

WITNESS
10

TEAGUE'S OUTBURST SOBERED ROBERT. BUT IT DID nothing to alter the profound change of heart that had taken place. His entire outlook on God's work within humanity was being transformed. He had come to realize that God the Father was the wooing, loving, and forgiving *Abba* of Jesus Christ, not the hell-threatening tyrant of the theology in which he had been so meticulously steeped since childhood. The explosion which had gone off in his heart in Teague's cell could be reduced to a simple truth which changed everything: Jesus Christ did not come to save humankind *from* God, He came to lead everyone *to* God.

The principles he had been familiar with for years now took on deeper and wider meaning. God's Fatherhood became near and real. The Savior was not one warding off arrows of wrath behind a shield called atonement. Rather He was an Elder Brother sent to take us home to the forgiving arms of our Father Creator. God's Fatherhood began to embrace him with its light and warmth.

In that light now blossomed a love for Damon Teague that entirely changed the way Robert thought of him. How effortless it was to fulfill his promise! The prayer was such a simple yet profound one: *May he come to know you as Father as I have come to know you as Father.*

He only hoped there would be time left for Damon Teague to allow God to answer his prayer. In the meantime, Robert's Bible was alive with renewed depth of meaning. He read through his New Testament three times in less than two weeks, the Psalms once, astounded to see what he had never seen before—the totality and infinitude of God's loving grace. The Gospels, and especially the words of the Master, became newly precious and vibrant with meaning he had until now failed to perceive. Yet there it was in black and white.

How could he have never seen it all before!

God was a good and loving and forgiving *Father*! Jesus told us so!

Daily Robert prayed that somehow the Holy Spirit would work a miracle in Damon Teague's heart. Now more than ever he knew that the work was *God's* to do. He could force no door open. He could but be prepared when and if it was opened from the inside. As difficult as it was, he knew he must bide his time in patient prayer and readiness.

The scheduled day of Teague's hanging approached. The Baltimore papers were full of it. They had gotten wind of Robert's visit to Teague's cell and did everything possible to persuade Robert to make public what he and the condemned man had talked about. But Robert remained silent.

The day before Teague's execution, a messenger arrived at the Paxton home. He handed Robert an envelope with his name hastily scrawled on it.

Robert opened it. The handwritten message was brief:

He wants to see you.

Heyes.

Robert was on his horse and on his way within minutes.

When he walked into Damon Teague's cell this time he knew instantly that there had been a change.

Give me your words to speak, Lord Jesus, he breathed

silently. *Put in my mouth only what you want him to hear.*

Teague still sat on the side of his bunk. Rather than an expression of anger and defiance, his face wore a look of defeat and sadness. For the first time Robert saw fear in his eyes. And with it also perhaps even remorse.

"I, uh . . . I'm ready to listen to whatever you have to say to me," he said quietly, almost humbly.

"What about?" asked Robert.

"About God, I suppose," said Teague. "They tell me tomorrow's the day I'm going to die."

"Does the idea of death trouble you?"

"Wouldn't it frighten you to know you were going to die?"

"I don't know—I hope not. God is good. What can be frightening about going to meet Him?"

"I'm not sure I'm ready to meet Him," laughed Teague bitterly. It was a laugh without humor. "I'm not looking forward to it."

"Why not?"

"What do you mean? Are you joking? Look at me . . . what I've done. There could hardly be a more suitable picture of a sinner than me. You know where they say sinners go."

"Jesus said He came to call sinners."

"Yeah, maybe so . . . but repentant sinners. I know how that stuff works. I've heard enough of your hellfire and brimstone. Don't forget—I've heard your own father preach. I know well enough that God's got no use for someone like me."

"Don't be too sure."

"You said before that you hoped I would discover God's love, or something like that. But how can I? *No one* could love me."

"Again . . . don't be too sure."

"You can't deny that I've been about as bad as they come."

"No, I wouldn't deny it," said Robert. "But God is the one who can make it all right."

"Make what right?"

"Everything—what you've done, who you are . . . your sin. He's your Father. He can make it right."

"How do you figure he's *my* Father?"

"Why wouldn't He be?"

"Because . . . like you say—my sin."

"God is still your Father whether you acknowledge it or not."

"I thought that was only for the saved."

"He gave you life, didn't He? Where do you think life comes from? Who else could be your Father than the Creator of all life, along with your earthly father, of course."

"Maybe so, but that hardly changes the fact that I've mocked Him all my life. What love could He have for me?"

"The love of an infinitely loving Father."

"My father wasn't very loving, that's for sure."

"Maybe he didn't know how to be. But God is the perfect Father."

At last the force of the word *Father* seemed to penetrate his mind with a fleeting glimpse of the ideal and perfect rather than the broken human image. Teague sat thinking.

"Instead of dreading seeing Him tomorrow," Robert went on after a moment, "you have the opportunity to look forward to it. It will be your chance to tell Him that you want to start recognizing Him as your Father, and to live for all eternity as His son."

But Teague could not dislodge the terrifying image of hell from his brain.

"Not many preachers would agree with your assessment of my prospects!" said Teague with a cynical laugh. "They would say that by tomorrow night I'll be on the fast road to hell, and that God won't be anywhere within sight. They'll say that that's exactly what I deserve."

"I won't argue that most would say that." Robert nodded. "I won't even argue that it's not what you deserve. I deserve it too."

"So *will* God send me to hell? Am I going to be burning in torment in those flames by this time tomorrow?" The desperation in Teague's face pierced Robert's heart.

"I honestly don't know," replied Robert seriously. "But if He does, it will be because He loves you, not because He condemns you. Even in hell, He will still love you."

"Not much good it will do me then!" laughed Teague with bitter hopelessness. "It hardly seems like what you can call love if He just sits by and watches people burn forever. Like I said, I'm not saying I don't deserve it. Just don't call it love when that's the *last* thing it is. That's what I always hated about religious people—saying things that make no sense—talking about God's love and sending people to hell in the same breath."

"Who says He just sits by and watches?" asked Robert. "The Bible says that even in hell, He will be with you. Maybe there will be more going on there than you think."

"I've never heard that before."

"Neither had I," said Robert. "I just discovered it recently. In the book of Psalms, it says that if we make our bed in hell, He will be there with us."

"You said before that you thought my soul would rot in hell."

"I was wrong to say it and I'm sorry," said Robert. "My words that day only revealed the evil in my own heart, not God's. I truly am sorry and I apologize."

"The evil . . . in *your* heart?" laughed Teague. "What evil have you ever done?"

"I am a sinner, Mr. Teague, just like you. We all are. There was a time when I hated you. According to the Bible, that makes me a murderer too. I deserve to go to hell just as much as anyone else. I had to face my own sin too. That meant I had to learn to forgive you."

The force of Robert's admission struck Teague more fully as the remarkable thing it was than it had before. He was quiet a moment or two. Because he had opened the door of his own heart and had begun to hunger for something to satisfy the torment in his soul, Robert's words were slowly getting through.

"Is what you're saying," he went on, "that you *don't* think that I'm going to be burning in hell tomorrow when that door opens and I drop down and my neck breaks?"

The brutal honesty of the question stunned Robert.

"Again, I really don't know," he answered quietly. "I can't claim to understand everything. I am young. I'm just learning about the ways of God myself. All I know is that I think God has work to do in your heart that you haven't let Him do yet. I don't know when or where He will do that work, or what that work will be like. But He wants to help you acknowledge Him as your Father and accept your place as His son. That's why He created you and gave you life in the first place. That is all He has ever wanted. That's why His son Jesus came—to help sinners like you and me live like God's children. Jesus went into hell after He died and brought souls that His Father still loved back out with Him. That love of the Father for His children is what life means, though not many discover that meaning. I am only just beginning to understand it myself. But I do know you can receive His forgiveness and begin anew."

"But there's no time," said Teague. "I am going to hang tomorrow."

"Then there is a whole day for God to work," said Robert.

"That's not much, after a whole ruined life."

"For God that is an eternity to turn a soul around and set it on the road to life and freedom and peace."

Teague stared down at the floor, his head between his hands. It was not an idea he could grasp. *Freedom and peace—*

what could they have to do with him!

"Would you like to live in God's family?" asked Robert at length.

"It's a little late for me to be thinking of that," replied Teague.

"But would you?"

"I suppose . . . yes, I would."

"Then begin. It's not a matter of how *much* time God has," Robert went on, "but what direction we are going. If we are going *toward* Him, then a moment is an eternity. God is not bound by time like we are. If it were your last breath of life, you can still cry out to Him. In an instant you can give yourself to Him. All I'm saying is, why not turn your life around now? Even if you have but one more day on this earth, God has already forgiven you. It's done. You need only accept that forgiveness, and then say to Him, *Your will be done in my life.*"

It grew silent. Teague was thinking hard. Thoughts of Abraham Lincoln and slavery and the Confederacy were far away. For the first time in his life, he was thinking about his obligations as a man to his Creator. It was obvious that he had failed in that obligation. But . . . *was* it too late? Or *might* there still be time? The thought was too stupendous to take in.

Might there actually . . . could it be . . . was there really room in God's heart . . . for him!

The Beginning

11

As if reading his mind, Robert now spoke.

"Do you know about the two men who were executed with Jesus?" he asked.

"Only what everyone knows, I suppose."

As Robert began to recount the ancient tale, alive with poignant power in the cell of a man likewise condemned to death as the three so long ago, Teague listened with a heavy heart. His expression was one of impending finality, yet he was strangely warmed by Robert's portrayal of the Savior's love.

"You see," said Robert at length, "He utters not a word of questioning, no doctrinal analysis, no preaching to the man, not a word of condemnation, not a word about his past sins. He only says, *Come home with me.*"

By this time Teague was wiping at his eyes.

The cell grew silent and remained so for a minute or two.

"I . . . want to tell you," said Teague at length, "that I'm sorry . . . you and your whole family."

The rusty hinges of the door called repentance had finally begun to break free.

"Thank you," said Robert softly. "I know that will mean

a great deal to my father and mother, and sister, as it does to me."

"I know I don't deserve it, but . . . but I hope that you will someday be able to find it in your heart to forgive me."

"I told you the last time I was here that I forgave you some time ago, Mr. Teague. Realizing that God loved and forgave me in spite of *my* sin helped me see how much He loved you in spite of *your* sin. I hope you get a chance to meet my sister one day. I know she will forgive you, just as I do. I think you will like her."

The idea stung Teague with remorse. At last the tears began to flow.

"I've hardly slept in weeks," he said. "Oh, God . . . I killed *your* sister! I am so sorry! I've killed other men too. It is so crushing that I cannot stand it. Can you imagine the terrible guilt of knowing you have killed innocent human beings? The guilt is overpowering. Can you imagine what it is like to hate who you are, to look in a mirror and see the devil himself? It will be a relief to die and have it over with. Even the torment of hell could hardly be worse than this!"

"But rather than just having it over with, wouldn't you rather have it made right?"

"Of course, who wouldn't—but how?" Teague sobbed. "I can't go back and undo the evil I've done."

"There is one who *can* make it right. Death is nothing to Him. He conquered death."

"I know who you mean," nodded Teague.

"Remember His promise on the cross. The salvation He offers was not only for those listening, not only for the repentant thief . . . it was for you and me too. He died for *you*, Mr. Teague, so that you could know His salvation too. All you have to do, like the thief on the cross, is acknowledge your sin, and then ask Him for His salvation. Tell Him what you are, that you are sorry, and ask Him to forgive you and change you."

"I suppose you mean pray a sinner's prayer like the hell-fire preachers are always talking about."

"Call it whatever you like." Robert smiled. "I would rather think of it as crawling into your Father's lap, telling Him you are sorry for being bad and asking Him to help you be good."

"Do you think . . . I mean, did He really die . . . for *me*?"

"Yes He did. Had you been the only person on the face of the earth, He would still have died for you."

"But . . . but why—how could He possibly . . . why would He do such a thing?"

"It's just what I told you before—because His Father *loves* you."

At last the power of the word broke down the final barrier in Damon Teague's heart, and God's love rushed in.

He broke down in sobs of remorse.

"God . . . I am so sorry!" he wailed. "Forgive me for what I am and what I have done. I have been a sinful man. But . . . if it is not too late . . . I want to start over . . . help me and heal me of this horrible evil."

He continued weeping as the cleansing tide of repentance flowed through him.

Several minutes went by. Gradually he calmed.

"I deserve nothing, God," Teague prayed, still sniffing and wiping his nose and eyes, "but if it's not too late to begin over again, I am ready to let you see if you can do anything with me. I don't see what you can accomplish in a day, but if young Paxton is right and that's all it takes to make a beginning, then please begin with me. Jesus, like the thief on the cross beside you, I ask you to remember me tomorrow."

Again a long silence followed. Robert did not want to fill it with his own words.

When Teague spoke again, Robert silently rejoiced that he had begun to look forward. He was no longer thinking of hell and death, but about the next phase of *life*. The will of

God can only be known by doing, and this *do* Teague was ready to face.

"You say a day is enough for God to make a beginning," he said, "even for someone like me. But how . . . what am I to *do*? What do I *do* today and tonight in the hours I have left? How am I to begin?"

"Believe in Jesus Christ and then do what He says."

"How can I possibly do that? I've got no time to learn what you know about Him."

"He said to give yourself up into the will of His Father, who is also our Father. There is time to do that. Give yourself into the care of God the Father."

"But how?"

"The whole of Jesus' life and teaching can be summed up in five simple words—*Not my will but yours.* You can pray that same prayer in a moment. Then God will show you what He wants you to do."

"It doesn't seem like enough."

"It is a beginning, therefore it is everything."

"That's all there is to it?"

"That *all* is everything. It is no small *all*—the repentance of the prodigal and the forgiveness of the Father."

"And then what?"

"Begin to think differently," replied Robert.

"About what?"

"About yourself and about God, about who you are to Him and what He is to you. Begin to think of Him as your good and loving Father, and of yourself as His rebellious child who has decided to begin obeying Him. Ask Him to show you yourself as you are. Continue, as you have, to ask His forgiveness for the wrong you have done. Then do your best to accept His forgiveness—though this may be the hardest thing of all—and to realize that He loves you in spite of what you have done."

Teague nodded.

"You cannot make restitution for your sin out in the world," said Robert, "to those you have hurt. You are right—it is too late for that. But you can make restitution in your heart and ask God to take care of those you have hurt. Ask Him to show you how. Pray for them and ask God to bring goodness to their lives. If there is anyone you hold a grudge against, you must forgive him as you have asked God to forgive you. In all these ways you will be doing your part to help God make a beginning in you."

"You mean people like you . . . your family?" said Teague. "Should I pray for the people I killed?"

"You can do that, but especially pray for their loved ones. And pray for yourself, that God will continue to change the attitudes in your own heart. Pray to be given deep love for them. It is never too late for that. Forgiveness and life can blossom in an instant."

"I see," nodded Teague humbly.

"Turn your cruelty into compassion. Turn killing into life. Turn evil into good. Turn bitterness into forgiveness. Turn defiance into submission. Turn hatred into love. All this you can do in your heart. You can ask Jesus to help you. He will come into your heart himself and help you."

"How does He do that?"

"He made a promise before He died that His own Spirit would come to dwell within us. That is a remarkable thing when you think about it. He can help us become God's obedient children from the inside. He can work a miracle of healing within you. There may be just one day, but that is enough time for God's miracle. A day is an eternity for God."

Teague sighed and smiled a thin smile. "It is a lot to think about," he said.

"You will remember what God wants you to remember. He will bring what we have talked about back to your mind."

"I hope you're right."

"By such beginnings, you will be ready to meet Him

tomorrow. You will be able to say to Him, *I'm sorry I didn't come to you sooner, Father. I have sinned against heaven and against you. I am not worthy to be called your son. But if you will help me, I want to become your son.* And then He will say, *Oh, my dear boy . . . you have indeed been a prodigal. But all that is behind us now. Welcome home!*"

Again Teague began to weep.

"In short," Robert concluded, "in the time you have left, talk to God and do what He shows you to do. Ask for His help. Talk to Him as a Father. Let Him whisper into your heart. Prepare to meet Him as a wayward son returning home to His Father's house. That will be the best possible use of a day you have ever had in your life."

"I will try, Paxton . . . with God's help, I will try."

Robert smiled. He sat awhile longer, but knew he had said enough. When Teague's questions were finally done, he rose.

"I'll leave my New Testament with you in case you feel like reading," he said. "—Here, I'll put this marker in the place where it tells about the thief . . . and also about the prodigal who went home to his father's waiting arms."

He extended his hand.

"I think you are now ready to be alone with your Father," he said.

"Thank you, Paxton," said Teague as they shook hands vigorously. "I will try to do as you say. This is all new."

"God will help you."

"I can't thank you enough. You have every right to hate me. . . ."

He looked away and his eyes again filled with tears.

Robert waited. Teague took two or three deep breaths, then turned back to face him.

"Thank you . . . that's all I can say."

"Guard!" Robert called. "I am ready."

"Spend your last hours talking to your Father," he added. "And listening to what He tells you. Then make what restitution in your heart He shows you to make. Do that and you will be ready to meet Him."

The guard's footsteps sounded behind them.

Robert stepped forward and embraced Teague, then turned and left the cell.

SCAFFOLD

12

ROBERT HAD NOT EXPECTED TO GET MUCH SLEEP THE night before the hanging. But he awoke feeling surprisingly rested. He wondered if Damon Teague had fared as well.

He was the only member of his family who planned to witness the execution. He left the house early in a sober and prayerful frame of mind.

He arrived and took his place outside the jail where the scaffold had been built. A sizeable crowd had already gathered. He glanced up where the rope hung from the topmost beam in ominous readiness.

Fifteen minutes later the door opened and a small procession emerged from the building. Teague's hands were bound behind him and he was led by several officers. They led him up the steps of the scaffold. Teague glanced up toward the rope. Then his eyes drifted over the crowd, apparently looking for a face among the several hundred spectators.

The official spokesman for the State of Maryland stepped forward.

"Damon Teague," he said in a loud voice, "inasmuch as you have received a fair trial and have been found guilty by a jury of your peers of murder in the first degree, and have been sentenced to hang by the neck until dead, by law I now give you the opportunity to make a last statement before the sentence is carried out."

Dozens of reporters were on hand anticipating an inflammatory speech of defiance and denunciation of the Union, blacks, Christianity, Reverend Paxton, and Abraham Lincoln. They were in for a surprise.

The crowd quieted in expectation.

"Thank you," said Teague calmly. "Yes, I would like to make a statement.

"I want to publicly express my sorrow for what I have done," he went on. "I am guilty of all the crimes for which I was charged and I am deeply and truly sorry.

"I know there is nothing I can say, much less do, to deserve or expect the forgiveness of the Paxton family and the other families and individuals that my terrible actions have hurt. I hope they may someday find it in their hearts to forgive me anyway. I want to publicly thank Robert Paxton for having the courage to confront me with my sin and having the compassion to forgive me. We had a long conversation just yesterday about three other men who were executed a long time ago. He helped me gain strength from their example for what I am about to face today."

As Robert listened, tears filled his eyes.

"I have prayed to ask God to forgive me," Teague went on, "and to deal with me justly as I deserve. I ask the same from all those I have hurt. I know that I deserve to die and I want the judge and jury and all the witnesses against me to know that I bear them no ill. They did what was right and I accept their sentence as just.

"I commend my soul to God. May He be merciful to me, a sinner. I am at peace."

He glanced toward Robert with a sad smile. Robert saw the words "I'm sorry" form on his lips.

Then Damon Teague bowed his head.

The hangman stepped forward and placed a black cloth hood over Teague's head and shoulders. He fitted the noose over the bag and drew it tight at the neck. The man now took several steps away from him, then reached for the lever attached to the hinge of the door beneath Teague's feet. . . .

TRAIN
13

When and how Katie and I finally actually decided to go north to Philadelphia to visit Aunt Nelda, I can't say exactly. It just grew on us gradually that it would be a good thing to do. We talked quite a lot about it with my papa and Uncle Ward through the winter after Henry and Josepha were married and Jeremiah had gone north to find work.

Of course, there were more letters back and forth with Aunt Nelda too, and lots of questions. Jeremiah's being in Delaware probably added to my own enthusiasm. Both Katie and I began to get excited about the trip north. It would be another adventure together, but unlike anything we had ever done before.

So gradually our plans formed and we made arrangements to go to Philadelphia for our visit in May of 1870.

Letters of anticipation began to pass more frequently between me and Jeremiah. Katie had been writing back and forth to the North a lot too in the months leading up to our trip. I wasn't the only one looking forward to visiting someone! She kept most of her thoughts to herself. But I knew she had a big long letter that had come only a week before.

As the time grew closer we looked forward to the trip more and more. Pretty soon it seemed like we were talking about nothing else. We knew we'd feel better about going if the planting was done before we left. So we worked hard to get the crops in as soon as the weather turned and the spring rain and sun's warmth made the earth just right. The harvest the year before hadn't been very good and prices were down. We hadn't been able to pay all our taxes and were hoping for a better harvest this year so we could get caught up again. I didn't know what it cost for the school we were going to visit, but it had to be a lot and I didn't see how we could possibly pay for it if we couldn't even harvest enough cotton to buy food for us all and pay for the other things Rosewood needed and pay the taxes. But everyone insisted that there would be money for school if we decided we wanted to go.

What I didn't know at the time was that our taxes had nearly doubled in the last few years and were just about more than Rosewood could afford unless Papa and Uncle Ward hired a lot of men and doubled the acreage we grew crops on. We had done pretty well for amateurs, I suppose. But there wasn't a true farmer among the men, Papa or Uncle Ward or Henry, who really knew how to get the most out of a large plantation like Katie's father had, or her uncle Burchard or probably William McSimmons. We were just a family of people who happened to be here and happened to own Rosewood because Katie's father and mother had been killed.

Under the circumstances, we had been pretty proud of ourselves for what we'd done.

But was it enough?

Would it be enough for the difficult times that lay

ahead for Rosewood? And was this a time when Katie and I wanted to be away?

They were questions I didn't know the answers to right then.

Whatever the future held, we were going on a trip to see Aunt Nelda. That much at least was certain. Then we would come back and we'd get the cotton harvest in and pay off the taxes with hopefully plenty to spare.

Then we'd worry about the future.

At last it came time to actually start packing. That's when the excitement really began to set in! My carpetbag was packed two weeks beforehand. Then unpacked and repacked another ten times after that!

Finally the big day came when we were to leave for Charlotte to board the train for Richmond, and then north on to Philadelphia. The train was to depart in the afternoon, so we left Rosewood at dawn. Josepha and Henry were up to see us off. Josepha handed us a basket so full of food we all laughed. Then Papa and Uncle Ward took us in the buggy to Charlotte.

Papa and Uncle Ward tried to be excited for us. But once when we were standing on the platform I saw Papa look away and brush at his eyes. It stung my heart to see a grown man having to fight back tears because of love for me. That is a pretty incredible thing.

Then the time came.

"You two be good," said Uncle Ward, giving us each a hug.

"That goes for me too," said Papa. He took me in his arms and hugged me tight. As I stepped back he kissed me on the cheek. By then I had tears in my *eyes!*

Then he did the same with Katie.

"All aboard!" called out a uniformed man up toward the front of the train.

We all hugged again, then Katie and I went to the open door closest to us, stepped up, turned and waved one last time, and stepped inside. We hurried into the coach to get a seat by the window on the side where they were standing so we could see them.

A minute or two later the train began to move. We waved frantically as long as we could, but in another minute they were out of sight and we sat back down.

Our adventure had begun!

We looked at each other and smiled as if to say, "Well, this is it!" then turned to look out the window as the city faded and we entered the countryside. I suppose we were both so full of thoughts and emotions that we couldn't talk. That's the great thing about best friends, you don't have to talk all the time. The friendship deepens just as much through silence as with words.

That's how I felt then. Just to know Katie was beside me, enjoying the same sights, maybe feeling and thinking some of the same things, was enough.

"It's almost like it's a new chapter of our lives, isn't it, Mayme?" said Katie at last. "We've read the book up till now and here we are. But we haven't read the next chapter yet."

"What kind of chapter do you think it will be?" I said. "An adventure, a romance, a mystery?"

"I guess we have to keep reading—just keep being who we are to find out. Maybe all three!"

"I wonder what the school is like."

"Me too. Aunt Nelda is so looking forward to our visit. She's been alone for so long. I wish I hadn't waited so long, but for some reason I was almost afraid of her. I can't imagine it now. It must have been hard for her to have been widowed for so long. I wonder why she never married again."

I thought about Katie's words for a minute, and couldn't help thinking about Papa.

"Maybe it's that the Daniels family only gives their love once," I said. "After he lost my mama, Papa never had eyes for anyone else either."

"Do you really want to spend three years at school away from Rosewood, Mayme?" Katie asked.

"I don't know. It does seem like a long time."

We were quiet awhile longer, enjoying the clickety-clack of the tracks beneath us.

"I hope everything goes all right at Rosewood," said Katie after a bit. "I can't help feeling a little guilty for leaving them alone. There's a lot that we do every day—the chickens, the cows, making the cheese and buttermilk, the washing. Josepha can't do it all."

"They'll all pitch in and probably enjoy it!" I laughed.

"I'm just glad we got the planting done and that we'll be back in time for the harvest."

"I have the feeling they're going to miss us. I could tell."

"Me too. They were trying to act happy for our sakes. But they were sad."

"Things are sure changing at Rosewood, with Emma and William gone, and Jeremiah gone, and now with us gone . . . it's going to be pretty quiet around there."

"Just like it used to be when we were alone together, remember?"

"You think I will ever forget!"

"I suppose not. I never will."

"Remember when Papa first came? It was all women and him. Now it's all men but Josepha."

We laughed at the thought.

"If I know her," smiled Katie, "she'll keep them in

line. Wouldn't you love to see that—Josepha bossing the three men around!"

We laughed again and then it grew quiet. I took out the most recent letter I had received from Jeremiah. I had written to him about our visit to Aunt Nelda's and I read in his letter again that wild horses wouldn't be able to keep him away from Philadelphia when we got there. When I next looked over at Katie, she was absorbed in the long letter she'd gotten last week.

SEPARATION
14

We had been on the train probably about half an hour, talking and looking out the windows and going back to our letters. We were sitting with our letters in our laps when we heard the door open behind us and the conductor came along asking for people's tickets. Katie folded the pages in her hand and we both pulled out our tickets to get them ready.

The conductor reached us, looking at both of us with a stern expression.

"What are you doing here?" he asked, looking down at me.

"I have . . . here's my ticket," I said nervously. The look on his face was enough to make anyone nervous!

He took it and clicked it with a little metal thing in his hand, glanced at Katie, took her ticket and did the same, then looked back at me.

"Get your things, girl," he said, "and come with me."

"That's all right," I said, misunderstanding him at first. "I am fine here."

"I should say you are!" he said. "But you aren't staying here. Now I said come with me!"

"Why, where are you going?" I asked.

"You can't sit here. This carriage is for whites only. You'll have to sit in the colored car at the back of the train."

Katie and I glanced at each other. Neither of us knew what to do.

Finally Katie stood up and picked up her carpetbag and satchel.

"Let's go, Mayme," she said. "I'll come with you. That will be the simplest thing to do."

She stepped out into the aisle where the conductor was waiting.

"I'm sorry, miss," he said to Katie. "I cannot allow you to do that. No coloreds in the white car, no whites in the colored car."

"But we have the same tickets," said Katie.

"That doesn't matter, miss.—Now, girl," he said, looking at me again, "come with me now before I have to forcibly remove you."

"It's all right," I said, looking at Katie. "I'll be fine."

I got my things and stepped out to go with the man.

"Well, it's not all right with me," insisted Katie. "You can't do this," she said, continuing to argue with the man. "We have the same tickets. There's no slavery anymore, or haven't you heard? You can't treat her this way!"

By now other passengers were looking at us and it was becoming a scene.

"Sit down, lady!" yelled a man several seats away. "The nigger girl doesn't belong here."

"That's right, miss," said the conductor. "Now if you don't sit down and behave yourself, I'll put both of you off at the next stop."

I could tell that Katie was irate, but finally saw that there was nothing she could do. I looked at her and smiled and tried to reassure her that I didn't mind.

She sat down, still fuming, and I followed the conductor along the narrow aisle. I glanced back as the conductor opened the door at the back of the car. I smiled again. Katie tried to smile too, then I saw her pull out her letter and start to read again.

❧ ✵ ❧

Forever Changed
15

As Katie read, tears streamed down her face.

I looked away at the last instant, but the terrible bang of the trapdoor opening, and the gasps of the onlookers as the poor man's body fell through the scaffolding and the rope yanked taut on his neck . . . they are sights and sounds too horrible to speak of, yet ones that will remain with me forever.

Oh, Rob . . . Rob! Katie whispered as she broke into sobs.

That he may have deserved it according to the law is not sufficient to quiet the unrest of watching a man die and knowing that I was personally responsible. Not solely responsible, of course. I recognize the intellectual arguments that can be marshaled against my feelings of guilt when they surface as they often do. But such arguments do not meet the agonies of such a memory. Certainly I am comforted by his change of heart at the end. As he was at peace in death, I too am at peace, though the memory of his death remains a burden that I carry with me daily . . . and one I carry alone.

Later that day, Detective Heyes came to our house

and asked for me. He handed me back my New Testament, a watch, and a worn and folded letter that Teague had saved for years. He said that Teague had asked him to get them to me. The letter was from his mother, from years before, and it broke my heart every time I read it. But when I was up to it, I went to visit her, told her my story, and tried to offer her what comfort I could.

Katie put aside the letter and took out a handkerchief. She dabbed at her nose and eyes and stared out the window.

"Something to eat, ma'am?" said a voice beside her. She glanced up. In the aisle stood a well-dressed man pushing a cart with food and drinks. "A sandwich, perhaps, and coffee or tea?"

"Oh," said Katie, "oh . . . I don't think so just now.—Thank you," she added with a smile.

She drew in a long breath as the man continued toward the other passengers. She blew her nose, and again picked up Rob's letter.

You once asked me how a minister's son turned out to be a sheriff's deputy. So when you told me that you were coming to Philadelphia and I realized there was a good chance that we might be able to see one another again, I thought it time that I told you the whole story. You deserved to know. Whether you will want to see me after learning everything I have told you . . . that will be up to you. My mind will be relieved just to know that at last I have answered your question thoroughly, and you know most of what there is to know about me.

In a way, however, this is only the beginning of the story, though the most important part. I suppose you could say that my part of the story began in the cell of Damon Teague, or at least the part of the story about how the experience affected me . . . and changed me. I hadn't really considered my feelings much until the man was jailed. I was so young, just seventeen when my sister was shot. That is an age when hate can flourish if given the chance, and as I have said, I allowed it to grow in me. I can now look back and truly thank God, not that my sister was killed or anything like that, but thank Him for using the entire experience to expose those flaws in my own character that I was unaware of, to confront me, I suppose I should say, with my own sin. That is not a pleasant confrontation for any man or woman. But I am grateful for it. Because it enabled me to begin looking with truer perspective into my own life and, I hope, to begin growing in some small measure toward the Christlikeness that is the only goal and objective of the Christian life. I feel I am finally beginning to understand a little of what being a Christian *really means—which is nothing more nor less than allowing God to make us more like Jesus himself. Had all these things not happened, who knows how long I may have continued in my blind self-righteousness? I might indeed have become a minister of renown, but if I had never truly known myself, what would it have been for? Only so much wood, hay, and stubble.*

Please do not misunderstand me—I love and respect my father more than words can say. I attribute none of these deficiencies that I discovered in myself to him. I believe his call to the pastorate was genuine and I believe his ministry to have been an enormously fruitful one. But I realized that as things stood at that point in my life, I had serious reservations about following in his footsteps. I saw *something when I looked into Teague's eyes that day that changed my whole perception of the Christian message. I came to realize that perhaps the gospel as normally perceived was no longer one I could devote my life to. In those moments I saw, I felt, the enormity of God's love and infinite forgiveness. I realized that I did not want to preach that the Son came to save us from the wrath of the Father. Heaven forbid such a thing to be true! But that changed perspective was not one that I felt would find a welcome home within the organized church. It seemed to me that I could do more good out in the world where a message proclaiming the goodness of God, rather than His vindictiveness against sin, would be welcome. Even among my own family, when I attempted to tell them what I had experienced in Teague's cell that day, the first response was one of suspicion. The truth of an infinitely forgiving Father, I am discovering, to my surprise and dismay, is not a welcome message among Christians. Yet out among the Damon Teagues of the world, among those who know something about sin firsthand, it is a message that gives hope and enables many to respond to God as I believe He truly is.*

I know this has been a terribly long letter. I did not really set out to pen my autobiography when I put the Dear Katie *on the first page! I only wanted you to know the struggle I have been through, and why. I still wrestle with much of what I have told you. The man's face still haunts me. I still miss my sister. Many* what ifs *remain.*

All these events I have recounted at last led me to the decision not to pursue the ministry, at least for the present. In a decision that my mother and father had a very difficult time with, I decided to join the army for what remained of the war, but on the Union side. I went north to Philadelphia and volunteered my services to watch and guard and take care of the prisoners. I knew I could not fight, on either side. Nor did I feel called to become a chaplain. But I hoped I might be able to help in some way with those who had been captured. Probably my experience with Teague in the Baltimore jail had more than a little to do with it.

When later Detective Heyes left the Baltimore police

department and ran for sheriff in Ellicott City, I was stunned when he asked if I would be his deputy. By that time the war was over and I was home again with my family and working at insignificant jobs, still pondering what I wanted to do with myself. His offer sent me into a new round of prayer and reflection. I had to reevaluate my future and my ministerial vow all over again. As I did I began to see that God needed people in many walks of life, not just in the pulpit . . . even in the office of a small-town sheriff. So I accepted his offer.

That was about a year before I first met you and your uncles. After several years in Ellicott City, Sheriff Heyes decided to take the job in Hanover as assistant sheriff for York County, just north of the Pennsylvania border, as I told you about, and I decided to accompany him and remain his deputy. I thank God that I have never had to kill, and I hope I have done some good.

It is all right with me if you show what I have written to Mayme. I know how close you two are.

Perhaps I should be embarrassed to have gone on for so long with this autobiography. *But truthfully, if feels so good to have told you all that. Whatever your response, I feel an enormous sense of relief. I thank you for being a patient and, I hope, understanding listener.*

Yours faithfully,
Rob Paxton

On the Train

16

As for me, I had no idea at the time of all the emotions Katie was going through from reading Rob Paxton's letter about everything that had happened to him. I knew that she had a long letter from Rob, but I had no idea what was in it. When Katie let me read it later, I was as moved as she had been. What an incredible story. But at the time I knew nothing of it because I had troubles of my own!

The conductor had been rude and brusque to me as he took me away from Katie. He grabbed my arm and pulled me along the aisle and through several more half-empty cars of white people to the last car on the train—the colored car. He opened the door and shoved me inside, then slammed the door behind me.

The car was crowded with twice as many blacks as there were seats. It was hot and stuffy and already smelled pretty bad. None of the windows opened.

Fifty or more black faces turned to look at me as the conductor stuffed me through the door. None of them wore welcoming looks. One more person meant less space and less air for the rest.

"Who dat, Mama?" said a little boy a few feet away, pointing at me.

"I don' know, son, jes' somebody dat wuz sittin' where she wuzn't s'posed to, I reckon."

"Why she do dat, Mama?"

"I don' know—maybe she thought she wuz better'n da rest ob us."

I wanted to shrink out of sight! I smiled sheepishly and gradually most of the faces turned away. I squeezed my carpetbag down on the floor between my feet and tried to look out the window as I stood there.

The fun train ride Katie and I had looked forward to didn't look like it was going to happen. Now the hours dragged slowly by. It was so stuffy and hot in that car crammed so tight and full of us blacks. My back hurt from standing, though I wasn't the only one. Some people were talking, some were just looking out the windows. The few children in the car were chattering away like children do and I was reminded of Emma's William, the poor dear boy. But after the reception I'd received when the conductor pushed me in, I wasn't particularly anxious to talk to anybody. Listening to those around me, I knew I would sound different and I was afraid they'd make fun of me or something because I was more tan than black and I was dressed nice and didn't talk like most former slaves. So I kept my mouth shut and kept to myself.

The train stopped in Raleigh. Everyone got out for water and necessaries. I hoped to see Katie, but the conductor and a couple of his men herded us behind the train by ourselves where there was a little woods and a stream for us to use. The outhouses at the station were only for whites.

As we returned to the train I saw Katie approaching along the platform. We hurried toward each other.

"Oh, Mayme, I'm so sorry about this!" she said, giving me a hug. "It's just terrible."

"It's all right . . . not so bad, really.—A little crowded!" I added with a laugh.

"It makes me so mad! I've spoken with every person who works for the train company and every one of them is rude to me. They treat me like I'm—"

She stopped and her face got red.

"I'm sorry, Mayme," she said. "I didn't mean that. Well, I meant it, but I didn't mean it like it sounded . . . you know what I mean!"

"I know what you mean, Katie." I smiled. "It's all right. They do treat blacks different."

"What was the war all about and what Mr. Lincoln did?" she went on. "They have no idea what being free means. If Rob were here, he'd do something!"

"Did you finish his letter?" I asked.

"Yes . . . oh, Mayme—"

Katie's eyes filled with tears.

"What is it?" I asked.

"It's the most amazing story. Poor Rob—what he has been through. He said you could read it if you want to."

"Do you think I should . . . I mean, he wrote it to you. Do you want me to?"

"Yes, I think so. In fact, I think Rob would like you to."

"If you want me to, I'd like to," I said. "Maybe when we get to Aunt Nelda's."

"He reminds me of Micah Duff," said Katie.

"In what way?"

"I don't know . . . in how his life with God and his faith is so personal. He prays about everything. Most men aren't like that!"

"Did he . . . say anything . . . you know—about you and him?" I asked.

Katie smiled.

"Not too much," she answered, "only that he hopes we can see each other when we are in Philadelphia. He'll be less than a hundred miles away."

"Are you going to?"

"I hope so," said Katie. "I would like to see him, of course. I thought I knew him before, even though it's just from our letters. But after reading his letter I realize there was so much I didn't know about him."

"Hey, what's going on there!" a voice yelled at us. "—You . . . you colored girl—get back where you belong!"

Now Katie's eyes really flashed with a fire I'd hardly ever seen in her before.

She spun around to see the conductor walking toward us.

"She is where she belongs," said Katie, and it was obvious she was upset. "I came here to talk to her. She hasn't moved an inch. She has every right—"

"Look, little lady," interrupted the man. Now he was mad too. "I've just about had all the tongue from you I intend to take!"

He grabbed Katie by the wrist and yanked her along the platform.

She cried out in pain.

"Ow . . . ow, that hurts . . . stop it!"

I was so furious I wanted to run after him and kick him or something. But I knew that anything I tried to do would only make it worse for both of us.

Paying no attention to her, the man pulled Katie after him back toward the front of the train.

"If I see the two of you so much as looking at each other again," he said as they went, "I will throw you both off the train. Even if it's in the middle of nowhere. You don't want that, little lady—there's bands of kidnappers

roaming these parts, snatching up the coloreds who are traveling north and selling them overseas. No, sir, you don't want to be left behind. They would get a handsome price for a pretty white girl like you and that nigger friend of yours. So you just keep to yourself!"

I returned to the colored car with the rest of the blacks. Poor Katie, I thought. This was going to be harder on her than me.

The rest of the day was all right, though I got awfully tired standing there staring out the window. We stopped another time or two but I didn't dare look for Katie.

We stopped overnight in Richmond. When we pulled into the station and got out, I went inside with a group of the other blacks. I didn't want to be anywhere near Katie where the conductor might see us and get after us! We saw each other from a distance and went outside to the street before greeting each other.

"I'm glad that ride is over!" exclaimed Katie.

"Me too!" I said. "That car was so stuffy . . . and I had to stand the whole way!"

"Oh, Mayme . . . I'm so sorry."

"Oh, well . . . we're here now."

There were lots of horse-drawn cabs at the station for people who had just got into the city on the train. We went to one and Katie told the man where we wanted to go. He hesitated, looked at me as if he didn't much like the idea of a colored girl sitting in his buggy, but then just nodded and said, "All right, then . . . get in."

Katie and I laughed and giggled and talked all the way to the hotel, making up for the whole day we had been apart. We had been planning the trip for long enough that we'd had time to write to several hotels and find one that would let a white girl and black girl stay together. Since we had made our arrangements ahead of time, that was one thing we didn't have to worry about. But my papa and Uncle Ward had been very stern about not wanting us to leave our hotel room after dark. We arrived in Richmond a few minutes before four o'clock in the afternoon and got to the hotel and had our room key by four. Then we went out and walked around the city for an hour—they'd said we could do that—and then went back to the hotel.

We also needed to send a telegram back home, care of Mrs. Hammond, telling Papa and Uncle Ward that we were safe in Richmond. That was another thing they told us to do so they wouldn't worry. They had planned to return to Greens Crossing from Charlotte and wait in town until the telegram came. But they said not to telegraph them until we were safely in the hotel for the evening.

We went to the man at the desk and Katie told him we wanted to send a telegram. He said he would take care of it. Then Katie wrote down the message:

> *ARRIVED SAFELY IN RICHMOND. THE HOTEL IS NICE. WE'LL BE IN OUR ROOM ALL EVENING. WE LOVE YOU. KATIE AND MAYME.*

Then we went upstairs and locked ourselves in our room. We had brought enough food with us for the day on the train and supper in the hotel that evening, and it was as good as a feast. We laughed and talked and read all evening. Being in a big city in a hotel together—even if we were in our room—was an adventure and we were so excited we couldn't even think about going to sleep.

But our train through Washington and on to Philadelphia left at nine-thirty the next morning, so we had to get some sleep so we would be able to get up and to the station in time for the second day of our journey.

PHILADELPHIA
17

We got to the station the next morning in plenty of time. We hoped that maybe we would be able to sit together. But as we left the station and walked out across the platform to the train, there was the same conductor helping people into the first several cars—white people, that is.

We had hoped never to see him again!

He glanced up and saw us from a distance, so we knew there wasn't even a chance of trying to get on together. So we said good-bye again.

"Please don't worry about me, Katie," I said. "I'll try to find a seat this time. Promise me you will try to enjoy yourself."

"Only if you do too," said Katie.

"All right, I promise!" I said. "However crowded it is . . . I will enjoy myself!"

"Good. Then I'll see you in Philadelphia!"

We parted, Katie to the front of the train, and me again back in the direction of the last car.

Since I was earlier than before, I found a seat. But then people kept coming and coming and pretty soon the car was full again and men had to stand in the aisles. An old black woman sat down on the seat beside me and smiled. By the time the train left the station, the car was as jammed as before. I recognized about half of them from the day before, but there were lots of new passengers too.

Just before I boarded, two mean-looking men came walking along the platform. They were looking at the train, especially where all the cars connected. One was white and one black, but the conductor didn't say anything to them *about talking together! I thought at first that they must be train workers or mechanics or something from the way they were looking around underneath the train. But when it came time to go, they got on the train with everybody else.*

We'd been on our way again about an hour when the mean-looking black man came into our car and found a place to stand. He had no luggage and spoke to no one. But it got a little quieter right after he came in. He didn't have a very nice look.

After about another hour he turned around and left the car again. I didn't know why he was free to come and go when none of the rest of us were. But I wasn't about to ask!

❦

The train arrived at the Philadelphia station late that same afternoon. Aunt Nelda was waiting. Katie stepped down to the platform, saw her aunt, and ran toward her with a smile. They greeted and hugged.

"It is so good to see you again, Katie!" said Aunt Nelda. "I'm glad you had a safe trip."

She glanced about.

"Where is Mayme?" she asked.

"She's at the back of the train," said Katie, pointing along the track. "They made her ride in a Negro car."

"I can't imagine such a thing," said Aunt Nelda as they started walking toward the back of the train. "There is no segregation like that here in Pennsylvania."

"Well, there must be in North Carolina and Virginia," said Katie. "We talked to each other after the first stop yesterday, but the conductor got upset with us and threatened to put us off the train. So when we got on this morning, we went to separate cars and haven't seen each other since. It would have been a lot more fun if we'd been able to be together, but at least we're here now."

They reached the end of the train and glanced around looking for Mayme. Most of the people were moving across the platform toward the station. By then no one else was getting off the train. A conductor, though not one Katie recognized, stepped down onto the platform from one of the cars and walked toward them.

Aunt Nelda approached him.

"Excuse me," she said, "where is the Negro coach?"

"Ma'am?" he said with a puzzled expression.

"The car with the blacks in it," said Katie.

"I'm sorry, miss," said the man, "I'm not sure what you mean. We have no Negro coach on this train."

By now Katie was thoroughly confused. She glanced about in every direction, expecting Mayme to appear any moment. But slowly the platform continued to empty of people.

"Is it all right if I go look inside the train?" she asked.

"Anything you like, miss," said the conductor. "This train's not going anyplace till morning."

"I'll walk back toward the front," said Aunt Nelda, "—give me your carpetbag. I'll carry it and meet you back at the front."

Katie stepped up through the open door into the last coach of the train and slowly wandered through it, looking for any sign of Mayme.

But the car was empty.

She opened the door and passed through into the next car. A young black man was picking up paper and sweeping the aisle.

"Excuse me," said Katie, "did you see a black girl . . . about my age?"

"No, ma'am—everybody dun got off an' dere ain't nobody here but jes' me, ma'am."

Katie continued on, through the next car . . . and the next. Except for an occasional train worker, all the cars were empty of passengers.

Finally she reached the front of the train. She stepped back out onto the platform where Aunt Nelda was waiting for her.

"Did you see her?" asked Katie.

"No," replied Katie's aunt. "I walked all the way up the platform, but there was no sign of her. She must have slipped past us and gone into the station."

They left the train, crossed the platform, and walked through the wide double doors into the station. The huge room was filled with people coming and going. As the recently arriving passengers greeted the people who had come for them and gathered their things, slowly the crowd diminished in size. Katie and Aunt Nelda walked about together for a while, then separated and continued to walk back and forth throughout the huge hall.

Half an hour later, the room was mostly empty except for a few remaining passengers and train workers. They walked toward each other from opposite sides of the room.

"I'm frightened, Aunt Nelda," said Katie with a look of desperation. "Where could she be? What could have happened to her?"

"I don't know, dear," said her aunt. "I'm concerned too. Let's go talk to the stationmaster."

No Trace

18

KATIE AND HER AUNT MADE THEIR WAY TO THE office of the stationmaster. Aunt Nelda explained the situation.

"We can't find her anywhere," said Katie frantically. "But she was on the train with me. They put her in a car of blacks at the back of the train. The conductor was very rude about it."

"I'm sorry, miss," said the stationmaster, "but the train that just arrived from Washington had no coach designated for Negroes. The Negro cars only come as far north as Washington. Beyond that, blacks are seated in the cars along with the other passengers. Where was it you came from?"

"Charlotte."

"Through Raleigh, Richmond, and Washington?" the man asked.

"That's right."

"Hmm . . . there was some trouble reported between Richmond and Washington."

"What kind of trouble?" asked Katie anxiously.

"Actually . . . it's an embarrassment for the railroad."

"Why . . . what happened?"

"It seems—this is very unfortunate—but it seems . . . that one of the cars was lost."

"*Lost* . . . how could a car be lost from a moving train!"

"They're not sure exactly. Apparently it came unconnected from the train."

"Was it the last car . . . the Negro car?"

"I'm afraid so, miss."

"What about the people onboard?" asked Katie's aunt.

"That is the strange part," answered the man. "We received a telegram saying the car was discovered, but that all the passengers had vanished without a trace. There was no sign of them."

"But what are you doing about it?" asked Katie in disbelief.

The man shrugged. "What can we do? We assume the passengers continued on to their destinations on foot. It would be useless to attempt to track them down."

"But what if something happened to them?"

"We are a railroad, miss. We are not equipped to send posses after missing passengers when they leave the train. There is just not much the railroad can do under the circumstances."

By now Katie was getting angry again. Her experience with officials of the railroad had not been a pleasant one.

As she and her aunt left the stationmaster's office and walked back out into the deserted station, Katie looked all around again, then finally began to cry.

"Aunt Nelda," she said through her tears, "what are we going to do!"

"Why don't we go home, get you settled, and have something to eat," said Aunt Nelda. "It's nearly night and we cannot do anything more here. We've left our names with the stationmaster. They will notify us if anything turns up. In the meantime, if Mayme should telegraph us, we need to be at home. Does she know how to send a telegraph?"

"I don't know," said Katie. "We sent one back home

from Richmond last night. So she can figure it out."

"Does she have any money?"

"A little. And that reminds me—we were supposed to send a telegram home when we arrived in Philadelphia too. Uncle Templeton and Uncle Ward will be expecting it."

"We don't want to worry them," said Katie's aunt. "Let's think about it overnight and decide what to say to them. They'll be less concerned hearing nothing than for us to tell them we can't find Mayme!"

"Maybe you're right. Oh . . . this is so terrible. And if I know Mayme, wherever she is, she'll be more worried about me than she is herself."

"We'll come down to the station again tomorrow when the northbound arrives and see if she's on it."

Katie sighed and wiped at her eyes. It didn't sound like a very satisfactory plan, but there was nothing else they could do. Dejectedly Katie followed Aunt Nelda from the station to her waiting carriage.

There was no telegram waiting for them when they arrived at Aunt Nelda's house.

They returned to the station again the next day. But there was no sign of Mayme, nor word of any kind.

She had disappeared without a trace.

ROSEWOOD
19

AFTER WAITING AROUND GREENS CROSSING FOR SEVeral hours before receiving the telegram from Katie and Mayme at Mrs. Hammond's store, Ward and Templeton Daniels rode back to Rosewood in the chill of early evening.

The following day Rosewood was quiet. Too quiet. Neither of them felt like doing much, but they had to keep busy to keep it from feeling too dreary with their two girls gone . . . and to keep themselves from worrying. But neither relished the idea of another ride into town.

"Elfrida will keep the next telegram for us," said Templeton. "By tonight they'll be with Nelda anyway. They'll be fine."

"They're just about grown-up," said Ward, nodding. "I reckon it's time we stopped nursemaiding them."

"It's hard to do with your own daughter."

"That I wouldn't know," laughed Ward. "I'll have to take your word for it."

Just then Josepha walked into the kitchen.

"You two 'bout ready fo sum lunch?" she said.

"And another pot of coffee," said Templeton. "I've been sipping at this cold breakfast pot all morning."

Josepha began bustling about with the fire in the stove and

before long the smell of brewing coffee filled the kitchen. Then she set about slicing bread and cheese.

"What's that husband of yours up to today?" asked Ward.

"He's still workin' on dat bookshelf," replied Josepha. "He's still determined dat I's gwine hab a nice shelf wiff books on it. I ain't got no books!" she added with a laugh. "But I's gwine hab da finest bookshelf in Shenandoah County!"

Ward and Templeton laughed with her.

"When a man's in love, there's nothing he won't do for his lady," said Templeton.

The words seemed to sober Josepha. Her hands went still on the bread counter and a faraway look came into her eye. She thought a moment.

"You really reckon dat's true, Mister Templeton?" she asked after a minute.

"I do indeed, Josepha."

She shook her head, almost in disbelief, and let out a long sigh.

"Laws almighty, dat's a strange an' fearsome thing," she said. "A man in love wiff da likes er me . . . my oh my, dat's sum amazin' thing, all right. But . . . I reckon he is at dat. He's a good man, ain't he?"

"Henry's one of the finest men I know," said Templeton.

KATIE'S BOLD DECISION

20

WHEN THERE WAS NO WORD FROM MAYME ON Katie's second day in Philadelphia, and when the railroad was apparently doing nothing to locate the missing passengers, Katie was nearly beside herself with worry.

They couldn't do any of the things they had planned. They couldn't do anything at all except sit . . . and wait . . . and hope to hear something. The clock on the mantel ticked by the seconds, but the hands moved slower than Katie thought was possible. It seemed that every hour when she glanced at the clock, only five minutes had gone by!

To pass the time and try to console herself, she had been reading Rob Paxton's letter through again. Suddenly an idea came into her brain like a bolt of lightning.

"Aunt Nelda!" she said excitedly. "Can you take me to the telegraph office?"

"Of course, dear. Have you decided to tell Templeton and Ward what has happened?"

"No, not that," said Katie, already going for her coat. "I want to send a telegram to someone else."

"Who?"

"Rob Paxton—our friend that I told you about . . . the sheriff's deputy."

"Ah yes . . . the young man from Baltimore."

"Yes, but he lives in Hanover now. I suppose it's bold, Aunt Nelda," said Katie, "but I don't know what else to do. Maybe he can tell us what we should do."

"It is certainly worth trying," said Katie's aunt, now rising also. "Then afterwards I can show you a little around the city to help us take our minds off it for a while, while we wait to see if there's a reply."

Sheriff John Heyes left the only decent dining establishment in Hanover, Pennsylvania, after a satisfactory lunch, and walked along the boardwalk back toward his office. As he passed the telegraph office, he heard his name called out from inside.

He stopped and went inside.

"Sheriff, I'm glad I caught you," said the man behind the counter. "I was just about to come down to your office. I've been wanting to talk to you."

"What is it, Tim?"

"This just came in for your deputy."

He handed him the customary yellow envelope containing a telegram.

"For Rob, you say . . . not me?"

"It's to him, all right."

"Must not be official business, then."

"Didn't sound like it, Sheriff. Of course, he'll have to tell you about it . . . I can't, you understand."

"I'll see that he gets it right away."

"By the way, John," said the man, "I wanted you to hear this from me—I just got word that my son's going to stay up in New York State for a good long while. Landed him a good job and his family is happy there. You know I built that little new house, figuring I'd move there when my son and his family took over the main house. But that's not going to happen now, so I've decided to sell my place and move north to join them."

"You . . . Tim Evans, the original pioneer of Hanover! You can't leave here, Tim!" laughed Heyes. "The town wouldn't know what to do with itself. You were the town's mayor a while back as I recall, long before I moved up here."

"I was, and I've served six times," said Evans, "whenever they couldn't find anyone else to take the job!" he added, laughing. "But time marches on, John. I'm not quite ready to retire yet, but I want to be with my family and a good telegraph man can always get work. They're also doing a lot up there with new inventions—electricity, pumps, heating systems, ways to heat a house in the winter other than just a fireplace in every room—pumping heat through pipes through the house from one central fire that will heat the whole place. I'd love to get in on something new like that while I'm still young enough. It's a good time for a change for me. And I need to be near my family."

"You'd hardly need to work if you sell your spread. What is it . . . a hundred acres?"

"Actually more like two hundred with the old Quaker claim," replied Evans.

"That's right, I'd forgotten. There's an old house out there, isn't there? Is it still standing?"

"Yeah, the place had been in a Quaker family from back in the days when Pennsylvania was nearly all Quaker. The house and barns aren't in very good shape, but I've tried to keep it in one piece."

"Three houses on two hundred acres—that ought to qualify you to get a good price," said Heyes.

"We'll see. I just hope to find someone who will love the place the way my wife and I loved it before she passed away. We built the new house with our own hands, but now it seems time to let it go. It's one of the hardest things to do in the world, you know, John, letting go of a lifelong dream."

He glanced toward the sheriff and smiled a melancholy smile. "But I know it's the right thing," he added. "So . . . that's why I have found myself wondering if perhaps . . . well, I have heard you speak of getting out of the law business and settling down to a quiet life of ranching . . . so I thought it might be just right for you."

Heyes laughed, but it was obvious that Evans' words had hit something deep inside him.

"You are a shrewd man, Timothy Evans," he said. "I doubt I could ever meet your price. No one gets rich on a lawman's wages. But the thought of taking off this badge and settling on a spread like yours is tempting indeed. I can't think of anything I'd like better. And that young deputy of mine is sharp enough to take my place. He could probably run against me . . . and win."

"He never would."

"I think you're right."

"He's completely devoted to you, John."

Heyes nodded, then chuckled lightly. "I suppose he is at that," he said. "He's a good kid. I'm lucky to have him."

"So you'll think about it?" persisted Evans.

"I'm not ready to retire yet. But now I don't suppose I'll be able to help thinking about it," laughed Heyes. "Anybody else know?"

"No," said Evans. "I don't want this spread around. If I decide to sell at all, it's got to be to the right person. It matters a lot to me who lives in my home and who winds up with that old Quaker place."

"May I tell my deputy? Decisions I make affect him in the long run."

"Sure."

The sheriff continued on his way, entered his own office, and handed the envelope to the young man seated behind the desk.

"Looks like you've got a telegram, Rob," he said.

"Me," said Deputy Paxton in surprise. "Who from?"

"Don't know."

Rob opened the envelope, took out the yellow sheet, and read the message. The look on his face certainly did not indicate that it was good news. He handed it to Heyes.

Dear Rob, Heyes read. *Arrived at aunt's in Philadelphia. Mayme put in colored car at back of train but never arrived. Looked everywhere. They say car came loose from train. All people disappeared. No word from Mayme. Very worried. What should we do? Send word to Nelda Fairchild, 37 Bingham Court, Philadelphia. Yours, Kathleen Clairborne.*

"What do you make of it?" asked Heyes.

"I don't know," replied Rob. "You think it could have anything to do with those reports we've heard about disappearing Negroes and the Caribbean slave market?"

"It could be. But the whole thing sounds pretty far-fetched."

Rob thought a moment, then reached for a sheet of paper and pen. "I'm going to write Katie a short reply," he said. "And then—I'm sorry to do this to you on such short notice . . . but I'm going to have to take a few days off."

"Starting when?"

"Starting now, I'm afraid, Mr. Heyes," answered Rob. "I've got to catch the train to Philadelphia. Meantime, can you see what you can dig up on that black-market slave thing? Seems like there was a suspected transport spot on the Virginia coast somewhere."

"I'll see what I can find out," replied Heyes.

Peculiar Rescue
21

Katie wasn't the only one who didn't know where I was. Neither did I!

It happened some time after the train had left Richmond the day before, as we were going up a steep hill, we slowed way down. The big black man I had noticed who had come into our car and then left didn't come back. Outside I heard some clanking metallic noises, and after that it seemed like we were going slower than ever.

Then finally we stopped completely.

I had been sitting near the front of the car and looking out the window. Now I turned around to look out the little window on the door we had all come through at the front of the car. But instead of seeing the door of the next car of the train a few feet away across the open platform between the cars, all I saw was open sky and trees and the train track.

I was confused at first. Then I looked closer. The rest of the train was a hundred yards away up the track . . . and still going!

We had come unhooked from the train!

My looking around had only taken a few seconds.

Almost the same instant as I saw the back of the train through the window, I realized that we were no longer stopped—we had started to go backwards down the hill!

Most of the rest of those in the car were also realizing by now that something was wrong. We weren't with the train anymore!

Everyone began looking around and asking questions, and as we picked up speed—backwards!—some of the men started to get alarmed. Before much longer children were crying and a few women were starting to scream and the men were yelling and looking around trying to figure out if there was something they could do.

But there wasn't. We were flying down the hill backwards with no brakes, and if we came to a sharp curve or if another train came along the tracks, we all knew we were done for.

We were racing down the hill faster than I could imagine a train being able to go. People were screaming and praying and crying for help. I was scared to death that any minute we were going to fall off the tracks and roll down a cliff and all be killed. Everyone was in a panic except for the old woman who was sitting calmly beside me.

"How can you be so calm?" I asked her, though I could hardly make myself heard. "Aren't you afraid?"

"What dere ter be feared ob?" she said.

"That we'll crash. That we'll fly off the tracks or run into another train."

She started chuckling.

"We ain't gwine fly offen dese tracks, dearie," she said.

"How can you be so sure?"

"Because I take dis train norf every munf an' I

knows every inch er da way. An' dat hill we wuz comin' up is as straight as an arrow all da way from da bottom. Ain't a curve in sight. We's jes' gwine go faster'n faster straight down till we git ter da bottom, den we'll slow down an' stop an' den dey'll figger out what went wrong. Dere ain't nuthin' gwine happen ter us—we's jes' gwine be a little late, dat's all."

"What about another train?"

"Da nex' train along here ain't fo two hours er more. Jes' relax, dearie, an' enjoy da ride—even effen it's in da wrong direction," she added with a laugh.

What she said helped, but I still couldn't help being afraid, especially with all the screaming and pandemonium around us.

But she was right.

After a while, gradually, I felt our speed start to slow down. You could both feel it and hear it from the clacking of the wheels along the tracks. Everyone calmed down. As the car slowed and stopped shaking back and forth so violently, we all began to think that maybe we would make it alive through the day after all.

Soon the slowing became all the more noticeable. Slower . . . slower . . . slower we went, until again, just like at the top of the hill, we were just inching along.

Then finally . . . we stopped.

But this time we stayed stopped. And there we were, dead still on the tracks in the middle of nowhere.

It was quiet for a few seconds. Everyone glanced around. Then some of the men began to stand up and look outside.

"What's we s'posed ter do now?" said one of them.

"Ain't nuthin' we kin do," said another. "We's stuck here until dey comes an' gits us wiff anuder train."

"What could er happened?" asked a third.

"We come loose, dat's what. Muster been dat

blamed hill dat done it. Dis car muster been too heavy an' it jes' come loose."

Suddenly the door opened and who should appear but the big mean-looking black man who we'd all thought had gone back into the front of the train.

"All right," he said, "come on, all er you—git out."

Everybody looked around, not quite knowing what to do.

"Come on, I said . . . out. I'm tellin' you—ain't no time ter lose. We gotta git out afore da nex' train comes an' runs into us. Den we'll be in a fix. Come on, I's here ter help y'all."

"Ain't no train gwine come soon nohow," said the old lady next to me. "I don't know what's goin' on, but it ain't dat!"

But she rose with everyone else as we slowly filed out the door and stepped down to the ground. In three or four minutes the car was empty, just sitting there on the tracks with everyone milling around. If there was another train coming, you sure couldn't hear it. It was completely quiet.

I was still standing next to the old lady. She was the only person who had spoken to me the whole time. She was still mumbling about there not being another train for hours.

Before very many minutes had passed we did hear a sound. But it wasn't a train. It was the clatter of two large wagons, each pulled by a team of four horses, rumbling toward us from across an empty field, seemingly coming from nowhere.

Gradually they got nearer, then finally stopped. The first one was driven by the mean-looking white man I'd seen at the station before. How he'd gotten there I couldn't imagine.

"You see now," said the black man, "help's come already."

"The man's right," said the white man. "We're here from the railroad. They sent us to rescue you and take you to get on another train."

"Effen dey's from da railroad," muttered the woman standing beside me, "den I's Martha Washington!"

"All right, let's go . . . all of you—load in. We've got orders to get you to the train."

"Beggin' yo pardon, suh," said one of our fellow passengers, "but I's thinkin' dat perhaps me an' my family, we'll jes' stay here wiff da stranded car till dey comes fo us here."

A few nods and mumbled comments went around the group.

"I'm afraid that won't be possible," said the man. "They told us to bring you all to the new train. They don't want anyone staying here. They said it won't be safe for you to stay here."

"Meanin' no disrespect, suh," said another. "But I think I'll be stayin' right here too wiff da others."

More murmurs spread through the group.

Suddenly a look of anger erupted on the white man's face. He pulled out a gun and pointed it straight at the passenger's face. At the same instant, the driver of the second wagon pulled out a rifle.

"Look, you fool!" the first man shouted. "I told you to get in the wagon. All of you—or we start shooting!"

"I done tol' you dey wuzn't from da railroad!" mumbled the woman as she ambled with the rest of us toward the wagons. Slowly we all climbed into them with our carpetbags. It was very crowded. But that was the least of my worries.

❧ ✲ ❧

Getting Worried
22

When everyone was aboard, the wagons clattered back off across the field and into a wood where we came upon a dirt road that we followed for the rest of the day. As we left the open field, several heads turned around and looked back as the lone train car sitting there on the track faded out of our sight. Whether we were frightened yet or just confused, it was hard to say. I think most of us sensed that something funny was going on. But blacks in the South had been so trained to take orders and do what they were told and ask no questions that we just went along.

Knowing the men had guns was another reason to do what they said!

None of us had the courage to ask any questions after the man's outburst and threat with the gun. What could any one of us do? Each of us was just one of twenty-five or thirty others.

If I'd thought the railroad coach was crowded, I discovered it was nothing compared to those two wagons. We were packed into the back of those things so close we were squeezed against each other on all sides. We had no idea where we were headed. At least we had fresh air, but now the sun was beating down on us. It was dusty and hot.

"Where do you think they're taking us?" I whispered to the lady beside me who seemed to know so much about the trains.

"I don' know, dearie," she whispered back. "But whereber it is, it ain't no train boun' fo Washington."

"How can you be so sure?"

"'Cause dere ain't anuder one. Dat back dere's da only track from Richmond ter Washington."

We rode for several hours. There were no towns, only a few farmhouses in the distance, and for sure no trains. It was a rugged, hilly country and that explained why there weren't so many farms and cultivated fields. We were going east mostly, I thought, or northeast. Eventually the sun began to set out over the hills behind us. Still we kept going till it was nearly dark. Finally the two drivers pulled up.

"We'll camp here for the night," he said. "Come on, get down. There's a stream over yonder and a sack of bread that'll feed you all, and a blanket for everyone. Stay close to the wagons, except for the stream. Don't wander off. We'll be watching."

He sounded more like a plantation overseer than a train employee!

"I's cold," said a little boy.

"We'll make a fire, son," said the big black man. "Den you git yo mama to git you under one ob dem blankets."

The whole thing seemed more and more wrong by the minute! The thought crossed my mind, of course, but now I began to grow downright worried—how would I find Katie once all this was over? She would have no way of knowing the black car wasn't even with the train anymore! When they stopped at Washington, where we were supposed to change trains for Philadelphia, would she look for me after what the conductor said, or figure that we would both get on the new train on our own? Would they tell the people that all us blacks were gone? Or would Katie try to avoid getting in any more trouble with the conductor by just going into the station and then getting on the train for Philadelphia?

Suddenly there were a lot of questions . . . and worries!

Whatever happened, by the time Katie realized I wasn't with her, she might be all the way to Aunt Nelda's. We would have no way to find each other! She would have no idea where I was . . . and I didn't either! I didn't even know what state we were in! I thought we might be in Virginia, but couldn't be sure. If Katie went all the way to Philadelphia before she discovered me missing, at least I would know she was at Aunt Nelda's, though I had no idea how to get there myself. Katie had the directions and address in a letter in her satchel.

As I later found out, Katie did go all the way to Philadelphia before discovering I wasn't there. Just as I was thinking about her, she was thinking about me. Worrying too.

As I lay down that night after nothing but bread to eat, and still cold even with the thin blanket they gave us, using my carpetbag for a pillow, I don't mind saying that worrisome thoughts kept me awake half the night. I couldn't help remembering what the conductor had told us about bands of kidnappers roaming about, and I prayed as hard as I'd ever prayed, God, help Katie and me to find each other again.

The whole thing was starting to remind me of Josepha's adventures on the Underground Railroad!

But that was twenty years ago. Slaves were free now. So what was going on?

It was a long, hard, cold night on that ground. But most of us managed to get some sleep, dozing and waking and dozing again. I woke up tired but knowing I'd had some sleep at last. The morning was grey and wet and chilly. My stomach was rumbling from hunger.

The three men roused us up, kicking at those who were asleep, gave us more bread, gathered up the blankets and threw them into the wagons, told us to go and do our business and drink our fill in the stream, and then to load back up in the wagons.

By now a few of the men were starting to ask some pointed questions. I don't know if they'd forgotten about the guns, but they were asking questions anyway.

"We wants ter know where we's goin'," said one man. "We ain't seen no train nowhere."

"And you're not going to see no train," said the white driver.

"Den where's you takin' us? You tell us or we jes' won't go."

"You'll go, you old fool," the man shot back, "or I'll shoot you dead and you can stay here for the buzzards and we'll go on without you."

That silenced the man but did nothing to stop the murmurings. Though they were just whispers, the worries and anxieties spread through the whole group in both wagons during our second day together.

We went through a region where there were quite a few farmhouses and nicely cultivated fields. On two or three barns I noticed something that seemed familiar, like I'd heard about it before, a strange kind of weather vane made out of a horse's head. But I couldn't remember where I'd heard about them. I didn't think I'd ever seen a weather vane like that before.

It was familiar.

But I couldn't remember why.

News and Secrets

23

When Mrs. Hammond's carriage appeared at Rosewood, she drove right up to the big house in search of the Daniels brothers.

She stopped and got down and saw Ward walking in from one of the fields. He tipped his hat and greeted her as she approached.

"Mrs. Hammond," he said. "This is an unexpected visit."

"I know the two of you have been anxious about a telegram from Kathleen," she said. "I thought I ought at least to let you know that nothing's come from her yet—other than the one from Richmond the day after they left."

"I see . . . hmm, that's a mite puzzling."

Templeton came out of the house and walked toward them.

"Elfrida . . . how are you today?" he said.

"Hello, Mr. Daniels."

"She said there's still nothing from Katie," said Ward.

"I'm sorry," said Mrs. Hammond. "But I thought you ought to know. I do have one other delivery—a letter for Mr. Patterson . . . I believe it's from his son."

"Henry will be delighted," said Templeton.

"Personally delivered mail . . . that is service!" said Ward.

"I don't usually do that, of course—deliver the mail, but . . . I thought perhaps there might be news of Kathleen and Mayme."

"Well, we're glad you came," said Templeton. "Josepha will be thrilled to see you. She's been wanting to show you around their new place.—I'll walk you down."

"Thank you. May I leave my buggy here?"

"Of course," said Ward. "I'll give your horse some water and feed."

"Thank you."

With the letter in hand, Mrs. Hammond followed Templeton toward Henry's and Josepha's new home that Henry had worked to enlarge and modernize during the previous summer. Josepha saw them coming from the kitchen window and hurried outside.

"Elfrida!" she said. "What a nice surprise. Come in, come in!—Hello dere, Mister Templeton," she added.

"I'll leave you ladies to visit," said Templeton, turning to go. "If there's anything in that letter we need to know about, you let us know."

"What letter's dat?" asked Josepha, leading Mrs. Hammond into the house.

"A letter for Henry . . . from his son." She handed Josepha the envelope.

"From Jeremiah?—Henry!" she called into the house. "We got us a visitor . . . an' you got a letter!"

A moment later Henry appeared.

"Good day ter you, Miz Hammond," he said. "You brung a letter fo me?"

"Hello, Mr. Patterson . . . yes, I did."

Josepha handed him the letter. Henry sat down at the kitchen table and began reading while Josepha took her guest about the house.

They came back into the kitchen about ten minutes later.

"Mr. Daniels had hoped perhaps there was some word

about the girls from your son," said Mrs. Hammond.

"Nuthin' like dat," said Henry. "Only dat he hopes ter see dem when dey's in da Norf, dat's all. But he wrote dis a week ago. Dat was before dey lef'. It's jes' 'bout his work an' a few folks he's met an' askin' me how long I figures he ought ter stay dere an' work, an' dat kind er thing."

He rose from the table, letter still in hand. "Miz Hammond," he said, "you mind effen I hab a word wiff you in private before I take dis up an' let Mister Ward and Mister Templeton hab a look at it?"

"No . . . I, uh . . . of course."

Henry walked outside. A little perplexed, Mrs. Hammond followed. Josepha watched them go . . . even more perplexed than their visitor!

She watched from the open door while Henry and Mrs. Hammond walked slowly toward the big house. Henry was speaking in low tones while Mrs. Hammond listened, nodding occasionally.

Slowly Josepha walked down the steps and began to follow, straining to listen. Henry glanced back and saw her.

"What you two talkin' 'bout?" said Josepha.

"Nuthin'. Jes' neber you mind," said Henry.

But Josepha continued toward them.

"Now, Seffie," said Henry, "you jes' go back in dere an' min' yo own biz'ness."

"Well . . . I neber!" said Josepha.

Henry glanced back, chuckling at her pretended outrage.

"Now you jes' git, Seffie," he said. "I gots biz'ness wiff dis lady dat ain't none er yo biz'ness."

"What you mean, Henry Patterson, by tellin' me ter git? I's git when I's good an' ready!"

She turned and went back to the house in a huff, Henry still chuckling to himself as he watched her go.

He and Mrs. Hammond spoke together another minute or two, then parted, Henry to the big house to share Jeremiah's letter with his two friends, and Mrs. Hammond to rejoin Henry's wife, whom she hoped not to find in too bad a temper.

She knew Josepha would ask what she and Henry had been talking about. But she had promised Henry to divulge nothing.

Later in the afternoon as Mrs. Hammond was preparing to leave, Ward offered to ride back into town with her. She blushed slightly, and said it wouldn't be necessary. She was going to make a small delivery to Mr. Thurston before returning to town.

VISITOR TO BINGHAM COURT

24

IT WAS SHORTLY AFTER LUNCH WHEN THE KNOCKER sounded on the front door of 37 Bingham Court, Philadelphia.

Nelda Fairchild rose, left her niece in the sitting room, and went to answer it. There stood a tall, good-looking young man in his early- to mid-twenties. His request surprised her.

She returned to the sitting room.

"It seems, Kathleen," she said, "that it's for you."

Katie glanced up from the magazine she had absently been trying to concentrate on, a look of confusion on her face, then stood and followed her aunt to the open front door. The sight that met her eyes stunned her nearly into speechlessness.

"Rob!" she gasped.

Suddenly, without realizing what she was doing, she rushed forward, breaking into tears, and embraced him. Instantly she found her tongue.

"I didn't know what to do!" she said. "I couldn't think of anyone who could help but you. I'm sorry, I didn't mean for you to come all this way. But I'm so worried about Mayme, and—"

As suddenly as she had rushed forward to greet him, Katie now realized what she had done. Abruptly she stepped back.

Her face turned bright red and her hand went to her mouth.

"I'm . . . I'm sorry," she said. "I wasn't thinking. I was just so surprised and happy to see you, that . . . I forgot myself."

"It's all right," smiled Rob. "I am happy to see you too. I have been looking forward to it for a long time. Though I was concerned that after my letter you might not even want to see me.—You did get my letter?"

"Yes," replied Katie. "But why would that make me not want to see you?"

"I don't know," said Rob. "I wasn't certain how you would respond. I divulged more of myself than I ever have to anyone. I don't know, I suppose I just didn't know what you would think."

"I think it is a wonderful letter," said Katie. "I've read the whole thing four times. I cry every time. But . . . what am I thinking to keep you standing there.—Come in! I can't believe you came all this way just from my telegram."

"You sounded desperate," said Rob, following Katie through the door.

"I suppose I am," said Katie, leading him inside. Aunt Nelda was waiting in the sitting room.

"Aunt Nelda, this is my friend Robert Paxton, whom we sent the telegraph to.—Rob, this is my aunt, Nelda Fairchild," said Katie.

"Hello, Mrs. Fairchild," said Rob, smiling and offering his hand.

"I am happy to meet you, Mr. Paxton," said Nelda. "Kathleen has told me about you. But your telegram of reply yesterday said only that you would make inquiries and see what you could learn. You said nothing about following your telegram here. You almost might have delivered it yourself!"

Robert smiled. "I suppose I could have at that!" he said. "I took this morning's train from Baltimore. Katie and I have been writing and have talked about seeing one another when she came to visit you. So I thought I might as well come and hear about Mayme's disappearance firsthand."

"Well, I am certain Katie is greatly relieved to have you here. We have had no idea what to do.—Have you had anything to eat? Would you like some lunch?"

"Actually, that sounds very good, thank you," replied Rob. "I confess, I am a little hungry."

"Good. We just finished, but the lunch things are still out. Would you care for tea? We will join you in that."

"Thank you very much, Mrs. Fairchild. That will be perfect. In a sheriff's office all I usually get is coffee. But I do enjoy a good cup of tea."

"I'll go get started in the kitchen," said Nelda, "while you two young people visit."

When she was gone, Rob looked at Katie and smiled. "It is so wonderful to actually see you again. I'm sorry it is under these conditions. It has been far too long. You are looking very well . . . older, a little worried . . . but very well."

Katie smiled. "It is good to see you too," she said. "You look different too, in a way. Maybe it's just that you're older too. It's been two or three years since we saw one another. After reading your letter, I feel I know you much more than I did before."

Rob grinned. "Maybe you can write me a thirty-page letter sometime and tell me *your* life story!"

"I'm afraid it wouldn't be as interesting as yours."

"I doubt that very much. What you and Mayme did—now *that's* an exciting story!"

"I suppose so," smiled Katie. "I'm so used to it by now that I forget. And it seems like such a long time ago."

"Speaking of Mayme," said Rob, "why don't you tell me what happened."

A Quiet Talk at Dusk

25

Robert Paxton and Kathleen Clairborne were walking together in the dewy dusk of a Philadelphia evening. They had spent most of the afternoon together since Rob's arrival, though much of it in the company of Katie's aunt in trips back and forth to the telegraph office. Sheriff Heyes and Rob had sent several communications back and forth, with some interesting results. Rob was planning to leave Philadelphia in the morning, and to meet Heyes at Hanover, then ride together to the Virginia coast.

"Do you really think you and Sheriff Heyes will find them?" asked Katie.

"The leads are thin," replied Rob, "but we have to try. There have been numerous reports of kidnapped Negroes being sold as slaves. These slave traders never really slowed down even during the war—they just went underground."

"I still cannot believe it. The thought of it is too horrible!"

"I know, but true. Federal authorities have been after these slave traffickers for more than a year. But they never get word until after the fact, when it's too late. There have been rumors about a place called Wolf Cove on the coast of Virginia. But this is the first time they've learned about a potential kidnapping beforehand. I mean, not before the kidnapping itself but before the people are shipped away. If I hadn't heard from you, no one might have found out about this one either until it was too late. Sheriff Heyes has contacted the authorities in Washington. They're already on their way to West Point on the York River."

"Is that where you're going too?"

Rob nodded. "I take the train back to Hanover in the morning, then the sheriff and I will ride the rest of the way by horseback. We have to hurry—it's a race against time."

They walked on awhile in silence.

"When will I see you again?" asked Katie softly.

"Believe me, if . . . I mean when we find Mayme, I will bring her to you personally!"

"Good . . . I feel better already just knowing that you are involved . . . knowing that *something* is finally being done. I can hardly stand not knowing where she is!"

Later that afternoon as she and Rob were talking, Katie said, "I was really moved by your letter."

"Why . . . in what way?" said Rob.

"I was telling Mayme about it before we got separated on our way here . . . I think it was how you make God so much a part of everything in your life. That seems like a very unusual thing."

"Even for a minister's son?"

"I don't know," Katie said, smiling. "I've never known a minister's son before."

"Actually, it might be *more* unusual for a minister's son," said Rob.

"Why would that be?"

"It's easy to get too used to the words of spirituality, too comfortable with the churchiness. It can become stale when you've never known anything else. I suppose that's what the experience with Damon Teague did—I realized that so much of my faith had been nothing but words. It forced me to turn those words into reality."

"From your letter, it didn't sound like it put everything to rest."

"Very perceptive," said Rob with a smile. "And you're right. I still struggle with much of what happened. I wonder about the ministry, if I made the right decision. I know I disappointed my father, yet at the same time I think he understands."

"I thought you said your parents didn't understand."

"They understand the reasons for my decision on the level of wanting to bring God to people out in the world. They respect that. What they never could understand, and still don't, are the theological questions the whole experience raised in my mind and heart."

"How do you mean, *theological questions*?" asked Katie.

"That after watching Damon Teague die, I knew I could never again preach what I would call a traditional gospel message—the oft-heard, *Repent or God will banish you to hell for eternity*. What God will or will not do in the way of unrepentant sinners, I do not know. But that message, which has been the mainstay of the church for so long, is not one I could preach any longer. When I realized that, I realized at the same time that I was not prepared to give my heart to the ministry."

"So you changed your mind about the ministry when you watched Mr. Teague die?"

"It was the entire experience—losing Jane, the hatred I recognized within me, then the conversations with Teague. But mostly it was that moment in his cell when I knew the hate had been taken out of my heart. When I looked into Teague's eyes, and God stabbed me with such love for him that I was able to truly forgive him . . . I tell you, Katie, I was forever changed. And I could never get past the overwhelming truth that I forgave him *before* he repented. It was not a conditional forgiveness. I truly felt forgiveness come alive within me, and it would have remained alive within me even had he never repented. That is the astonishing thing. Love, a divine change of attitude I can't take credit for, brought me to forgive Teague, whether he knew and accepted it or not. The rest is up to God."

"I think I see," said Katie slowly. "The fact that you were able to forgive him, no matter what he said or did, is a small picture of God's love and forgiveness."

"Exactly! God's forgiveness is infinitely more than mine could ever be. . . . And truly understanding how far God's love reaches is what I fear my mother and father just aren't able to grasp."

"It seems so simple. How could anyone not see it?"

"You underestimate the power of doctrine to hold people tight," said Rob. "When the fabric of a church, and the belief system of that church, is all a person knows, they cannot see beyond it. They *fear* looking beyond it. Had I not had the experience I did inside the cell of a condemned man, perhaps I would never have seen beyond it either."

"I can hardly believe that, Rob," said Katie. "You seem like the kind of man who would have seen it eventually."

"I hope I would have. But very few people have the opportunity to look into the eyes of one who has killed someone close to them . . . and love them. That is a—"

Rob stopped and looked away. After a few seconds Katie realized he was crying. She reached out and gently touched his arm.

"Rob . . . Rob, what is it?" she asked.

He turned and she reached out her arms to comfort him.

"Oh, Katie," he said, weeping, "it was so awful . . . the moment he fell! It still haunts me!"

They stood for several long peaceful moments until Rob's emotions calmed and he stepped away.

"Now it's my turn to apologize!" he said, trying to laugh

as he steadied himself. "But I don't really want to. It feels good to have you in my arms."

Katie did not reply. She thought she was in heaven.

"Do you really have to go so soon?" she whispered.

"We have to find Mayme."

"Could I go with you?"

"What if it's dangerous? And we need you here in case Mayme shows up, or tries to contact you. I think it best that you are here."

Katie sighed. "I'm sure you're right. But it's been so long since I've seen you, and now you're leaving again."

Rob gently stepped back, holding Katie's shoulders by his two hands. "Don't forget, it's been just as long since I've seen you."

He looked intently into her eyes and opened his mouth to say something more. He drew in a breath, then paused for a second. Finally he let it out, as if deciding what he had to say would best be left until another time. At last he smiled.

"Well," he said, "I should be on my way to my hotel."

They turned and began walking back toward the house. They went about half the distance in silence.

"I'm really so sorry about Mayme," said Rob after some time. "I wish we had been able to see one another under different circumstances. I've wanted to see you for a long time. But I just didn't know exactly . . . I mean . . . we were so far away, I couldn't just show up for a visit and say"—he continued in a pretended southern accent—*"Hi, I'm here to visit Miss Clairborne."*

"Why not?" she said, laughing. "You've been to Rosewood once before."

"I didn't think that's how things were done in the South."

"We're not really Southerners."

"Your tongue sure had me fooled!"

"You know what I mean. My mother's people, Aunt Nelda and my two uncles—they were all raised here, in

Pennsylvania. But I didn't think much about it until recently."

"Really—I didn't know that. Where?"

"I'm not sure exactly. Out in the country somewhere. My grandparents or their parents—it gets confusing, you know—had a farm someplace. I think they were Quakers, but my mother and aunt and uncles weren't. Pennsylvania's the state that was settled by Quakers, isn't it?"

"That's what the history books say."

"But no matter where my people came from . . . and even though I *sound* Southern, you could still have come for a visit."

Again it was quiet for several seconds.

"I suppose the real reason I didn't," said Rob, "was that I wasn't sure what you would think . . . you know about everything that happened."

Katie drew in a deep breath. Her heart was starting to pound a little faster than normal.

"I . . . I would have loved a visit," she said softly, desperately trying to keep her voice from quivering.

"And I had to tell you about my sister and Damon Teague," Rob went on. "I felt . . . I don't know, almost like I was keeping secrets from you. We had written so many times, but I had never had the courage to tell you everything. I was so worried after my letter that you might not understand."

"I hope I do, Rob . . . I *think* I do."

"I think you do too, and it means more to me than I can say. So many of these things are spiritual burdens that I have to carry alone. Just to know someone else shares a burden like that, and understands as much as anyone can understand what is in another person's heart . . . just that alone eases the burden of it tremendously. I've really not had anyone to share it with. Some of my ideas seem foreign and strange to people in my dad's church. I know maybe I'm wrong about some things. I'm still young and growing. But it is hard having no one to talk to about what I'm thinking and feeling. I don't feel that I am carrying what I have to carry alone anymore."

"I . . . I will try to carry it with you, Rob," said Katie. "That is . . . if you want me to."

"There is nothing I want so much."

They reached the house and went inside. By now it was dark and the night was growing cold. Rob said his good-byes to Katie's aunt, and then departed for his hotel in the city.

"I will send you word the instant I learn anything," he said, as he and Katie parted on the porch. Then he descended the steps and disappeared into the night.

Katie waited until she could no longer hear his retreating footsteps, then returned inside, brushing her hand at both eyes as she went.

FATEFUL VISIT

26

WHEN THE VISITOR TO ARRIVE AT ROSEWOOD WAS invited into the house for a serious talk with Ward and Templeton Daniels, it was a conversation that would, in the months that followed, change the lives of everyone in the Rosewood family forever.

Their visitor from town sat down. They offered him a cup of coffee, but after a brief sip and nearly imperceptible grimace, he set the cup aside.

"So, those two girls of yours are gone, eh?" he said.

"Yeah, and it's too quiet around here!" laughed Templeton.

Behind them the door opened.

They glanced up to see Josepha walk in, followed by Henry.

"Are we glad to see you!" said Templeton. "We need a fresh pot of coffee. We've been drinking what's left from breakfast and it's not too good."

"Hello, Henry," said Mr. Watson.

"You didn't gib Mr. Watson my ol' stale cold coffee," asked Josepha, glancing at the cup in front of their guest as she walked toward the cook stove.

Ward nodded. "It was all we had."

"Well, you jes' wait a minute or two till I put on a new

pot.—You din't by chance bring no mail from town fo us from dem two girls?" she asked, turning toward Mr. Watson.

"No, I'm sorry, Josepha," he replied. "I didn't think to check."

"Still no word yet!" she said, half to herself. "It been too long. Dey shoulda wrote by now."

"I'm sure they're fine," said Templeton. "Probably just busy, that's all. They're probably having such a good time trying on store-bought hats and dresses that they just forgot to telegraph us."

"I still think it's been too long. I don't like it."

"From that look on your face, Herb," said Ward, "I'd say you got something serious on your mind."

Herb Watson tried to laugh with him, but without much humor in his tone.

"I suppose you're right," he said.

"Anything you got to say, you can say to us all."

Watson nodded. He might as well just get down to the business of his call.

"I'd hoped, as much as I didn't want to do it, that letting your boy go," he said, glancing in Henry's direction, "would take care of things. But I'm still getting pressure. And unfortunately, with the law on their side . . ."

He did not finish. Except for Josepha at the stove, the kitchen fell silent.

"Come on, Herb, out with it," said Templeton at length. Just give it to us straight."

Watson sighed.

"I guess what I'm trying to say is that maybe it would be better for everybody if you'd get your lumber and supplies elsewhere—just for a while, until things settle down."

"You don't want to sell to us?"

"Come on, you know it's not like that. But I'm being pressured, and . . . well, why should we intentionally alienate them? There are other places."

"What about our cotton, Herb?" asked Ward.

"I don't know—that's still several months off. It's only May—let's worry about that when the time comes. But there's talk you shouldn't get the same price as the other farmers."

"How can they do that?" asked Ward. "You set the prices."

"Only partly, depending on what I'm going to be paid by the consolidator in Charlotte. Then I judge according to quality. They figure theirs is better cotton—at least that's the excuse they use."

"But it's a lie, Herb. You know that our cotton is as good as anyone's."

"Well, that's true. But their kind can do anything they want. I can't very well let them put me out of business. That'll just hurt everybody."

"What happened?" asked Templeton in a more serious tone than was generally his custom.

"One of Sam's cronies saw Henry coming in a week or two ago, for that order of lumber of yours. More threats started immediately."

"Like what?"

"Nothing serious, but they made it plain enough what they think of my doing business with coloreds and those that harbor them. It was made clear enough that it wouldn't go well for me if I didn't put a stop to it."

"Is that all, Herb?"

Watson sighed. He was a tolerant man. This went against everything he believed in. When he finally spoke, it was with a sad voice of resignation.

"Well, you'd better be prepared for a low yield on your crop, that's all," he said slowly. "The likelihood is that you're not going to get but half what you're expecting, maybe even less. They're going to be watching."

The brothers looked at each other with expressions of concern and surprise.

"If we don't sell this fall's crop of ours, and for a top price, we'll never meet our taxes," said Templeton. "We were short last year and they gave us a year's extension. But they won't look kindly on us being short again."

"Yeah, I know that. But I don't know what else to do. They could ruin me if I don't go along. They could burn me out and ruin all the other growers too."

"We're going to have a good year, Herb. We got ten acres more planted than last year."

Ward shook his head and drew in a deep breath. "They're trying to squeeze us out," he said. "It's beginning to look, after all we've put into this place, like they might finally do it."

"I'm sorry, boys," said Watson. "I'll think on it and see if there isn't something I can come up with."

He rose to leave.

"Don't you want a cup er hot coffee?" asked Josepha.

"Thanks, but I've got to be getting back. Sorry to put you to the trouble, but this wasn't a very pleasant errand. I feel like a scoundrel having to say what I did."

"It's not your fault, Herb," said Ward.

"By the way," Watson said, "how is your boy doing, Henry?"

"Doing good," answered Henry. "Though he ain't much ob a letter writer."

"He's found himself work in Delaware," added Templeton. "He's making pretty good money, trying to save enough to marry that daughter of mine."

"I'm glad to hear it. Give him my regards when you write to him."

"We'll do that."

"Sometimes I think we all ought to pack up and join him," sighed Ward. "Probably save everybody a lot of trouble."

"We can't give in, Ward," said Templeton. "We've got to fight this. We've weathered plenty of crisis times before now."

"We always had the cotton to bail us out. And I'm not sure it's worth it if it gets someone killed."

"Well, thanks for letting us know, Herb," said Templeton. "I'm sorry our troubles keep landing on you."

"Nothing's landed on me yet. I just hope we can figure out a way to keep this mess from landing on everybody."

As Herb Watson headed back to town, and Henry and Josepha made their way back to their own house, the two brothers sat back down in the kitchen that had once been so full of life and activity. The whole house seemed far too big, far too silent, and far too empty for just the two of them. It seemed deserted.

More had changed around here than just the attitude throughout the South toward Negroes. Rosewood had changed too. They weren't so sure they liked it.

I Take Matters Into My Own Hands
27

By the second night since we had been taken from the railroad car, the men especially were getting restless. I had the feeling they'd try something before long. But they were worried about the women and children and the guns. I lay awake thinking about the weather vane. About halfway through the night I remembered why it was so familiar to me. I remembered it from Josepha's stories about the Underground Railroad. Josepha hadn't got this far north, of course, but she said the places where they'd stop and get help used horse weather vanes like that for a sign. They marked the homes of white religious people who talked old-fashioned and who'd sometimes help runaway slaves.

We weren't runaway slaves, but we were sure in trouble. I wondered if blacks could still get help at those kinds of places.

It was the middle of the night. In the distance I heard two of the men with guns whispering to each other. If I could just get close enough to hear!

Their backs were turned. They couldn't see me. I

tried to roll toward them, moving slowly so that if they looked in my direction it would look like I was asleep inside my blanket. I had to scrunch my way around some of the others who were sleeping. But eventually I worked my way close enough, an inch or two at a time, where I could lay pretending to be asleep and make out about half of what they were saying.

". . . three more days . . ."

". . . ship waiting?"

". . . think any of the men'll cause trouble?"

". . . might have to kill one or two . . . shut the rest of them up . . ."

". . . old woman . . . won't bring much anyway."

". . . much you think we'll get . . ."

". . . close to three, maybe four thousand."

The other whistled under his breath.

". . . desperate for workers. . . . last load . . . came away with a thousand . . . just my share."

". . . get to the river . . . safe then . . . barge down to coast . . ."

I couldn't be positive, but that sure sounded like they were taking us someplace . . . and planning to sell us. I could barely breathe—slavery was supposed to be over! I couldn't believe that I'd heard what I had just heard!

We had to do something! But what could I do? I was just one girl.

Now I really couldn't sleep!

I thought about trying to wake up one of the men. But whatever I thought of to do reminded me what they'd said about killing a few of us. If they heard me talking in the middle of the night to anyone, they would be suspicious and might do anything. So what should I do?

The two men finally got up and wandered around a

bit, keeping guard and checking the horses, and the night grew silent. I suppose I dozed a little, and by morning I had come up with a daring scheme.

I had to try to escape and get help!

The way I figured it, if I didn't, nobody would because nobody else likely knew what I had overheard. And I couldn't talk to any of the other people about it without possibly getting us all in trouble. If I acted on my own, at least if anything went wrong, it would only go wrong for me.

Whether all Negroes looked alike to whites I didn't know, but the big mean-looking black man who was with the kidnappers . . . I knew we didn't all look alike to him. He'd looked at me a time or two in a way I didn't like. So he knew my face, that's for sure. How could I get away without him noticing that I was gone?

Morning came, everyone stirred and began getting up, going to the woods, eating more of the stale bread, wandering back and forth from the stream. The three men watched as we went, but not so close that they saw every move we made, especially as people went into the woods to do their necessaries. Nobody talked much, because the men were listening too. Knowing that the men might shoot if anyone started something, I couldn't imagine any way for all of us to escape together, or to get the guns from all three of them at once without something going wrong.

But one person might be able to escape. So that's what I had in mind to try to do—escape myself and then worry about how to get help or rescue the others after I was out of danger.

I went slowly to the stream with a group of others, pretending to be sleepy and not paying attention to anything. But out of the corner of my eye I was watching the big black man. I knelt down, washed my face, *took a long drink, then got up. The man wasn't looking right then, so I followed a group of three or four women toward the trees. But I continued to keep the three guards or kidnappers or whoever they were in sight without it being too obvious. Gradually I went a little further from the others into the woods. Then I hid behind a tree that was just about as wide as me. I stayed there till I heard the other women go back. I waited a little more, then snuck a look around the edge of the trunk. The black man was talking to somebody.*

Hurriedly I darted a few steps further back among the trees until I found another trunk to get behind. I kept doing that until I was far enough away that I couldn't even see anyone or the wagons. By then I knew that they couldn't see me and that I was safe unless I made a noise or unless the mean-looking black man realized I was missing and came looking for me. If that happened, I'd be in big trouble!

So I crept back through the woods as fast as I dared, without stepping on twigs or making any sound. I got so far away that I could barely hear their voices in the distance. Then I stopped and waited. I was safe for now, unless any of them came looking for me.

Several minutes went by . . . then five . . . then ten.

I heard a faint yell that sounded like a driver calling to horses. Then I thought I heard the sound of wagon wheels grinding and wagons clattering into motion.

Gradually everything became silent. Had they really left without me? The old woman would know I was missing because we had talked quite a bit during the two days. I just hoped she didn't say anything about my not being there.

I waited another ten minutes or so, listening for any hint of noise. Then I crept out of the woods and into a field.

There wasn't a person or wagon or anything to be seen. They were gone and I was alone and I didn't know where.

The Wind in the Horse's Head

28

After hiding in the woods and waiting for the wagons to leave and realizing I'd escaped, suddenly my stomach reminded me that I should have grabbed a chunk of bread before heading off to the stream and the woods.

I was hungry!

I had successfully pulled off the first part of my plan and had gotten away from the three men and the wagons of blacks.

Now what?

I hoped to find a farmhouse, one of those with a horse weather vane. We had passed one a few miles back before stopping last evening. If I could just find it!

I started slowly running, following as best I could the wagon tracks I could faintly see in the grass and dirt. I still had no idea where I was. The terrain was much hillier than it had been after leaving Richmond, even hillier than the place where we'd gone up the hill and they had unhooked the car from the rest of the train. There was farmland and grazing land, but a lot of woods and forested land too. I hoped I didn't run into any bad people! I hadn't been out like this alone since the day my family had been killed and I'd wandered my way to Rosewood. I was older now and I knew that some people did bad things to young women.

I ran and walked for half the morning, stopping for drinks of water along the way. In three days, all I'd had to eat was the stale bread they'd given us. So I was famished and exhausted within a couple of hours.

Finally in the distance I saw smoke rising from a couple of farmhouses, so I struggled to keep going.

At last I reached the house I remembered seeing the afternoon before. I glanced toward the roof of the barn. There was the weather vane glistening in the sun—the metal outline of a horse's head painted black. I hoped Josepha was right about these people being friendly!

What if the friendly religious people didn't still live here? That was a chance I would have to take.

I drew in a breath and tried to gather what courage I had left. Most of my courage I'd used up escaping. By now I was too tired to feel very brave! I walked up to the front door, took another deep breath . . . and knocked. A minute later a white lady dressed in a long grey dress came to the door.

"Yes, may I help thee?" she asked.

"Hello," I said. "I . . . I, uh, saw your weather vane up there," I said, pointing to the barn. "Do you, uh . . . still help colored folks who are in trouble?"

A look of astonishment spread over the woman's face.

"Wilber!" she called into the house. "Wilber, 'tis a

Negro girl who inquires about the wind in the horse's head."

A man's foot sounded from inside, then the woman's husband appeared and came to the door.

"I see," he said, looking me over, and then glancing past me out into the yard. "Art thou alone?" he asked.

I had never heard anyone speak like that before, but I understood what they meant. "Yes, sir," I said. "But I am in trouble, sir. I was kidnapped with a whole train car full of other blacks two days ago. They were taking us somewhere in wagons. I saw your house when we passed yesterday and I knew about the horse weather vanes from a friend and lady who used to be a slave and who went on the slave railroad—"

"The Underground Railroad!" exclaimed the woman. "But that was years ago!"

"Yes, ma'am. I used to be a slave too. But the men who took us from the train two days ago treated us like we were still slaves. They had guns and frightened us so much that everyone did what they said. But I escaped this morning, and I remembered your house and the weather vane, and that's why I came here."

The woman and I both looked at the woman's husband. He thought for a moment.

"It seems, wife," he said, "that the railroad may yet be needed again. We have heard of these abductions. What thinkest thou? Dost thou think perhaps it is time for me to pay a visit to our neighbor?"

"Perhaps the tidings of which we have heard are indeed true. Yes . . . why dost thou not visit the good man, while I see what I can find for this nice young woman to eat?—Art thou hungry, my dear?" she asked, turning again to me.

I smiled timidly. "They didn't give us much to eat,"

I answered. "Yes . . . I am very hungry."

"Good," the lady said with a smile. "Then come with me while Wilber goes to our friend and they think what is to be done. Thou art safe now. But we must pray for the others."

New Friends
29

The lady scarcely had me sitting at her kitchen table and starting to set before me fresh bread and milk and strawberries and cheese, when I heard her husband galloping away outside.

She introduced herself as Mrs. Brannon and said that she and her husband were Quakers, which I figured was why they spoke like they did. I remembered what Katie had once said about thinking her family used to be Quakers or something. She was as nice as she could be and made me feel completely at home. I almost forgot how worried I was about Katie.

Mr. Brannon returned about two hours later. Another man was with him. They dismounted and came straight into the kitchen.

"Wilber," said Mrs. Brannon, "our young friend's name is Mary Ann . . . Mary Ann Daniels."

"Hello, Mary Ann," he said. "I am sorry I had to leave thee with such haste. But it was important that our neighbor hear what thou hast to tell us."

He turned to the man who had come with him, a tall, almost imposing but peaceful-looking man, whose smile immediately put me at ease.

"Hello, Miss Daniels," he said, extending his hand. "My name is Richmond Davidson. I live just over the ridge to the east. Mr. and Mrs. Brannon and my family were involved in what was called the Underground Railroad, helping fugitive slaves get to freedom in the North. Since the war there has been no more activity of that kind . . . until recently. There have been rumors—unsubstantiated until now—of the kidnapping of unsuspecting Negroes and selling them in an illegal slave trade to the sugar plantations of the Indies. So why don't you tell us exactly what happened."

I told them about the train and everything that had happened since, including what I'd overheard the night before, which was why I decided to escape. Even though I was with total strangers, I felt completely safe and at peace. That's the kind of men Mr. Davidson and Mr. Brannon were. I felt as secure as if I'd been with my own father.

"You are a brave young lady," said the man called Davidson.

He glanced at Mr. Brannon. "We've got to get some men and go after them, Wilber," he said. "We have to rescue those people and find out who's behind this."

"We ought to be able to overtake them if they are pulling wagons and we are on horseback."

"It is now about one o'clock," said Davidson, thinking. "If they left shortly after daybreak, that means they have six or seven hours on us. But you're right, Wilber, we should be able to catch them, if not by nightfall, certainly by tomorrow."

"I heard one of them say three days," I said, "and something about a ship waiting."

Davidson thought again.

"What should I do?" I asked.

"If you don't mind remaining here until we return,

Miss Daniels," said Davidson, "we may need you to identify the men."

"Couldn't I go with you, sir?" I said. "I want to help. I'm worried about the people I was with. Some of them were old, and there were a few children too."

"You are a plucky one!" he laughed. "You remind me of my daughter-in-law. Hmm . . . now that I think about it, that might indeed be best. We need to be absolutely positive before we make any accusations, and you are the only witness we have."

He turned toward Mr. Brannon.

"If they're heading for the Mattaponi River, we'll have to head over the ridge and cut them off before they get to West Point."

"We could go downriver and wait."

"I would rather intercept them before the river. Once on the water, the risk increases. And we'll have to have more than just the two of us . . . the three of us, I mean."

He thought to himself again.

"I'll ride home and get a few of my men. You saddle a horse for Mary Ann.—Can you ride, Miss Daniels?"

"Yes, sir."

"Good. Then the two of you meet me at Greenwood in a couple of hours."

Perfume and Problems

30

WARD AND TEMPLETON DANIELS CLATTERED INTO Greens Crossing in one of the small Rosewood wagons for what supplies they could get from Mrs. Hammond. In the distance they'd heard the sounds of building where the new livery stable was going up. They stopped at the general store for their supplies and mail.

"Morning, Elfrida," said Templeton as they walked in.

"Good morning, Mr. Daniels . . . Mr. Daniels," said Mrs. Hammond. "I try not to snoop too much at the mail, but after receiving no telegram, I must confess that I have been watching closely for any word from either of those two girls of yours. But I've seen nothing . . . have you had any—"

"No word yet, and we're a little concerned," said Templeton.

"It's mighty quiet out there without them," added Ward.

"Well, they are with their aunt and I am certain they simply forgot."

"I hope that is all it is," said Templeton, though his tone did not make it sound as if he was convinced.

"Well, give Josepha my regards," said Mrs. Hammond, handing them their mail.

"And a newspaper too, if you don't mind," said Ward.

"Of course, how could I forget?"

"She says to tell you to come out for another visit. She enjoyed having you the other day."

"I just may do that—perhaps this Sunday after church."

"She would like that."

Behind them the bell above the door jingled. They turned.

"Ah, Thurston!" exclaimed Templeton, shaking the newcomer's hand as he approached. "Here we are neighbors and we have to meet in town. In for supplies too?"

"A few," replied Mr. Thurston. "But first I just stopped by to pay my respects to this lady here.—Good morning, Elfrida," he said, tipping his hat as he greeted Mrs. Hammond.

Mrs. Hammond smiled. "Mr. Thurston," she said, then ducked her head.

"Well, we'd best be getting on," said Ward. "—Good day to you both."

They left the store and climbed back into the wagon.

"Did my eyes deceive me," said Ward, "or did I see Mrs. Hammond's face get red when Thurston walked in?"

"I didn't notice." Templeton grinned. "I was too distracted by that smell all over him. Thurston's boots and trousers always have the reminder of his cows about them, but just now . . . whew! He smelled like he spilled a bottle of lilac water all over himself!"

"I would never have suspected it of our widower neighbor!" chuckled Ward. "Thurston and Mrs. Hammond—that really does beat all. Wait till the girls hear about this!"

"I just hope we get the chance to tell them," said Templeton, reminding them of their troubles. "And now with all that, we've got to go cap in hand and kowtow to Taylor."

"I know you make light of my past life as a gold seeker, and I reckon I've made light of your life as a dandy, but you know what really gripes me?"

"What's that, brother Ward?"

"That when a man turns honest and tries to do right and work hard, like we've been doing, all the money goes to the tax man and the bank. I'm not sure honesty and hard work *do* pay after all. There's just no reason, as hard as we work at that place, why we should be in financial trouble. Something about it's just not right."

They pulled up in front of the bank.

"Here we are," sighed Ward, shaking his head. "All roads for the honest man lead to the bank," he added cynically, "where they'll try to take away everything you've worked so hard for . . . if the tax man doesn't take it first."

"Come on, Ward," laughed Templeton. "We're not quite that desperate yet. Let's see what we can figure out."

They went inside and were soon seated at the manager's desk.

"I'm sorry," said Mr. Taylor, "but I won't be able to give you boys another extension on your taxes. If they're not paid by September, I'll have no choice."

"We'll have our harvest in by then. It looks like it will be a bumper crop."

"When one plantation has a bumper crop, so does everyone else. Then the price naturally drops. Don't put too much faith in the size of your crop. The way I hear it, the price on *your* cotton might actually be suspiciously low."

"Where did you hear that?" asked Ward moodily.

"I don't know. The farmers talk about the various crops around the county. Some do better than others. Some fields don't produce quality cotton is the way I hear it."

"Even average prices will bring in enough to pay up our back taxes and pay off the bank in full," said Ward.

"*If* you get average prices."

"Why wouldn't we?" asked Templeton pointedly.

"I hope you're right," said Taylor. "I've done all I can for that place of yours through the years—helping Kathleen after her family was killed. I want to help, you understand. But when people get behind on their taxes, that's when banks tighten up. Helping out once . . . that's understandable. Everyone has tax problems some time or another. But two years in a row . . . that's when the people I am responsible to get nervous. Because when a place is seized by the government for taxes, a bank can get left out in the cold. I'm just concerned about what I've been hearing, that's all. . . ."

"Don't worry, Mr. Taylor, we'll have our taxes paid."

On the Trail of the Kidnappers
31

Rob Paxton returned to Hanover, where Sheriff John Heyes had news for him. He had heard back from the federal authorities. There was indeed an active investigation under way into the illicit slave trade, but thus far every potential lead had turned out to be a dead end. They had not yet been able to successfully learn of a kidnapping early enough to stop it.

They hoped this time would be different.

Reports had surfaced during the preceding months concerning two potential pickup sites on the Virginia coast, both with heavy former ties to the Confederacy and presumably used for centuries for piracy and smuggling. The one was called Wolf Cove, the other, about twenty miles south, Rum Harbor. Both were isolated and difficult to get to, which added to their appeal to smugglers. The York River had a deep channel where a seagoing vessel might lay anchor without fear of the tides as close as three hundred yards from shore. A skillful captain could ride in close on an incoming tide in the dead of night and drop anchor, a barge of unsuspecting victims could be loaded on by skiff back and forth from shore, and his ship be gone and steaming on the outgoing current beyond sight of the American coast on its way south by first light of the following morning. How many former black slaves had seen their short-lived freedom snatched from them by this new evil, and who now toiled in the sugar and indigo plantations of the Caribbean and Indies, was anyone's guess.

"I've had enough dealings with the federals," said Heyes as they discussed their options while they saddled their horses, "not to depend on them being anywhere when they say they will. If they're there, fine. But I wouldn't want to stake your young black friend's life on it. So I say we go on our own and hope we have backup. But if not, and if we can intercept them, you and I will have to think up something on our own."

"What's your plan, Sheriff?" asked Rob, cinching up his strap and checking his stirrups.

"We don't know which of the landing sites they will use," answered Heyes. "I don't see anything else but for us to split up and hope the federals show up in time at both places. If they don't, we're going to have to try to crack this thing ourselves. But we've got to stop them before they get to sea. By then, it'll be too late and we'll never get the people back."

Heyes took out a coin. "You want to call it?" he said. "Heads, Rum Harbor . . . tails, Wolf Cove."

"Fair enough."

Heyes flipped the coin in the air.

"Tails," said Rob.

The coin fell to the ground.

"Tails it is," said Heyes. "All right, you've got your map?"

Rob nodded.

"Then you make for Wolf Cove and I'll ride for Rum Harbor. If it's still light when we arrive and there's no sign of a ship offshore, we'll search upriver for a mile or two to see if we can find where they're waiting. If I still find nothing, then

I'll make my way north to you. If you find nothing, you make your way south to me . . . keeping an eye on the horizon all the time. If there's any sign of an incoming vessel, we have to let that guide us to the pickup site. All right, then?"

They mounted and swung their horses around in the direction where they would start together.

"Good luck, Sheriff," said Rob. "Once we part, I'll see you somewhere on the coast."

"If not, we'll work our way home on our own. Let's go!"

Too Late
32

When Mr. Brannon and I arrived at the home of his neighbor, Mr. Davidson and his men were waiting for us. I barely had time to get off the horse for a short rest before it was time to go again.

"Are you sure you wouldn't rather wait here with me?" Mr. Davidson's wife asked me as we were getting ready to go.

"Thank you, Mrs. Davidson," I said, "but I feel like I ought to be with them. I might be able to help in some way. With all these men, I don't know how. What can a girl like me do? But, since I was there when they kidnapped us, you know—there might be something they need me for."

"I understand, dear. Well, you just be very careful. I hope I shall see you again . . . safe and sound.—You take good care of her, Richmond," she added to her husband.

"I shall indeed, Carolyn!"

There were about a half dozen men altogether. Mr. Davidson led the way but kept me near him the whole time. I could tell he felt as protective of me as my own papa would have been.

From what I had told them, Mr. Davidson and Mr. Brannon seemed to have a good idea where they were going and where they hoped to intercept the two wagonloads of people I had been with. But like Mr. Davidson had said, we were six or seven hours behind them already.

We rode all afternoon, and pretty hard. My bottom was sore and I was getting tired. As the sun began setting, gradually we slowed and the men quieted. A few of them were talking amongst themselves. I knew we must be getting near the river.

We continued on for another twenty or thirty minutes. Then Mr. Davidson signaled everyone to stop.

"Let's go the rest of the way on foot," he said quietly. "We're only about a quarter mile from Hotchkiss Landing. If they were planning to load a barge, it's the only spot between here and the coast. Tie your horses here."

The sun had just about set so the shadows were long as we crept through the trees. I couldn't help being a little scared, even though I was surrounded by nice men. Slowly we made our way along the river at the top of the bank overlooking it below. If anything was going on up ahead of us, I sure couldn't hear it. All was still and quiet. The crickets had started their evening song and we could hear frogs down at the water's edge.

"There's the wharf and the landing up ahead," whispered Mr. Davidson.

"Do you see anything?" asked Mr. Brannon.

"No . . . nothing yet. Let's keep moving."

Five minutes later we emerged from the woods and came out into the clearing of the place called Hotchkiss Landing. We looked all around, but there was no one in sight.

A couple of the men ran up to the wharf and looked around.

"They were here, all right!" one of them called back. "Here are fresh wagon tracks, footprints all around—must have been a lot of people."

Mr. Davidson shook his head in disappointment. "We missed them," he said.

"Hey . . . over here," called another. "Here's the wagons and the horses!"

We ran behind a little stand of trees to where the horses were tied to two rails on either side of two troughs. The horses were calmly munching and drinking from them. One was filled with water, the other with feed.

"They must be planning to come back for them."

"By the looks of this sweat," said Mr. Brannon, stroking the neck and back of one of the horses, "they haven't been here long. These horses are still warm."

"Look!" cried another who had wandered out onto the end of the plank wharf.

We ran toward him and out over the water. He was pointing downriver in the distance.

"There they are!" he said.

We all followed the direction his hand was pointing where we could just make out a flat barge heading into a curve. In another few seconds it disappeared from sight.

"Just as we suspected," said Mr. Brannon. "They're on their way to the coast."

"We can't have missed them by half an hour, maybe less."

"Then we've got to overtake them," sighed Davidson. "I know you're all tired, but I do not see that we have any choice. We've come too far to give up now. There are a lot of people's lives at stake."

"What do you suggest?" asked one of the men.

"We'll have to circle far enough from the river so

they don't see or hear us," said Mr. Davidson. "Otherwise they'll be ready for us when they land."

"That's going to be hard riding at night."

"The current's slow. It'll take them till morning to reach the coast. And it looks like we'll have half a moon," added Mr. Davidson, glancing up at the sky. "We might be able to get there an hour ahead of them. But there's no time to lose. Let's get as far as we can in what little daylight we have left. Let's go!"

Stranger in a White Neighborhood

33

THE SECOND UNEXPECTED VISITOR TO ARRIVE within two days on the doorstep of the Fairchild home at Bingham Court had attracted more than his share of stares walking through this well-to-do white section of Philadelphia. This wasn't the South, but there were still some things that weren't done. Like single young Negro men walking past nice white people's houses.

But he had come too far to be put off by a few stares. He slowed as he scanned the numbers on the homes, then at last approached Number 37, walked up the steps, lifted the iron knocker, and let it drop.

About twenty seconds later, the door opened.

"Beggin' yo pardon, ma'am," said the youth, "but unless I's mistaken, you's Miz Fairchild. I seen you when you wuz visitin' at Rosewood, ma'am. I don' know effen you remembers me, but—"

He had no chance to finish. Katie had been listening from inside the open door. With a shriek, she rushed past her aunt and attacked their visitor with the embrace of a bear.

"Jeremiah!" she exclaimed.

Taken as much by surprise as was Katie's aunt Nelda,

Jeremiah nearly stumbled backward down the stairs.

"I can't believe it . . . how did you get here!" said Katie. "Oh, it's so good to see you!"

As liberated as Nelda Fairchild was in the matter of relations between the races, Katie's display was a little much, even for her.

"Aunt Nelda," Katie said, still unable to curb her excitement, "you remember Jeremiah . . . Jeremiah Patterson—Henry's son. He's like a brother to me. He lives with us at Rosewood."

"Yes . . . yes, of course," said Nelda, fumbling for words and unconsciously glancing about to see if any of the neighbors might be watching. "How, uh . . . good to see you again. Won't you, uh . . . please come in."

"I knows I's takin' a dreadful liberty comin' here like dis, ma'am," said Jeremiah, following them inside. "But I's been jes' countin' da days," he added to Katie, "when I knowed da two ob you would git here. I knowed from Mayme's letters. An' I's jes' couldn't wait an extra day ter see her. I had ter come."

In her enthusiasm, Katie had momentarily forgotten. But now she remembered. Her excitement vanished.

Nelda and Katie glanced at each other. Katie didn't know what to say.

By now they were inside the house and Jeremiah was glancing about. He was wondering where Mayme was!

"An' where is dat girl ob mine!" he said, still beaming broadly.

"I'm afraid there is some bad news, Jeremiah. Mayme's not here."

"Not here! Why . . . didn't she come?"

"We left together, but something happened on the train . . . we got separated, and when I reached Philadelphia, Mayme wasn't on the train."

"Well, where is she, den?"

"Jeremiah . . . we don't know. We haven't heard from her. She's missing."

Jeremiah slumped into a chair, for the moment more disappointed than worried.

"Would you like something to eat?" asked Nelda, slowly recovering her surprise at having a young black man sitting in her parlor.

"Thank you, ma'am," said Jeremiah, "but I's not so hungry jes' now. Dis ain't good news . . . no dis ain't good news nohow."

Gradually Katie told him what had happened, about what the stationmaster had said, and about Rob's visit.

"Dere must be somefin' we kin do!" said Jeremiah at length.

"But we don't know where she is. Rob told me to stay here in case she came or sent word. And now I don't even know where Rob is!"

"Den I's stayin' too. Dey kin fire me from dat job effen dey wants, but I ain't leavin' here till we find my Mayme!—Beggin' yo pardon, ma'am," he said, turning to Katie's aunt. "Does you know someplace dat ain't too far from here, a boardin' house or hotel where dey'd put up a colored man?"

Katie glanced hopefully at her aunt, but wasn't sure what she would say.

"Uh, well . . . there are hotels, in the colored part of the city," she began. "But that is several miles—it would be a long walk for you. And . . . it seems . . . well, uh, Jeremiah . . . if you would like . . . that is, to stay here with us, I, uh . . . have several extra rooms, and . . . you would be welcome."

"Dat's right kind er you, ma'am. I'd appreciate it more'n I kin tell you. But that'd be too much. I could stay in yo carriage house. You shore you doesn't mind?"

"Not at all," said Nelda. She appreciated the young man's tact. She smiled. "After all, I uh . . . I understand that you and Mayme will be married one day."

"I's hopin' one day not too long from now, ma'am. Dat's why I's up here workin', so's I kin save enuf dat we kin afford ter git married."

"Well, as I was saying, that almost makes you one of the family, doesn't it?"

"Thank you, ma'am. Dat's real good er you ter say."

NEAR WOLF'S COVE

34

ROB RODE HARD.

He and Heyes had separated about ten miles from the coast, and Rob was now riding as fast as he dared toward Wolf Cove. He only hoped he would not be too late.

There had been no sign of the federal authorities.

Dusk closed in, then night. But he continued on by the light of a partial moon. According to the map, he should be two or three hours from the sea. He should reach it in the early hours of the morning.

Two hours later, on the crest of a small hill about half a mile away, Rob suddenly saw the outline of several riders in the light of the moon. Quickly he reined in and stopped. They were moving in the same direction toward the sea. He must be extremely careful now. He must track them without a sound, without their suspecting he had caught them. But he must also close the ground between them enough to listen, to find out who the ringleaders were. Since he was alone, when he made his move he had to be absolutely sure of himself.

For another hour he tracked them, drawing steadily closer. Besides the half dozen riders, he saw no sign of the captives and heard no sound of wagons. Were they on foot?

Twenty minutes later he realized he had lost them.

He dismounted, tried to get his bearings, then struck out slowly on foot in the last direction where he knew he had seen them. They couldn't be more than two, maybe three hundred yards ahead. They had probably stopped to camp for the rest of the night until the ship arrived.

He crept along inch by inch, listening and smelling to detect any hint of a fire. Yes, there it was! A whiff of smoke . . . faint, but straight ahead of him. They must have made camp.

If only Heyes were here! The two of them could circle around and get the drop on them from opposite sides. It had probably been a mistake to split up, but now, how could he—

Suddenly a figure sprang out of the undergrowth to his right.

Before he could react, Rob found himself caught in the clutches of a powerful man, his wrist clamped behind his back with such force that any attempt to escape would break his arm. Another man stepped in front of him, holding a pistol to his chest. A third relieved him of the reins of his mount.

"I think you had better come with us, son," said the first.

"We've got him," another called softly into the darkness. "He was following us all right. He seems to be alone."

Shoving him forward, his arm still wrenched painfully behind his back, Rob found himself walking into a clearing where half a dozen men stood or sat around the small campfire he had just smelled.

Beside one of the men stood a girl. His eyes immediately went to her. In the darkness, he could not be sure, but—

She looked up, saw him, and gasped in astonishment. She jumped to her feet and rushed forward.

"Mr. Davidson," she exclaimed. "I think . . . I'm not completely sure in the dark, but . . . this man looks like Rob Paxton!"

"I *am* Rob Paxton," said Rob.

"Then what—"

"Is that . . . is that you, *Mayme*?" said Rob.

❧ ✲ ❧

"Yes . . . yes, it's me!" I cried. "What are you doing here!"

"Trying to find you!" laughed Rob.

"Me! How did you know that I needed finding!"

Another man walked up. "Apparently you men can release him," he said. "Miss Daniels, perhaps you can explain what's going on."

"I don't know!" I laughed. "All I know is that this isn't one of the kidnappers! He is a friend of ours!—How did you know I was out here in the middle of nowhere, Rob? How did you know I wasn't with Katie?"

"I saw her."

"You've been with Katie!"

"When you didn't arrive in Philadelphia, she wired me and I came looking for you. The sheriff and I thought that you might have been involved with a string of kidnappings we had been hearing about. We had leads pointing down in this direction, specifically to Wolf Cove. That explains me . . . but what are you doing here?"

"We're looking for the kidnappers too. I managed to escape and these people helped me, and now we're trying to rescue the others."

Mr. Davidson had been listening to everything we were saying, trying to figure it out, just like I was. He now stepped forward. "I'm sorry for the rude treatment," he said. "We had no idea who you were. I am Richmond Davidson."

"I am pleased to meet you, sir," said Rob. "I am Robert Paxton."

The two shook hands.

"Then it seems," said Mr. Davidson, "that the most prudent course of action at this point is for us to join forces."

"I'm only one man," said Rob.

"But one who almost managed to sneak up on us without being detected."

"Almost," laughed Rob. "But it turned out that you won that little battle of wits."

Davidson laughed with him.

"Nevertheless, something tells me that you are a very resourceful young man."

I could not help thinking that as they each looked into the eyes of the other, even just in the flickers of a small fire, they saw something that created a lasting bond of camaraderie and friendship. I got the idea that, rather than being where they were, they would each like to be somewhere alone where they could sit down and have a long talk together.

But if that's what they were thinking, neither said so in words, only by their expression. And under the circumstances, such a time would have to wait.

Rescue

35

It was an hour or so after Rob had overtaken us. A couple of Mr. Davidson's men had gone on ahead from where we stopped to rest and had discovered the kidnappers where they had camped for the night at Wolf's Cove. The blacks were all huddled together. They could hear humming. Every once in a while the kidnappers yelled at them to shut up. But by now most of the black men suspected what was going on and that they were to be sold. They figured they would not be shot because there was no money for dead men nowadays. Had the kidnappers known what to listen for, they would have heard in the humming a dialogue about whether it was better to be a slave or be dead. The old woman had whispered to one of the men that I was gone. But they didn't know if I had escaped or if one of the men had tried to have his way with me, and they were trying to communicate about what would be the best way for them to escape too, without endangering the women and children. The ship hadn't come yet.

As soon as the scouts returned with the news, we doused the fire and hurried to the place as quietly as we could. By then I was so tired and sleepy. I had probably managed only a couple hours of sleep at the two or three places we had stopped to rest over the last day and night. Now that we had caught up with the kidnappers, we had to decide what to do to rescue the people I had been with on the train.

Mr. Davidson and his men and Rob were all whispering about what to do. The kidnappers were doing exactly the same as when I had been with the group—two of the men were on guard, while the other slept. They would soon herd their captives aboard a ship, and that would be the last these former slaves ever saw of the United States of America!

I had just heard Mr. Davidson say, "If only we could get some of them away without charging in. It would make it less likely that anyone got hurt."

I had an idea.

"Mr. Davidson," I said. "What if I snuck in close and lay down and pretended to be part of the group again, and slowly went to some of the ones who were furthest away from the kidnappers. I could whisper to them to try to crawl away toward the woods when the men were looking the other way."

"Hmm, it might be a little dangerous," he said.

"If they hear me, or come to see what I'm doing, I'll pretend to have just woken up. Most of the people aren't asleep anyway. They'll just think I'm one of the group and tell me to shut up. They might not even have noticed I'm gone."

"But you'll be placing yourself in danger again."

"You're going to rescue everyone anyway, aren't you?"

"We certainly hope so! I just don't like to see you at the mercy of those men again."

"I think it's worth a try," said Rob, who had been listening. "By the time they realize something's wrong,

we could have half the group with us and safe. We have to get the drop on all three of them at once. If the slightest thing goes wrong, some of these people could get hurt."

"I see what you mean," Davidson said, nodding. "And you are the only representative of the law we have here. So I bow to your judgment."

Rob thought a minute more.

"All right, let's try it," he said. "But, Mayme, you must promise that at the very first sign of trouble, you will quietly and carefully get back to us. Do you promise? For Katie's sake, I cannot let anything happen to you."

"I promise."

"In the meantime," said Mr. Davidson, "we'll sneak around so that we're ready to make a move when the time comes."

"All right, see what you can do, Mayme," said Rob. "But if you think there is any danger to any of those people, stop at once."

I nodded. "Mr. Davidson, do any of your men have a blanket?" I asked.

A few minutes later, with the blanket huddled around me, I crept toward the place where all the people were spread out on the ground, with a campfire at the far end where two of the men were sitting. When I got close where they might be able to see me, I lay down and, like I had before, rolled and inched my way slowly into the group. Then I lay still, tried to listen and see if I could recognize any of the people by the flickering of the light from the fire, then gradually inched my way into their midst.

The man next to me I remembered as a single man forty or forty-five years old. I thought he would be someone good to try to talk to first. If something went wrong, it would only be to the two of us.

I nudged at him gently. When he stirred I got as close as I dared to his face.

"Shh . . ." I whispered.

"But what—" he began.

"Shh . . . don't say anything," I whispered. "Can you hear me?"

"I reckon," he whispered.

Around the rest of the group, the men who were awake were humming and whispering so we could whisper ourselves without being heard.

"There are some men in the woods behind us who are here to help us."

"Where'd dey come from?"

"Never mind that. Can you help me try to wake up a few people and get them to the woods? We've got to be real quiet."

I left him to think about it. I rolled to my opposite side and did the same thing with a single woman I also remembered. She didn't have to be told twice. Within seconds she was crawling away—a little too hastily, I thought! But we were far enough from the fire that they couldn't see us clearly in the darkness and she made it to the woods safely. By then I faintly heard the man I had woken up waking up one of his friends. The next people beside me were a man and his wife. In another minute they were gone too. Then a few feet away I saw the old woman I had sat next to. I nudged at her. When she heard my voice she recognized me immediately.

"I wondered if you'd come back, dearie," she said, "or ef dey'd done somethin' to you."

"Shh . . . stay as quiet as you can," I said. "There are some men that have come to help us."

"Praise da Lawd! I knew somebody'd come!" she whispered.

"Can you crawl over that way?" I said. "They're waiting for you in the woods."

"I don't know ef I could wiffout dem seein' me. But I feel better jes' knowin' you's back. I'll jes' lay here an' wait. I's be fine. You go help da others."

She reached out and gave my arm a squeeze, then I crawled on a little further.

The first man was now humming and mumbling in song so faintly the kidnappers didn't even hear any change in his voice. But around the other group a few more of the men began to look around while they kept up their low singing and gradually word began to spread. The kidnappers probably thought we were all dumb, like cattle being led to slaughter, and though they occasionally yelled at us to quiet down, they weren't really paying much attention.

The two men on guard must have been sleepy too because some of the people the man and I woke up made a little too much noise when we startled them. And one little girl cried out for a second or two. But neither of the men got up and came looking to see what was going on. Eventually I think twelve or fifteen people made it safely to the woods, maybe even more—I couldn't tell exactly because it was dark. But I was slowly getting closer and closer to the fire, and finally one of the women I tried to wake up who had been sleeping real soundly got so startled she cried out.

"Hey, what's going on there!" one of the men said. He slowly stood and wandered toward where I was lying. "What are you doing there?"

For a moment I was terrified. Then I remembered that Rob and Mr. Davidson and his men were close by and were probably watching me and waiting for a chance to run in and grab the men. It was probably a stupid thing to do, and I did it without really thinking how dangerous it might be. But what went through my head was that it might help them if I distracted the men for a few seconds.

So I stood up.

"Nothing's going on," I said. "I just woke up and need to make a visit to the woods."

I walked straight toward him. "Is it all right?" I said.

"Who are you?" he said, coming toward me. "I don't remember you."

"I was on the train with everybody else—" I began, still walking toward him so he would keep looking at me.

Suddenly from the woods there was running and several men appeared and the man found himself surrounded and grabbed by Mr. Davidson and two of his men. He swore loudly, but they held him so tight, even as big and strong as he was, that there was nothing he could do. At the same time, several other men ran to where the big black man had been sitting by the fire. At the first movement he reached for his gun. But they grabbed his arm and yanked him to his feet before he could get to it.

But they didn't know where the third man was who was still asleep. Neither did I.

He had woken up as soon as the man who had heard me yelled out. Seeing the commotion and men running out of the woods, he rolled over and grabbed his rifle and swung it around and pointed it right at Mr. Davidson.

A shot exploded in the night.

Screams and shouts sounded from those who were still asleep, terrified to wake up to gunfire. With them came a huge yell of pain and terrible swearing. Everybody jumped up and people were running around and yelling in panic and confusion.

I looked toward where the shot had come from as the echo died away. There stood Rob with his pistol in his hand, about ten feet away from the man he had just shot in the arm.

Mr. Brannon and several of the black men ran out from the woods and grabbed hold of the wounded man, both to keep him from trying anything else and to bandage his arm to stop the bleeding.

Rob put away his gun and walked over toward me. I was looking at him with wide eyes of amazement. He was so cool and collected . . . and he'd just shot somebody!

"Are you all right?" he asked.

"I think so," I said. "My goodness!" was all I could say.

The people were scurrying around, still wondering what was going on while the men tied up the three kidnappers and everyone who had been hiding wandered in from the woods.

Gradually everyone calmed down as they realized they'd been rescued. The children were wide awake by now and chattering away and asking questions. Some of the people were asking Mr. Davidson and his men if they were from the railroad. All I really wanted to do was go to sleep! I was so tired. But I wasn't going to have a chance to do that for a while!

When they had the men tied up and the people calmed down, Rob and Mr. Davidson and Mr. Brannon had to decide what to do with all the people who had been kidnapped by the three men.

They asked the kidnappers when the ship was coming, but they were surly and belligerent and wouldn't tell them anything and insisted they didn't know anything about a ship.

It was an hour or two, maybe three, before daybreak. There wasn't much that could be done while it was dark.

Mr. Davidson talked to the people and told them who he was and what had happened. Most of them now remembered me and came up and talked to me like I was a hero for rescuing them, even though I hadn't really done much.

Then he told them that we would have to stay there till morning anyway, so they might as well try to get some more sleep, which sounded good to me! I talked to the old lady, who was quickly becoming my friend, for a little while, but it didn't take long for all the excitement to make me sleepier than ever. I lay down near the fire and wrapped the blanket tight around me. People were still murmuring in little groups and the men were talking about what to do. But my eyes were heavy and it wasn't long before I was sound asleep.

WAITING
36

I don't know how long I slept, but it was light when I woke up. People were milling around and talking—mostly about how hungry they were!

One of the men was on a bluff overlooking the ocean watching for the ship. We weren't far from the mouth of the river at the cove where they had brought the people ashore.

I got up and looked around for Rob. They told me he had ridden down the coast to find Sheriff Heyes to see if he had made contact with the men from the government.

By the time Rob and Sheriff Heyes got back an hour and a half or so later, the sun was up. Four men from the government had the kidnappers in custody. Everyone was talking at once trying to tell them about what had happened. The government men were waiting and hoping to be able to arrest the captain of the ship too, though now they thought that it probably wouldn't come until the next night. A couple of Mr. Davidson's men were just getting back from the nearby town of Yorktown with food for the people, who were starving for something more than bread to eat. And besides that, the bread had run out the day before.

"Well, Mayme," said Rob, walking over to me, "with everything happening so fast, I haven't had a chance to talk much with you. How are you? Are you feeling all right?"

"I was really tired," I said. "But I think I slept several hours. I'm feeling better now."

"Katie was very anxious about you."

"How is she?"

"Fine. Just worried about you."

He sat down and told me about his brief visit.

"She's quite a special young lady," he said at last.

"I think so," I said. "I don't know where I'd be without her. I don't even think it's too much to say that I owe my life to her."

"She feels the same way about you. And now that I've found you, we've got to get you back to her."

"What will happen to all these people?" I asked.

"Mr. Davidson made arrangements in Yorktown for transportation to the station in Richmond so they can continue on their way wherever they were going before this happened. He's spoken with someone from the B&O, and they've agreed to transport them without additional charge to their destination. By the way, who is Mr. Davidson anyway? He seems a most extraordinary man. How did you meet up with him?"

I told him how I had escaped and a little bit about Josepha and her story and about the horse weather vane.

"Everybody has an interesting story to tell, don't they?" he said. "How fascinating that Josepha's story would give you the idea how to get away and help these people."

"Katie tells me you have quite a story too," I said.

"She said I could read the letter you wrote to her if I wanted to."

Rob smiled almost sadly, then nodded. "Of course," he said, "you may certainly read it if you like. My story is for anyone it can help."

He paused a moment.

"All our stories ought to be that way," he added, "—to help people learn more about themselves and grow."

"I never thought of that," I said. "That makes every person's life really special and unique, doesn't it—if something in it can help another person grow."

"I believe that with all my heart, Mayme. I suppose that's what intrigues me about Mr. Davidson. I have the sense that he's a man with a story too, one that might change me in good ways if I knew it."

"Maybe you will find out about it someday."

"I hope so."

"He was a neighbor to the farmhouse where I went. The two men used to be involved in the Underground Railroad together. They hid runaway slaves at their two plantations and in caves and in the woods in between."

"Well, he's quite a man. I would like to know more about him."

Almost as if he knew we were talking about him, Mr. Davidson now approached us.

"Well, young lady," he said, "it looks like these people have you to thank for their freedom."

"And you too," I said. "All I did was slip into the woods and run away. You and your men, and you, Rob, actually rescued them. Though I have the feeling that before they would have let themselves be put on a modern-day slave ship, some of those men would have done something, but I don't know what. I'm sure they would rather have died than go back into slavery. I

think the men were planning something right when we came along."

"It was a group effort, all the way around," said Rob.

Mr. Davidson looked back and forth between us. "I am still a little uncertain how the two of you know each other," he said.

Rob and I looked at each other.

"You might say we have a mutual friend," said Rob. "Mayme and her friend were traveling on the train and Mayme was in the last car with these other people. When she didn't arrive, her friend, who is named Katie, wired me and I came looking for her."

I told him a little about me and Katie. Then he remembered reading about us in the newspaper back in 1867. Then he told us about his family and a little about their experience with the Underground Railroad.

"You remind me of my son," Mr. Davidson said to Rob. "I wish you both could meet him and his wife."

"What's his name?" Rob asked.

"Seth."

"A good biblical name," Rob said, nodding.

Mr. Davidson looked at him with an expression that made me not quite able to tell what he was thinking. Slowly a faint smile came to his lips.

"If I understand where you have come from correctly," said Rob, "perhaps we could meet him on our way back."

"You are welcome, of course," said Mr. Davidson. "But my son and his wife are away, in Kansas actually, purchasing several horses from an old friend of my son's father-in-law for our breeding stock."

"You have a horse ranch!" I said.

Mr. Davidson laughed. "That is almost exactly one of the first things my daughter-in-law said to me when she and I first met," he replied. "But to answer your question . . . not exactly. We grow cotton and wheat and other crops. The horses are more of a sideline, but we enjoy them very much. I hope you would both consider it a permanent and standing invitation to come visit. You know where we are, Mayme, if I may now call you that. I would love to have you meet my son and his wife."

"Of course," I said. "I always feel a little funny when anyone but my papa calls me Mary Ann."

He turned again to Rob.

"Our plantation is just outside the small town of Dove's Landing," said Mr. Davidson. "I do sincerely hope that we will see you again."

"I hope that will be possible," said Rob. "But before any of that, we have to get all these people on their way . . . and Mayme back to Katie!"

Sunrise Thoughts
37

An early May sun had just peeped over the horizon, casting long morning shadows over the fields of the North Carolina plantation known as Rosewood. A faint fog layer of less than four feet hovered over the growing young stalks of cotton as a reminder of the night's chill still hanging in the air. But both shadows and mist would soon be swallowed up in the burning heat of the strong sun rising to conquer the last remnants of night, as the sun of God's light will one day wipe out death and sin and all their temporary hazes, shadows, and griefs.

A man was slowly walking through the fields, his shadow stretching almost all the way back to the plantation house from which he had come three-quarters of an hour earlier.

He was not by nature an early riser. When he was younger, the night and its fleeting attractions had lured him for many years and kept him from knowing the joys of life's quieter and more solitary pleasures. But now, in this autumn season of his life, he was a man newly at peace. He had become a man of the soil, of the seasons, a man of family and friends and simple enjoyments. He had begun to see *into* things with true eyes, and thus had begun to be a true man himself.

Mornings like this often called him now. There was no time he enjoyed so much, walking throughout the plantation, watching its many-faceted life begin to stretch and breathe again after the refreshment of a night's sleep. The chickens were always first, then the stirring of the birds and their many morning songs, the rustling about of the cows, the renewed squawks of crows overhead . . . the opening of leaves, the bending of stalks toward the sun, the gradual drying of ten million drops of dew on just as many blades of grass . . . and then the gradual warming of the earth beneath his feet as the day advanced . . . these and a dozen subtleties that remained undefined to his consciousness, but which nonetheless his heart felt as he made his way through the morning, all combined to make his soul one with nature in a way he had never known before coming to this place. The cycle of the earth and its wonders drew him and spoke to him as he could never have imagined them capable of doing.

On this particular morning, however, their hidden messages spoke in a strangely melancholy tone. He suspected part of the cause. But there was more to it than that. For he had begun to wonder about the future. And as is their custom, his musings had imperceptibly become anxieties. And as is *their* custom, they had slowly crowded out the peace he usually felt at such times.

He had been as far as the river, then circled back around the ten acres they had reclaimed last winter and newly planted this spring in the cotton that was their money crop, and that they needed now more than ever. It seemed to be growing well and to the same height on his dungarees as the stalks in the other fields.

He had been walking perhaps fifty minutes, and the shadow reduced by the sun's rise to some six or eight feet in front of him, when another figure appeared from the direction of the barn. He stopped and waited.

"A fine morning, brother Ward," he said.

"You look pensive, even from a distance," his brother said as he approached. "Worried about the girls?"

"I do wonder why we haven't heard from them—but not worried, really," said Templeton. "Missing them, I suppose, though I know we have to realize that they have their own lives to live."

He drew in a long breath of the still chilly morning air.

"It's great to be alive, isn't it," he said with satisfaction, "and to have a place to call your own?"

"Who would have thought it—a couple drifters like us?"

"Fate does play its tricks—for good and bad. What's that they say about God's will? I remember Mama quoting it—something about everything working for good."

Ward nodded.

It was quiet a minute as the two brothers began walking side by side toward one of the adjacent fields.

"How serious do you think this thing is with Herb?" asked Ward at length.

Templeton sighed. "I don't know . . . I just don't know," he said. "We've got bills, we've got taxes coming due, we've got a fine crop coming on . . . yet one of our few friends around here, besides Thurston, of course, is getting pressure to steer clear of us. Yeah, I can't say it doesn't concern me. It does. But what can we do but wait?"

"Nothing, I suppose. Just wait to see how it plays out."

"A little like holding two jacks when the pot is getting a bit too big for comfort," said Templeton with a grin. But the smile quickly faded again. "Sometimes waiting's the hardest thing of all to do."

"Like waiting to hear from the girls."

"Yep."

They walked on and gradually circled back toward the house.

"I don't know, Ward," said Templeton at length. "Maybe it is the girls being gone, and growing up, and going to Nelda's to look at that school . . . I don't know, I've just been having a strange sense—I don't even know what to call it—like I may not have many more opportunities to walk through these fields."

"A premonition of death, younger brother? I don't know if I like the sound of that."

"No, I don't think that's it. It's more a sense that a change is coming and that we need to enjoy what we've got while we've got it. I don't know, what if the girls decide to go to that school and then they get married and stay up there? Jeremiah's got a good job up there now. What if he and Mayme decide to stay in the North?"

"They wouldn't . . . would they?"

"I don't know. There's going to be more opportunities for a kid like Jeremiah there, and less antagonism toward them because of their color. If I was black, that's where I'd go. Why would they want to stay around here the way things are changing? And then there is Katie's young man—he has a life and job up north."

"You've got a point there. But this is their home."

"Yeah, but home is where your people are. This hasn't always been home. There was that homestead Grandpa used to talk about. That was his home for a while. Then Rosalind came down here to marry Richard. Nelda got married and moved into the city. This has been Katie's home and a good home for the rest of us. I don't know . . . maybe everything's not meant to last forever. I just wonder what we'll do if they both wind up leaving someday. We're not spring chickens anymore."

"Speak for yourself, brother!" laughed Ward.

"I'm serious, though—what would we do if they did? Would we want to stay here without them? They're growing up, Ward. We've got to face it. Changes may be coming that we can't stop."

ROSEWOOD'S THREE MEN
38

WHATCHU LOOKIN' AT?" ASKED JOSEPHA, WALKING to where Henry stood with his back turned looking out the window above the kitchen counter he had so painstakingly made for her the year before.

"Jes' lookin' at our two men walkin' out dere—Mister Templeton an' Mister Ward."

Josepha came and stood beside him.

"Dey looks like dey's in da middle er some parful serious talk, all right."

"You notice how Mister Templeton always walks 'bout da place on mornin's like dis?"

"I seen him, all right."

"It puts me in da mind er dat Scripture 'bout faithful men—Be diligent ter know da state ob dy flocks, an' look well ter dy herds. Dey's come da long way roun', but dey's a couple er men dat's learned ter be diligent in what da good Lord's given 'em ter be about. I got a heart full er respeck fo dose two."

"Dey's shure been good ter us, an' dat's a fact," said Josepha.

Henry turned and slowly walked toward the door.

"Sumfin' tells me I oughter go out ter join dem," he said,

"dat maybe dere's things dey's be needin' ter talk ter me about. You wants ter come?"

"I'm thinkin' dat whateber it is, it's for Rosewood's men ter be talkin' 'bout. So I's jes' stay here an' let dem do it."

Henry nodded and left the house.

The brothers saw him coming and turned toward him.

"Morning, Henry!" Ward called.

"Mo'nin' ter you, Mister Ward . . . Mister Templeton. I hope I ain't intrudin'."

"Not at all!" said Templeton. "We're just enjoying the morning air and talking about what changes life might yet have in store for us."

"What kind er changes, Mister Templeton?" asked Henry.

"Oh, I don't know . . . getting older . . . what's going to become of the girls, that kind of thing."

Henry nodded.

"How old are you, Henry?" Templeton asked.

"Fifty-one."

"And Josepha?"

"She jes' turned fifty dis year."

"Well, I'm fifty-four and my older brother here's fifty-seven. That makes us all over fifty. Ward and I've been talking about the future and what's to become of us. What do you think, Henry—do you think Jeremiah and Mayme might stay in the North?"

"Don' know, Mister Templeton," answered Henry. "Jeremiah neber said nuthin' like dat before he lef'. It was jes' ter make some money so he could feel like he could support a wife. But things ain't too safe fo him here."

"I understand. But suppose they were to get married and settle in the North and have a child one day. That'd make you and me grandpas, and likely as not we'd want to be nearby."

"Dat's da truf. Ain't nuthin' Josepha an' me'd like more'n dat!"

"You see what I'm driving at, Henry? We're all at an age where we've got to face facts. I can't hardly see the three of us and Josepha bringing in a harvest together five or ten years from now."

Henry chuckled at the thought.

The three men walked in silence a minute or two.

"What got you an' Mister Ward thinkin' 'bout such things?" asked Henry at length.

"I don't know, Henry," Templeton replied. "I woke up this morning pensive, I suppose. I think mostly it's having the girls gone, and the visit we had with Herb Watson."

Again it was quiet.

"Dere is anudder solution ter dat problem," said Henry after a moment.

"What's that?" asked Ward.

"Me an' Josepha cud leave an' go up Norf somewheres. Dat'd git folks—"

"Don't even think about that, Henry," interrupted Templeton. "Rosewood's a family—all of us. Whatever happens, we stick together. It took us all a while—at least Ward and me—to figure out how important family was. Josepha was alone most of her life. You lost your family when you were still a young man. Now we've got each other, you and Josepha have each other. We've got kids and nieces and maybe even grandchildren someday. No—this family's together no matter what."

"Dat's kind er you ter say," said Henry, then began chuckling again. "Dere is one udder thing along dem same lines," he said.

"What's that?" asked Templeton.

"You an' me's got a son an' a daughter sayin' dey's gwine

be married one er dese days. Dat jes' 'bout makes us real kin."

"That it does, Henry!" laughed Templeton. "So we'll have no more talk of anyone leaving here . . . unless we all leave together!"

REUNION
39

The shriek that sounded when Aunt Nelda's front door opened nearly broke my eardrums.

"Mayme!" Katie cried.

She rushed toward me and grabbed me in her arms and just about squeezed the innards out of me, and within seconds we were both crying. At almost the same instant that Katie saw Rob behind me, I saw who was walking toward us from behind her. Almost as quickly as we had embraced we released each other.

"Jeremiah!" I exclaimed. "What are . . . I don't believe it!"

I ran through the door and into his arms next.

"I tol' you I wuz gwine come as soon as I cud," said Jeremiah as he stroked the back of my head with his big strong hand. "I decided not ter wait. So I jes' foun' my way here an' Katie tol' me you wuzn't here an' dat Rob had gone lookin' fer you."

"Oh, I just can't believe I'm seeing you!" I said. "I've missed you so much!"

Rob and Katie were also catching up on the front porch, although they did not have quite so much catching up to do. Then finally Rob and Jeremiah shook hands and got reacquainted from the one other time they'd met several years before.

The next few days passed like a whirlwind. It was hard to get back into the same frame of mind as when we'd set off for the trip. It wasn't as if that much time had gone by. But somehow because of what happened it seemed that everything had changed. A crisis like that, I guess, brings people together. And even though it was Rob and me who went through the crisis, I suppose you'd say it brought Katie and Rob together more than anything. He didn't stay in a hotel this time. He stayed with Jeremiah in Aunt Nelda's carriage house two days, and he and Katie were together almost all the time and took long walks and talked and talked and talked.

The day after I got back, Jeremiah left to return to his job. But it wasn't far and we wrote to each other every day back and forth. He wasn't planning to work much longer but to go back to Rosewood in July or August to help with the harvest.

Then Rob left to go back to Hanover, and Katie and I were left alone with Aunt Nelda. Even though that's how we'd planned it, it seemed quiet, sad, and lonely for a few days. For the first time in our lives, Katie and I realized that we weren't completely enough for each other anymore. As much as we loved each other, we each needed our men too. It was an exciting thought, but in a way a little sad too, like I suppose growing up often is, to realize that the friendship we had cherished wasn't the only important thing in our lives any longer. But now we were young women, not girls—young women whose hearts beat with new kinds of love.

We visited around Philadelphia with Aunt Nelda and went to see the school, which had been our reason *for coming in the first place. It was fine, I suppose. It was mostly white girls, except for several black girls there as servants. I only saw one black girl in any of the classes. We didn't know what to think. We had so many other things on our minds—the coming harvest to get in, not to mention Jeremiah and Rob, who we were spending all our free time writing to—that the idea of starting a completely new life to attend a girls' school seemed strange and foreign.*

Of course, the moment I finally got to Aunt Nelda's, she sent a telegram back home to Papa and Uncle Ward telling them that all was fine and that both of us were with her and apologizing for the delay in contacting them but that there had been a slight problem we would explain in a letter.

That set their minds at ease for a while, but only until they got Katie's letter, and then mine a few days later. Once they knew the details, they wrote right back saying that they would personally come up to Philadelphia to get us. Aunt Nelda wrote back asking if we could extend our stay until Katie's birthday and why didn't they come up for that. They said fine and made plans to come get us in a few weeks.

The Old Farm
40

Aunt Nelda showed us all around Philadelphia and we even took the train to New York City for a day. I got a chance to see Jeremiah again. In one of Papa's letters to Aunt Nelda, which she shared with us, he asked about the old family farm and if she knew where it was.

"Where is it, Aunt Nelda?" Katie asked.

"I don't know exactly, Katie," she replied. "It's west of the city, out in the country near the Maryland border. I only saw it once."

"That's where Rob lives, isn't it—in a town called Hanover?"

"Now that you say the name," said Aunt Nelda, "I do believe it was outside Hanover. That would be a remarkable coincidence."

"Who does it belong to now?" asked Katie.

"I don't know. It passed out of the family years ago, in my grandparents' time—that would be your great-grandparents. They were Quakers, you see. My great-great-grandfather, Elijah Daniels, had come over with the elder Woolmans and John Borton on the Shield *in 1678. Pennsylvania was largely Quaker land then, since William Penn had been granted much of it from*

King Charles and bought still more land from Lord Berkeley and the Duke of York. The Woolmans and Bortons settled around Burlington on the Delaware River. But some of the adventurous ones struck out a little farther west into Penn's great track and that is how our people came to occupy and build their little homestead. My great-grandparents had eight children and my grandfather was the sixth. Everyone couldn't inherit the farm. He married and left. I'm not really sure how much longer it remained in the family. Our parents took us to look at it once—Rosalind and Ward and Templeton and me. But we were just children. We hardly paid any attention, not realizing that we were seeing our family's first home in the new world."

"Could we go see it, Aunt Nelda?" asked Katie excitedly.

"I don't even know if I could locate it, dear."

"But could we try?"

"I suppose there'd be no harm in that."

We set out two days later by train. Katie was so excited. She hadn't written Rob that we were coming and wanted to surprise him. We stayed in a hotel in York, then continued on and by early afternoon of the following day arrived in Hanover, where Aunt Nelda rented a horse and small buggy.

We asked someone in town where the sheriff's office was, then rode to it. Katie hurried through the door almost without stopping, a big smile on her face. Sheriff Heyes sat behind the desk.

"Miss . . . Clairborne, isn't it?" he said.

"Yes," answered Katie. "Hello, Mr. Heyes."

"And Miss Daniels," he added to me. "You seem to be recovered from your ordeal."

"I am feeling much better now," I said.

"Where's Rob?" asked Katie.

"I sent him down to Ellicott City for a few days. Then he was going to visit his parents."

"Oh no!" said Katie.

"You didn't come all the way from Philadelphia to see him?"

"Not exactly . . . but we wanted to.—Oh, Sheriff Heyes, this is our aunt, Nelda Fairchild."

"How do you do, ma'am," said the sheriff to Aunt Nelda, then turned back to Katie.

"I'm sorry, ladies," he said. "Rob will be mighty disappointed to have missed you, but like I said, he won't be back for a few days."

Disappointed ourselves, we left Sheriff Heyes and continued on our errand to see if we could find the Daniels family homestead. It was so exciting, especially for Katie. Neither of us had stopped to think much about our kin who had come over from England, or that they were Quakers. But knowing that Katie's family came from Pennsylvania, we might have figured it.

It took her several hours, but eventually Aunt Nelda saw a long road leading off the main road. There was an old half-rotted sign with the name Daniels carved into it. She pulled up the horse and stared all around. There were a few other farms about, one with a white man and black man working together leading a team of horses pulling a plough.

"I think this is it," she said softly. We all felt goosebumpy, like something strange was about to happen.

Slowly she urged the horse on and led it down the long dirt road. We came through some trees and into an open area where there was a large wooden house and barn. They were run-down, with boards off and windows broken. They didn't look like they'd been lived in for years.

I looked at Aunt Nelda. She was just staring with a

faraway look, then sighed.

"This is it, girls," she said. "This is the house where your Quaker ancestors first set down roots in this country. This is the Daniels' homestead. I am not certain how much of this house is original. Probably not much. But this is where Elijah Daniels built his first home in America."

We got down and walked around quietly. I peeked in the windows, though they were so dirty I couldn't see much of anything.

"Look at this," said Katie from over on one side of the house.

Aunt Nelda and I walked over to join her. She was standing in front of eight or ten grave markers.

"It's just like at Rosewood," said Katie.

"The Daniels' family plot," said Aunt Nelda. "Just imagine . . . there is old Elijah Daniels and his wife Mary . . . John Daniels, Ezekiel and Eliza Daniels . . . William and Sarah Daniels . . . this is truly amazing to see."

"It's sad to see it so overgrown," said Katie. "Maybe we ought to clean it up and pull away some of the—"

Just then we heard some banging from the direction of the barn.

"Somebody's here!" I said. "Maybe it's not deserted after all."

"Whoever it is, maybe they know something about the place," said Aunt Nelda. "I'm sure they won't mind us having a look around."

Aunt Nelda led the way around the house and toward the barn where the banging was coming from. A horse was tied next to a watering trough. The noise was coming from up on the roof, where a man sat nailing on some boards.

"Hello!" Aunt Nelda called up at him.

"Oh . . . good day!" he called back, glancing down to where we stood. "I didn't know I had visitors."

"I hope you don't mind," said Aunt Nelda. "My great-great-grandfather, I believe, built the original house here. I was just showing my nieces around—if you have no objection."

"Not at all . . . of course," said the man. "I don't live here myself. No one lives here. But the owner's thinking of selling, so he hired me to do some work on the roof."

"I see."

"Go ahead and look around all you like. The house isn't locked. Have a look inside."

As we went inside the house, which still had some of the old furniture in it, though dirt and cobwebs and broken windows were everywhere, Katie got so quiet I didn't know what she was thinking. She didn't say a word for probably an hour after we had said good-bye to the man working on the roof and had returned to Hanover. And by that evening we were on the late train back to Lancaster and then on to Philadelphia.

BALTIMORE

41

We had an enjoyable time with Aunt Nelda, but I have to say that by the end of it I was itching to get back to Rosewood and the country. Sitting around inside a city house can drive you crazy after a while and it was starting to do that to me! It was wonderful having so many books around and all the time in the world to read. But I also wanted air and fields and woods and streams and cows and chickens and pigs! I couldn't wait to get home!

We once again visited the school we had come to see. The headmistress showed us all around and took us into several classes. Both Katie and I looked with yearning at the maps on the walls, and Katie almost drooled to see the piano in the music room and to hear a violin playing in the distance. There was so much to do, so much to learn about!

The headmistress invited us to stay for lunch. That's when we first began to realize that maybe things weren't as totally different here in the North as we had thought. We sat down at a table with the headmistress and some other girls and were then served by quiet young black girls in black dresses and white aprons.

Every once in a while one of them would glance in my direction, but I never heard a word from one of them. There were a handful of black girls that attended the school, but they mostly kept to themselves. Even here whites and blacks were separated. Would we ever find another place where we could be like we were at Rosewood?

It was a week before Katie's birthday when Papa and Uncle Ward would come to celebrate and then take us home.

Rob wanted Katie to go down to Baltimore for a few days to visit with his parents and family. We had been so busy, but now, with so little time left, at last she did. We took her to the station and put her on the train, and then Aunt Nelda and I were left alone for the first time. I thought it would be awkward. I don't know why. You always expect folks to treat you different when you're colored. But I shouldn't have thought that about her!

We had a great time together. She was just like a mother to me. She taught me how to bake some of my papa's favorite foods and helped me make a pretty new dress.

We went downtown several times. Aunt Nelda took me to the Philadelphia library and showed me around the historic buildings where the founding fathers wrote the Declaration of Independence and the Constitution and things like that. I learned so much about our country's history from her. And she told me more about the family and really treated me like I was part of it, even though I was half Negro.

Once in a while she would get a faraway look and begin reminiscing about her sister, Katie's mother, and my mother Lemuela too. I came to realize that it wasn't only Katie's mother who had loved Lemuela, but the whole family.

The time I spent alone with Aunt Nelda flew by. I really came to love her like the dear aunt she was. She asked me lots of questions about Katie and me and how we had survived together at first, then about Papa and Uncle Ward. She sometimes got quiet. I wondered if she was almost envious of our life at Rosewood. It made me feel bad that we hadn't come to visit her sooner.

❧ ✵ ❧

In the meantime, Katie grew closer to Rob Paxton's family. She had met them before, but only briefly. Now she was older and it was becoming clear to everyone that she and Rob were serious about each other. Now that she knew so much more of the family's story and the grief of the loss of Rob's sister, it was a much different visit than before. She was no longer a stranger, and they welcomed her as if she was one of the family.

The night before Katie was to take the train back to Philadelphia, she and Rob were together in the small library of the Paxton home. Katie was absently perusing the spines of the books on the shelves.

"This sounds like an interesting book," she said. "*—Dealings With the Fairies*. What's it about?"

"I don't know," answered Rob. "I haven't read it. It's by a Scotsman my mother discovered a year or two ago."

"There sure are a lot of books."

Slowly they wandered away from the shelves, out of the library and downstairs, and finally outside toward the garden.

"My family thinks the world of you," said Rob as they went.

Katie smiled. "They've all been wonderful."

"Do you think you could ever be happy here . . . in the North?" asked Rob. "I mean . . . Baltimore isn't technically in the North, but you know what I mean—it's farther north than the Carolinas."

"I don't know," said Katie. "Our people used to be Pennsylvanians before we were Southerners, from near your town of Hanover like I told you about."

"It's still hard to believe I missed you," said Rob. "I wish I had been there to see the place with you."

"Aunt Nelda said our family used to be Quakers. But I've been a Southerner all my life. Rosewood *is* my life. I can't imagine ever leaving it."

Rob smiled.

"Maybe Greens Crossing needs a sheriff."

"The one at Oakwood is corrupt. He's in the KKK."

"Then maybe I should go down and run against him."

"I'm still not sure I like the idea of you wearing a gun," said Katie, "even if you did save that Mr. Davidson's life like Mayme said. It frightens me."

"I suppose we shall have to figure something else out, then. It's no secret that I am very fond of you, Miss Clairborne. I'm just trying to figure out what's best . . . what's best for you, for everyone. Just be patient with me . . . can you do that?"

"I can. I trust you, Rob."

He took her in his arms and she returned his embrace. They stood a long time holding each other in contented silence.

They did not need to know times and seasons and timetables. Their hearts had become joined as one. And for the present, that was enough.

Good-bye to the North

42

Katie's twentieth birthday party at Aunt Nelda's was festive and fun. Aunt Nelda and I baked a big cake and she had been teaching me about cake decorating and I decorated it with frosting and whipped cream and all sorts of little colored candies. It was beautiful, if I do say so myself. We had a gay time eating and laughing and singing to Katie.

But in another way, there was an undercurrent of sadness too. We knew that we would all be parting soon. We might never be together again in the same way like we were right then. Maybe birthdays make you pensive too. I think so. We told everybody about the first birthdays we had celebrated together at Rosewood. I think everybody felt sorry for us. But Katie and I remembered them with a quiet peace and joy. Katie's birthday reminded us, along with everything that had happened, that we were growing up . . . suddenly very fast. Maybe the sadness came from knowing that life continually brings changes and that you can't always tell what they're going to be ahead of time. Some of them are good changes. But life brings pain and hurts with it too, as we knew all too well. So even in the midst of the celebration, we knew that partings and change would come sooner than we wished they would.

Those partings started the very next day.

Rob, who had just come for the day, left early on the train back to Hanover.

Katie cried.

That afternoon, Jeremiah left to return to his job across the river in Delaware.

"You tell my papa an' my stepmama dat I'll be back next munf," he said. "By den I'll hab a good little bit saved away.—An', Mister Templeton," he added to my papa, "I'll be dere fo da cotton harvest."

"We appreciate it very much, Jeremiah," said Papa. "It will be the most important harvest Rosewood's ever had."

"My papa tol' me dat in a letter. So you kin count on me bein' dere. We'll git dat cotton in, Mister Templeton, don't you worry."

"Thank you, Jeremiah."

"When you come, you be careful you don't sit in a car that comes unhooked from the train," said Uncle Ward.

"I's try, Mister Ward."

He and I hugged each other and had a few private words together. Then I watched him go.

And then I cried.

The next morning Katie and I and Papa and Uncle Ward set off for the long trip back to Rosewood. It's funny how they'd been missing us, and we'd been missing them. Yet now the four of us were together again and something seemed missing. Even together, something was incomplete. I knew what it was. For Katie it was Rob. For me it was Jeremiah. We weren't alone anymore. Our lives were inter-

twined with theirs and whenever we were apart, it didn't feel complete. The family we had known was growing. I think Papa and Uncle Ward felt it too, maybe more toward Aunt Nelda than Jeremiah and Rob. After all the years, all kind of going their own separate ways, the bonds of brothers and sister had grown deeper in all three of them. None of them were married. Aunt Nelda had been but was now alone. For so long they'd had so little to do with each other. Yet now as they were getting older, they realized how deeply they loved each other.

But sometimes brothers and sisters don't know how to talk about those kinds of things so well. So as we stood on Aunt Nelda's porch saying good-bye, they just hugged and said things like, "Well, you take care of yourself." But what they were really saying without saying it was, "I love you."

Katie and I hugged Aunt Nelda and she kissed us both.

Then we loaded into the carriage. We no longer just had uncles, we had a dear aunt and a new woman-friend. We would miss her.

As Uncle Ward called to the two horses, Aunt Nelda turned back into the house.

Now it was her turn to cry.

The first day of the trip was quiet. We were all lost in our own thoughts. By the second day we began to talk, and by the third we were talking and laughing like our old selves. It wasn't that we forgot Rob and Jeremiah and Aunt Nelda, we just were able to have fun being together—the four of us—again.

It took us six days to get home.

"Well, don't keep us in suspense any longer," said Papa one day.

"What do you mean?" I said.

"Are you two going to move north to go to that girls' school?"

Katie and I looked at each other.

"I don't think so, Uncle Templeton," said Katie.

"Didn't you like it?"

"It was all right. But . . . I don't know, it seems that wherever we go, there's no place we fit in. It was like when we were on the train—when we're together, people look at us different. People don't seem to like to see a black girl and a white girl being best friends. Not that I wouldn't love to study history and geography and literature and music. But after all Mayme and I have been through together, learning etiquette and about how to dress and how to place silver for a fancy dinner just doesn't seem very important."

Papa nodded, then glanced over at me.

"I think what Katie is trying to say," I said, "is that after our visits we both realized that Rosewood is our home and that we're happier there than anywhere."

Papa and Uncle Ward had brought camping things and we camped and cooked along the way. Especially the way our money was right then, we couldn't afford hotels! Our train ride up to Aunt Nelda's had cost more than we could afford too, but they had insisted. But from now till the harvest, we would have to watch every penny.

"What did you mean, Uncle Templeton," asked Katie as we went, "when you told Jeremiah that this is the most important harvest Rosewood has ever had?"

He and Uncle Ward looked at each other. It was almost a look that said, "Should we tell them?"

"It's just that the finances are tight, Kathleen, that's all," said Papa after a minute.

"You mean because of the taxes."

"Yeah, that's mostly it."

"But we'll pay them off with the cotton."

"Possibly. But prices could be down. And . . . we're not completely sure Mr. Watson will be able to buy all our cotton."

"Why not?"

"He may have too much. Everyone is having a huge crop this year. It's just that there are a lot of things to think about and a lot that could go wrong."

"You're frightening me, Uncle Templeton. You sound so serious."

"I'm afraid it is serious, Kathleen."

He paused and took in a deep breath.

"Remember how it was when I first came, with Rosewood's debts?" Papa asked.

Katie nodded.

"It's crept back on us again."

"I know there are a few bills, but it's not that bad . . . is it?"

"I'm afraid so, Kathleen. Debt creeps up slow, but then it can eat you alive. The long and the short of it is that everything depends on this harvest. If we don't have a good one, I don't see how Rosewood can survive."

His words sobered Katie and me. We had no idea it was that bad.

"And that's why we've got to work hard to get the whole crop in," said Papa, trying to sound cheerful, "and make sure we beat the rain and make it the best harvest ever."

"We will, Uncle Templeton. I know we will. Rosewood's been in bad trouble before and we always find a way out of it, don't we, Mayme!"

Papa and Uncle Ward didn't say too much more about it. I could tell they were thinking. But I didn't know what.

❧ ✵ ❧

Harvest Time

43

We arrived back at Rosewood.

It was so good to be home. Everything looked great. The crops in the field looked real healthy. I'd almost forgotten how much I loved the place. I could tell Katie felt the same way. It was great to see Henry and Josepha again too and give them each a hug for Jeremiah and to be able to tell them that he would be home before much longer.

One of the first things Katie and I did was sit down at our writing desks and start letters to Jeremiah and Rob. We were so anxious to tell them everything that by that night we both had ink stains on our fingers.

July came and the summer advanced and the cotton and wheat put out their heads and the sun warmed the earth.

Jeremiah returned to Rosewood around the first of August, to everyone's rejoicing, especially mine! For the first time in a long time he spoke openly to me about marriage. But we didn't talk about it with anyone else. I didn't even talk to Katie about it. It wasn't exactly a secret, it was just something Jeremiah and I had to decide for ourselves. We had waited for so long—it seemed that way anyway!—that we didn't want to make a big to-do about it until we knew for sure. So it remained between us.

We began thinking that after the harvest might be the best time to get married—after all the uncertainty about Rosewood's future was finally over and the bills were paid and everyone was content and relaxed again. Jeremiah said he had made enough money that we could pay to live in the cabin he and Henry had lived in before and fix it up some and buy whatever we needed for at least a year, maybe more. Then if he needed to he'd go work in Delaware again for a few months.

The end of August came and Papa and Uncle Ward and Henry were out in the cotton fields every day inspecting the ripening crop to see when we should start picking. Henry was still the most experienced and they were waiting for him to say, "It's time." They had the wagons and packing boxes and space in the barn for storage in case it rained. Everything was ready. We just had to wait for the cotton itself to be ready.

There were visits to the bank too, and we could all tell that Papa and Uncle Ward were feeling stress and pressure about the money. But they kept promising Mr. Taylor that the harvest would take care of it. On top of that, tax time kept getting closer and closer too.

Then came a surprise to all of us. Suddenly Aunt Nelda arrived for a visit! She had taken the train to Charlotte and rented a horse and buggy to come the rest of the way to Greens Crossing and Rosewood. She looked different somehow. I don't know how to explain it, like she was determined about something. And we found out soon enough what it was when she sat down and talked to her two brothers.

"I know you've been having some financial struggles," she said. "You don't need to worry about me knowing because I know, that's all. I could tell from things you've said and the girls said, and there's nothing wrong with that. You are all the family I've got. So whatever happens, I'm part of it too. So I'm here to help with the harvest like everyone else. I don't know what to do. I've never picked cotton in my life. So you'll have to show me how. But an extra set of hands is bound to be some good, even if it's just fixing meals. I don't mind having a few blisters on my hands if it saves Rosewood from financial difficulties. You're my family, after all."

The three of them were alone in the parlor talking. But when they came out a while later, it was the closest I'd ever seen Uncle Ward come to crying. He was brushing at his eyes and they were red. What Aunt Nelda had done meant that much to him. From then on the three of them—the two brothers and their sister—were as close as the best of friends. There was nothing any of them wouldn't have done for each other. After all their years apart . . . it was so beautiful to see!

"And one more thing," Aunt Nelda said when they were talking, though I didn't find out about this until later. "I'm not wealthy by any means. When Horace died, there were some debts and I barely managed to keep the house and one small investment. Along with that, and taking in sewing work, I have managed to pay off the debts and the mortgage and to live comfortably. But before I left I took what I had in my bank account. I think you need it now more than I do."

She opened her purse and pulled out some bills and set them on the table.

"It's only a hundred and fifteen dollars," she said. "But it's yours."

The two brothers sat and looked at her stunned.

"After as lousy as we've been," said Uncle Ward, "—leaving and everything, never helping with the folks, not keeping in touch . . . you'd do that for us?"

"There are no perfect families, Ward," she said. "But families forgive and stick together. Yes, I want you to have it."

Aunt Nelda took her two bags up to what had been Josepha's room, and for the rest of the time it was her room.

Katie wrote Rob a long letter that same night telling him as much as she knew and why Aunt Nelda had come to help with the harvest. I don't know exactly what she said to him, but she must have told him that the situation was bad—like it had been before when she and I had almost lost everything because of the bank loans—and that we were all going to have to work hard to get the cotton crop in.

September came.

It was hot. Papa and Uncle Ward went to visit Mr. Thurston and he was planning to start picking with his men that same week. When they returned they said that Mrs. Hammond was there visiting, which was interesting. Papa had that sly grin on his face that said he suspected something.

Then finally the day came. Henry announced at supper that the cotton was ready. We would start the next day.

When I woke up and looked out the window, though the sun wasn't yet up, there was Papa walking in the fields one last time. Uncle Ward and Henry were hitching a team to the first wagon to take it out into the field to be ready as soon as we all finished breakfast.

And then the harvest, which Papa had said would be Rosewood's most important, began.

More Surprises

44

Rob Paxton sat in the sheriff's office in Hanover reading over the letter in his hand for the second time.

Sheriff Heyes walked in.

"What you got there?" he asked.

"I'm not sure," said Rob in a thoughtful tone. "It's a letter from Miss Clairborne. It's harvest time down there and . . ."

He paused and drew in a breath, still thinking hard.

"Tell me, John," he went on, "you ever picked any cotton?"

"Never in my life. Why?"

"I don't know . . . I've just got the feeling that they may need help. I think I may need to take another leave of absence."

"For how long?"

"A month or two. How long does it take to get in a cotton harvest?"

"You got me. But if you want the time, I'll give it to you, especially if that's what it takes to keep you. I don't want to lose you. It's been slow around here lately anyway. In the meantime, take this telegram to the telegraph office for me, would you?''

Rob rose and left the office.

''Hello, Mr. Evans,'' he said when he walked through the door of the telegraph office a few minutes later. ''Any luck selling your property?''

''Not yet. I'm waiting for the right buyer.''

I suppose we should have grown accustomed to surprises by this time.

But when the horse and rider approached Rosewood during our third day of picking, all of us were stunned. Papa was the first to see him, though Katie wasn't far behind.

She shrieked with joy as she ran outside and nearly knocked him out of his saddle.

"Rob . . . Rob!" she cried.

"I would say she is glad to see you, young Paxton!" laughed my papa, walking up behind her.

Rob dismounted and grabbed Katie in his arms.

"What are you doing here?" asked Katie excitedly.

"I have an item of business . . . actually two, to take up with various members of Rosewood's family. I thought they would be best handled in person."

"Oh . . . I can't believe it!" Katie kept saying.

"One of them was that I thought you might be able to use another set of hands with your cotton. From the looks of it," he added, glancing around, "I would say that I'm already too late."

"Not by much," said my papa.

"We only started three days ago, Rob," said Katie.

"Well, it's a right kind offer of you, son," said Papa.

"I hardly know what to say. My sister came down too... you met Nelda."

"Yes, right . . . she is here?"

"Came down to help with the harvest too. Jeremiah's home. With you—let's see . . . that will make . . . nine in all—that is if we get Josepha out in the fields! But nine pickers—goodness, this harvest will fly by! We've never had so many!"

"Well, great. I'm glad I can be of help."

"What do you think, Kathleen," said Papa, "—shall we put him up with Jeremiah?"

"Oh yes!" cried Katie. "Oh, Rob . . . oh, this is too wonderful."

"Well, come on inside. We are just getting ready to have some lunch before we get back out for the afternoon. You can join us, then Jeremiah can show you around and where you'll be staying. You ever pick cotton before?"

"Never in my life."

"Neither had most of us until a few years ago. Now we're all experts, eh, Kathleen?"

"I don't know about that, Uncle Templeton. Henry still picks more than any three of the rest of us . . . well, except for Mayme. She's fast too."

Katie was beside herself all afternoon to be picking Rosewood's cotton with Rob at her side. Now she was the old experienced field hand showing him what to do, just like I had taught her.

Jeremiah and I worked together, Katie and Rob worked together, Henry and Josepha worked together, and Papa and Uncle Ward and Aunt Nelda worked together, every little group talking amongst themselves, Papa and Uncle Ward delighting in showing Aunt Nelda what to do, like Katie was with Rob, as if they had been picking cotton all their lives.

It always took a little while to get our momentum going. We didn't seem to make much progress in the first few days. But pretty soon the cotton began to pile up faster and faster in the backs of the wagons.

A Talk About the Future
45

The night Rob arrived, Katie and I were together in Katie's room. Katie was in such a state like I'd never seen her. Rob was downstairs with her aunt and two uncles. We strained to listen but couldn't make out their words.

"What do you think they're talking about?" I said with a mischievous smile.

"Oh . . . I don't know!" wailed Katie, though she had been beaming ever since she'd heard Rob say at supper that he had something important to talk over with Aunt Nelda and the two men.

Finally we heard a voice from below.

"Why don't you two girls come down here?" It was Papa calling at us up the stairs. "That giggling is driving us crazy! You sound like a couple of schoolgirls!"

Katie didn't need to be told twice. She flew down the stairs three at a time!

"Rob here's been talking to us about a few things," said Papa. "The first, like he told us before, is that he has taken a leave of absence from his job for a month or so to pitch in and help us with our harvest. We said we were grateful for his help and told him that he is

welcome as long as he wants to stay."

He paused and glanced around at the rest of us.

"Then there was one other thing he wanted to talk over with us, didn't he, Ward?"

"That he did."

"You want to tell them about it?" Papa asked.

"No, you tell them."

"I'm not sure I'd be comfortable . . . kind of personal."

"What about you, Nelda?" asked Uncle Ward. "You want to tell them?"

"Not me," said Aunt Nelda with a smile.

"Hmm . . . actually, why don't you tell them about it, Rob," said my papa, throwing Rob one of his famous winks.

Rob smiled and looked at Katie.

"How'd you like to go for a walk?" he said. "It's a nice evening. I think there might even be a moon up by now."

He led the way toward the door and they left the house together.

I stood staring at Papa and Uncle Ward and Aunt Nelda.

"Well!" I said.

"Well . . . what?" said Papa.

"Aren't you going to tell me?"

"Tell you what?"

"Papa! Whatever it is that Rob talked to you about!"

"I think that's something you had better ask Katie."

Katie and Rob walked out into the peaceful evening. As they left the house and barn for the fields, the night sounds of the chickens and cows and pigs faded. The stillness of the night descended over them. All they could hear was the hum of crickets in the direction of the trees bordering the river.

As they walked Rob took Katie's hand in his.

"Your hands are rough," he said.

"Sorry . . . that's the cotton."

"Nothing to apologize for—I think it's wonderful. I admire you all—especially you and Mayme—for your hard work."

"Your hands will be dry and rough and broken and blistered within a week too."

"I will consider them a badge of honor to help get Rosewood's taxes paid."

"Did Uncle Templeton tell you about that?" asked Katie.

Rob nodded.

"Those two dear men . . . they're remarkable," said Katie. "They've grown to love this place as much as I do."

"I can tell."

"When I think of everything that's happened since Mayme first came, I can hardly believe all the changes. We were hardly more than girls then. Now . . . well, I suppose we're *almost* women."

"You are indeed . . . though without the *almost*."

"Maybe. But does one ever really feel grown-up?"

"I guess I'm still too young to know the answer to that myself."

"You're older than me."

"Only twenty-three."

"That's still older than me. And you've done some brave and exciting things."

"You don't consider what you and Mayme did here brave and exciting?"

"I don't know," said Katie with a smile. "Maybe bravery is easier to see in other people. When Mayme and I did what we did, I felt more scared than brave. When I read your letter, I thought you were so brave. Not only in the things you did, but also in the way you thought and the way you talked to God about wanting to live like He wants you to, and the way you prayed for Mr. Teague. At least . . . I don't know, don't you think *thinking* can be a brave thing too?"

"I never thought about that before," said Rob. "But now that you put it like that . . . yes, I do think so. I suppose it does take courage to think boldly about certain types of things."

Katie breathed in deeply. "It smells so nice, doesn't it? There's nothing like a summer evening."

"I can see why you all love it here. This is quite a place. So peaceful."

"At times like this," said Katie. "But it's not always so quiet and peaceful. We've had trouble with the people in the community—some of them, I should say."

"What kind of trouble?"

"There is a lot of resistance to what we've done."

"You mentioned the Ku Klux Klan before. I've heard of it. But do they really do things like burn crosses on lawns and hang people? Nothing like that happens up where I live."

"Mayme has a scar on her neck where some men tried to hang her. Jeremiah was taken from our barn in front of us all and almost hung. It was a terrible night I'll never forget. Papa and Uncle Ward just barely got there in time to save him. I could show you where they burned a cross in the grass in front of our home. Emma's poor little boy was drowned by men who work for one of the most important plantation owners in the county. Henry almost died last year when they burned the livery stable down. And like I told you, the local sheriff is part of it. It's terrible what they do."

"Why do you stay?"

"Because this is home. Where would we go? I've never thought about being anyplace else. I've lived my whole life at Rosewood." Katie sighed. "After what happened to Mayme on the way up to Aunt Nelda's, I have to admit that I sometimes wonder why we stay. Why should we put up with it? I mean . . . I suppose it might be all right for the rest of us . . . but poor Mayme and Jeremiah and Henry and Josepha. Sometimes they are treated so awful if makes me furious. What kind of future can they have here knowing that people despise them just because they aren't white? Mayme is so wonderful—I want better than that for her. Sometimes I wonder if it's worth it, trying so hard to make things work here when people are probably never going to change. It seems to be getting worse. There's such hate in their hearts. I don't understand it."

"Have . . . *you* ever thought of living anyplace else?" asked Rob.

"You mean . . . just me, without Mayme and the others?"

"Yes."

"No, I don't suppose I have. Why would I?"

"Because . . . what if your life and Mayme's . . . I mean, up till now you've shared everything, shared every moment . . . but what if it can't be that way forever? What if a time comes when God has something different for each of you? What will you do then?"

"Different . . . how?"

"I mean . . . families, husbands . . . different lives."

Katie's heart began to pound.

"What I'm trying to say," Rob went on, "is that I want to spend my life with you . . . that I love you and want you to be my wife."

A gasp left Katie's lips.

"Katie, I'm asking you if you'll marry me."

"Oh, Rob!"

Tears flooded Katie's eyes. Rob stretched his arm around her shoulders and pulled her close.

"Is that what you were talking to Uncle Templeton and Uncle Ward and Aunt Nelda about?" asked Katie when she had recovered herself a little.

"They are your guardians now. I had to get their permission."

"What did they say?"

"They gave me their blessing . . . they gave *us* their blessing."

"I'm glad. I know they like you."

"I asked you when we were at my parents' home to be patient with me. And you have been. I told you then that I was very fond of you. Now I want to say with all my heart, I love you, Kathleen Clairborne. Will you be my wife?"

"Oh, Rob . . . of course I will marry you!"

How long they walked without any more words passing between them, neither of them thought about. The moon, which had only been up past the horizon when they set out from the house was now well up into the sky. The crickets had gotten louder as they approached the river, then faded again as they turned toward the woods. At last it was Katie who broke the blissful silence.

"Is that why you were asking me about Rosewood and the future and if I could be happy somewhere else?" she said.

"Sure," replied Rob. "It's been on my mind all this time. We do live several states apart. We have lives that are different and completely separate. What are we going to do?"

"Remember when you asked what I thought about being a sheriff's wife?"

"Of course."

"Maybe I should ask what you think about being a plantation owner's husband?"

"You mean . . . *me* . . . make this cotton harvesting and cow milking and all the rest a lifetime occupation?"

Rob seemed stunned by the thought.

Katie laughed. "It's a good life," she said.

"Do you really own Rosewood?"

"Not exactly. My parents did, of course, but my mother signed it over to Uncle Ward and he split it up between the four of us—he and Uncle Templeton and Mayme and me. So eventually, I suppose, it will belong to Mayme and me. I always assumed when we married that we would build another house and that both of our families would stay at Rosewood."

"But don't you see, the danger would always be there—two families, one black . . . how could it ever work?"

"I thought that it would eventually get better. I guess I figured that it was because of the war and that eventually things would settle down."

"You said yourself that it's getting worse."

"I suppose you're right. That doesn't agree with what I said before, does it? But who says a girl has to make sense at a time like this!"

"What if white Southerners *never* accept that blacks are free, and *never* accept them as equal citizens? The things you tell me about what life is like here worry me. I'm not sure I would want to raise a family in such an atmosphere of animosity between races."

"So what do you think we should do, Rob?"

"I don't know, Katie. I would never like to take you away from your family. At the same time, I would do everything in my power to protect you from danger. How Rosewood and our own future fit into that . . . I can't say. And whether I could be content being a cotton plantation husband," he added with a smile, "—I suppose that's something I'm going to have to think about too! What if after this harvest, I hate the whole thing!"

Katie laughed. "You won't, Rob," she said. "I promise. You will love it. There is nothing so satisfying as getting in a harvest! I mean, you *will* hate it. We all hate it. You sweat and your muscles ache and it seems like the rows will never end. It is *so* boring and tedious! And every little ball of cotton seems so insignificant. Yet all taken together, pretty soon you've picked a whole pound . . . and then the individual pounds become a hundred pounds . . . and then a whole wagon is full . . . and gradually the field is finished and you move on and start in on the next . . . and it seems like it will never end. Yet when it is all done, you've got such a feeling of happiness and contentment and satisfaction to have planted something and watched it grow and mature and then bear fruit. And that's when you say, I love this place, I love this life!"

Rob turned and gazed at Katie's face beaming in the moonlight.

"Wow," he said, "you *are* a plantation owner! You do love this, don't you?"

"I do, Rob. And you will too. Earning your life, producing your own bread and cheese and vegetables straight out of God's earth . . . it must be how God intended man to live. It's such a pure life."

"Then perhaps, Miss Clairborne, the important thing now is the harvest. I'll get my hands rough like yours, and I'll learn to hate it, and maybe love it too . . . and *then* we'll worry about our future."

He bent down and kissed her tenderly.

"I love you, Katie. You have made me a happy man tonight."

"How could anyone be happier than I am at this moment?" sighed Katie. "I love you too, Rob."

Cotton and Omens
46

It was probably after eleven when Katie burst into the house, and Rob walked in the moonlight back toward Jeremiah's cabin.

We were all in bed and the lights were out. Whether anyone else was asleep I don't know. I wasn't. And once Katie dashed up the stairs and into my room yelling excitedly that Rob had proposed to her, lanterns went back on all through the house and whoever was asleep wasn't anymore!

Five minutes later Katie and I were in Aunt Nelda's room sitting on her bed and Katie was telling us all about it. Aunt Nelda was just as excited as we were. We were like three girls chattering away together. A few minutes later we heard footsteps in the hall, and then Papa and Uncle Ward knocked and popped their heads in and that's how they got the news.

Papa came over to where we sat on the bed and congratulated Katie and gave her a kiss, then turned to go downstairs.

"This is news that can't keep," he said. "I'm going down to Henry and Josepha's."

"But, Templeton," said Aunt Nelda, "it's the middle of the night!"

"If we don't tell them now, Nelda," he said, "even if I have to wake them up to do it, we'll get a dreadful scolding from Josepha at breakfast."

Katie and Uncle Ward and I laughed so hard. We knew he was right!

"Hold on, brother Templeton!" said Uncle Ward. "I'll join you."

A few minutes later we heard a few hoots and laughs and Praise da Lawds! from off in the distance, and we laughed again. When we finally got sleepy, Katie asked me to come sleep with her and I did. We talked quietly in her bed for another hour. That's when I first told her that Jeremiah and I had been talking about possibly marrying after the harvest.

"Oh, Mayme . . . that's wonderful!" she exclaimed. "You've waited so long and patiently."

But then gradually I could tell the news began to work on Katie in another way too. Funny as it seems to say it, telling her what I did made us both sad in a way. We both realized that the time of our special friendship, when we could be together completely and didn't have to share each other with anyone, was coming to an end. We both wanted to be married. But we didn't want to lose this part of our lives either. It was a consequence of falling in love neither of us had anticipated.

And then I told Katie that Jeremiah and I had talked about staying in Jeremiah's cabin and fixing it up. I thought it would make her glad that we would be staying so close and wouldn't be leaving Rosewood. And I think that part of it did make her glad at first.

But then she got quiet. She was realizing for the first time, I guess you'd say, that there weren't enough houses at Rosewood to go around. Henry and Josepha now had their place. Jeremiah and I would fix up Jeremiah's cabin. That left only the big house and it was only right that Papa and Uncle Ward keep living there. At least that's how I knew Katie would think. There would be no place left for her and Rob!

They could build a new house, of course. But right now there wasn't money enough, and that's when the idea came into Katie's head that maybe she was going to be the one to leave Rosewood, and how could that not make her sad, even if she would be with Rob? She didn't want to leave here and go to some little town in Pennsylvania and sit at home all by herself with nothing to do and be the wife of a sheriff's deputy. She didn't tell me all this that night, but over the next few days, from things she said, I figured out what was worrying her.

That didn't keep her from being happy. Part of her was ecstatic about really belonging to Rob. But being spoken for suddenly makes you start thinking about things in a whole new way, and some of those new things you have to think about can be a little fearsome. Being engaged means change. And sometimes change is hard.

We didn't make it out into the fields quite so early the next morning! But the whole place was abuzz and excited over the news about Katie and Rob. I don't know if anyone else besides Katie was wondering what it might mean, and whether it meant that Katie would leave Rosewood. If so, no one mentioned it. I suppose it was something we would have to think about sometime, just like Rob and Katie would have to think about it. Katie was the life and soul of Rosewood. How could there even be a Rosewood without Katie? No one wanted to think about such things now.

Katie didn't get much cotton picked that day. She

was too busy looking at Rob and the two of them talking and smiling. It was only Rob's second day and Katie was supposed to be teaching him, yet she was distracted as she could be! But the next day they did a little more, and by then the rest of us were going pretty good, and Henry was whizzing up and down the rows as if the rest of us were standing still.

The days passed and the piles of cotton mounted.

The conversations shifted as we moved along and passed each other in our rows. One day Katie and I found ourselves together again and were talking away like we always did. We looked up and saw Rob and Jeremiah in the distance also working together and laughing and talking. They spent the rest of the day working together and soon were becoming the best of friends. By then Rob could just about keep up with Jeremiah too.

Aunt Nelda was so funny, all dressed up in one of Katie's mama's work dresses and sun hats. She had been a city girl all her life, and now there she was with her brothers, the three of them, going a little slower than the rest of us, looking like they were having so much fun. I found myself wondering what it had been like when they were children playing together. Did Papa and Uncle Ward play boy stuff together while Aunt Nelda and Katie's mother played dolls and house, or did all four romp about outside and play and get into mischief together? To see them now, you'd think they'd been friends all their lives. And to be able to work side by side on something so important, that draws people together all the more.

No one had been into town from Rosewood in a couple of weeks.

"We's be needin' coffee an' salt an' a few other things, Mister Templeton," Josepha announced at breakfast. "Somebody's gots ter be goin' inter town one er dese days."

Templeton glanced around the table, not particularly anxious to lose any of the work crew for half a day.

"How about Jeremiah and I going in for it?" said Rob. "I haven't seen much of your town, nor met the famous Mrs. Hammond I've heard so much about. We'll be back within a couple of hours—what do you say, Jeremiah?"

"Fine by me," said Jeremiah, nodding. "What does you think, Mister Templeton?"

None of the blacks had gone to town in probably two months. But there had been no trouble for a long time and everyone hoped that the worst was behind them.

"Sure," said Templeton, "I suppose there's no harm in it. But just go into the store and do your business and come home. Jeremiah, I know you'd probably like to see how things are going at Watson's . . . but don't. When he's ready to hire you back, he'll let us know."

"All right, Mister Templeton. I understand."

As soon as breakfast was over, they saddled two horses and galloped off. They arrived at Greens Crossing about half past eight, soon after Mrs. Hammond had opened her doors.

"Mo'nin' ter you, Miz Hammond," said Jeremiah as they walked in.

"Hello, Jeremiah," replied Mrs. Hammond, glancing toward the young man with him.

"Rob, dis is Miz Hammond, she's a good frien' ter my stepmama . . . well, I reckon you's a frien' ter all ob us, ain't you, Miz Hammond?"

"I hope so, Jeremiah."

"Miz Hammond, dis here's Rob Paxton. He's from up norf by Baltimore. Lives in Pennsylvania nowadays."

"I am pleased to meet you, ma'am," said Rob with a smile and shaking her hand.

"Likewise, Mr. Paxton. Are you, uh . . . visiting here?"

"You'll neber believe it, Miz Hammond," said Jeremiah, "but you's lookin' at da man dat jes' proposed ter Miz Katie."

"Well . . . my goodness! That is wonderful news!" said Mrs. Hammond. "Congratulations, Mr. Paxton. And now I recall your name—you must be the young man who has been writing to Kathleen."

"Yes, ma'am," laughed Rob. "I suppose that would be me. I came down to help out with the cotton harvest and . . . well, as Jeremiah said, to ask Katie to marry me. I am happy to say that she consented."

"I am happy for you both. Have you set a date yet for the wedding?"

"No, ma'am. It has all happened rather recently."

"Well, that is one wedding I do not want to miss."

"I will make sure you receive the first invitation to be sent out," said Rob.

Mrs. Hammond smiled, clearly pleased.

"Now, Miz Hammond," said Jeremiah, "we's be needin' a few things an' we gots ter be gettin' back right soon. Here's a list from Josepha. She sends you her regards."

Mrs. Hammond took the list and within five minutes Jeremiah and Rob were leaving the store with several sacks under their arms.

As they turned up the boardwalk where their horses were tied, they saw three white boys approaching from the other direction.

"Uh-oh . . ." said Jeremiah.

"What is it?" said Rob.

"It's Deke Steeves," whispered Jeremiah. "Jes' don't say nuthin'."

Steeves and his two cohorts paused beside the horses and waited.

Rob and Jeremiah walked off the boardwalk into the dirt street and to the backs of their two horses, where they loaded the goods and mail into their saddlebags. Then they went to their horses' heads to loosen the reins from the rail.

Rob nodded and smiled. "Hello," he said, reaching for his reins.

Steeves stepped toward him. "Nobody must have told you," he said. "This is my own personal hitching rail."

"I see," said Rob. "No . . . no one told me."

"Well, now you know. What are you going to do about it?"

"I don't suppose there's much I can do about it now," said Rob, "other than to apologize and tell you it won't happen again."

"Little late for apologies, white boy," said Steeves, who was about the same age as Rob. "What are you doing with that nigger trash?"

"I am not exactly sure whom you are referring to," said Rob.

At the word *whom*, Steeves glanced at his friends with raised eyebrows.

"If you mean Jeremiah here," Rob went on, "he and I just picked up a few things in the store, and now we are leaving town."

"You'll leave town when I say you can leave town," Steeves shot back. "Now I asked what you are doing with *him*."

"And I told you. But if you really want to know," Rob added, who, in spite of his calm exterior, was rapidly heating up inside, "he is my friend."

Steeves laughed. "Then that makes you trash just like him! Don't it, boys?"

Steeves' companions laughed with him, although they eyed the two carefully. One of them had tangled with

Jeremiah before, and his tall white friend looked more than capable of handling himself.

"You see, boy," Steeves said, "since you ain't from around here, you need to learn how things is. And here white folks don't mix with the likes of him."

"It is a little different where I come from," said Rob, smiling.

"You making fun of me, boy?"

"Not at all. I'm a Southerner too, if you want to know. Maryland was my home, as confederate a state as North Carolina. But people in my state believe that the war is over and that it is time to move on. But again, I sincerely apologize for using your hitching rail."

Rob reached for his reins, but this time Steeves' hand on his arm restrained him.

"I think maybe you need to learn some manners," said Steeves. The menace in his tone was unmistakable.

Inwardly Rob sighed, more from frustration than fear.

"What do you say, boys?" Steeves went on. "Should we show them both that they ought to stay out of our town?"

At Rob's side, Jeremiah inched forward. Rob reached out an arm to stop him.

"What's the matter, white boy? Why don't you say anything? I think you're nothing but a coward!"

The next instant Steeves' fist was flying through the air straight at Rob's jaw. With a quick jerk of the head sideways, Rob avoided the blow. Losing his balance, Steeves stumbled off the boardwalk into the street. Enraged to look both impotent and foolish, Steeves recovered himself and rushed Rob with a full body blow and knocked him to the ground. The same moment his two friends, whether eagerly or not, rushed Jeremiah. Jeremiah was able to hold his own well enough against the two, and within a minute or two they began to back off. Neither of them were anxious to receive the brunt of his fist in their face. Rob, however, only tried to protect his face with his hands and therefore received bruising blows to his stomach, ribs, shoulders, and head.

Seeing his friends backing away and knowing he was only seconds away from being attacked himself by Jeremiah, a thought he did not relish, Steeves relented in his assault and stood, giving Rob one final kick in the ribs.

"Just as I thought," he sneered. "You're nothing but a coward. Who else would hang out with nigger trash? Come on, boys!"

Jeremiah helped Rob to his feet as the three walked off down the street laughing.

"You all right?" said Jeremiah.

"I wouldn't say that," groaned Rob.

"I wish you'd hab let me gib him what he's got comin'."

"It's better this way. Let him think I'm a coward—it's better than you and he squaring off. Then he'd have to get revenge and that's never good. They think we're a couple of fools and that's fine with me."

He felt his head and chest, winced a few times in pain, then brushed the dirt from his shirt and trousers.

"He's a powerful kid . . . I'm going to have some nasty bruises. But I managed to keep him away from my face. I don't think anything's broken."

Seeds
47

When Jeremiah and Rob arrived home, Katie ran out to meet them. When she saw Rob's torn coat and the gash at his hairline she halted midstride, with her hand over her mouth.

"I'm all right," Rob said, but he winced as he swung his leg over the saddle to dismount. Katie hurried to help him, taking his arm and leading him into the house. When he explained what happened, Katie sighed and shook her head.

"Welcome to North Carolina."

After Katie had bandaged the cut on his head and wrapped his chest to support a couple of tender ribs, Jeremiah came in from putting away the horses and handed her the mail they had picked up in town that day. There was another letter from Micah and Emma. Katie read it aloud that evening at the supper table.

> "Dear Katie and Mayme and everyone at Rosewood,
>
> "While we were waiting in Utah deciding which route to take to the West Coast, the most extraordinary thing happened. I saw a man in the distance. He had a grey beard and was, of course, older than I remembered him, but I chased after him and called out the single name, 'Hawk!'

"The man turned. It was indeed the Hawk of my youth who had stopped me that night on the streets of Chicago and turned my life around.

"His eyes scanned me but for an instant. Though I was now a man and he had not seen me since my youth, as is Hawk's way, he can see inside people with the most penetrating insight and vision. He knew me almost instantly. We embraced and I scarcely thought he would let go! When we stood back, his eyes were wet. Imagine—tears to see me!

"'I would like you to meet my wife Emma,' I said.

"They shook hands and he gazed deeply into Emma's eyes. She said she felt he knew all her history in an instant and the struggle it had been for her to recognize worth within herself. He simply nodded and smiled. It was enough.

"That is Hawk! He is always looking for what an individual can, and should, become. When he sees true becoming, as he perceived in Emma, he always rejoices. It is what he lives for—to see people grow. He had come west before the war, shortly after I knew him. He had mostly lived in the mountains and wilds among the Paiute Indians. He was in Utah at that time negotiating with government officials on their behalf.

"He was older but, if anything, wiser and even more committed to speak God's truth into the lives of those God sends to him. Of course, I told him my story and how his influence had set me on the road of responsibility, maturity, and spiritual growth. Again tears filled his eyes.

"Oh, how I wish you could meet him.

"Hawk urged us to accompany him to California. He said if we were determined to settle in Oregon, he would personally take us north from San Francisco or Sacramento. The way is not hard, he said, mostly through dense forests rather than high mountains.

"So when you receive this we will be on our way to California, with plans yet uncertain as to where we will end up. We will winter with Hawk and some friends he has near Sacramento, a man named Zack Hollister and his wife, a Paiute Indian named Laughing Waters—"

"Wait a minute," said Uncle Ward as Katie read. "Are those *our* Hollisters, Templeton? Didn't Drum Hollister have a kid called Zack?"

"I believe you're right," Templeton replied. "It's been a long time, though. You knew them better than I did."

He nodded at Katie and she continued reading.

"Hawk says that Zack and I had a lot in common when he was young. I asked what he meant and he just smiled. 'When you meet him,' he said, 'ask him to tell you his story. I'm sure then you'll understand.'

"Our long journey will soon be over. Winter will be upon us, but we will be in California. How we hunger for news of you all. But that will have to wait until we have an address where you can write to us. We are very happy, though we miss you. Emma sends you as much love as a letter can contain.

"Yours,

"Micah and Emma Duff"

❧ ✵ ❧

The following Sunday when we were taking a break from the harvest, Katie and Rob were sitting on the porch in the afternoon. I walked up and joined them. Pretty soon we were all three talking.

"I hope you don't mind, Rob," I said, "but Katie

showed me your letter—you know, the long one about what happened with that man who was hung."

"I don't mind at all," he said. "It's part of me. I have nothing to hide."

"It was . . . not like anything I've heard people talk about before . . . wasn't it, Katie?"

Katie smiled and nodded. "I hope you don't mind, Rob," she said. "We've talked about it quite a bit."

"It was a trying and difficult experience," said Rob. "I learned a lot about God, about myself, about sin . . . about so many things. If anyone else can benefit from what I went through, I will be glad."

"Ever since Mayme and I have been together," said Katie, "we've talked about the Bible and God and trying to obey Him and live like He wants us to. We've prayed together too, haven't we, Mayme? But I think your letter made us realize how much more there is to it if someone is really serious about living for God. Is that sort of what you were trying to say, Mayme?"

"Something like that," I said. "I think what stood out to me most was how serious and dedicated you were to doing what God wanted you to do. Besides Micah Duff, I've never known anyone who took their faith so personally and deeply."

"I understand," said Rob, nodding. "I suppose it is a little unusual. There are thousands of people in church every Sunday, but my guess is it's a smaller number for whom faith is real and personal and dynamic."

"I loved what you said about God being a good Father," I said. "Is that really true?"

"I believe it with all my heart."

"It's not how revival preachers talk about Him when they're trying to scare people about hell."

Rob smiled. "I know," he said. "It's a common prob-

lem. Especially for someone like me who grew up as much in church as at home. Now that I have come to know God so differently, and to see how much greater is His unconditional love for humanity than is commonly believed, it breaks my heart to realize that in many people's minds He is a giant ogre."

By then Henry had wandered up and was seated on one of the steps of the porch. Uncle Ward and Papa had been listening from the front room and had gotten up out of their chairs and were now standing in the open front door of the house.

"But don't you think it is because you're a minister's son that you know those things and take your faith so seriously?" I asked.

Rob laughed. "I'm sorry for laughing," he said. "I don't mean to take your question lightly. But if anything, just the opposite is the case. It's such a common misperception that some people are cut out to be more spiritual than others. God wants to be active in everyone's life, not only people who happen to be religious. I am just trying to live like I think He wants everyone to live. I see nothing special or out of the ordinary in it. I do as many selfish things and think just as many selfish thoughts as anyone else. But with His help, I'm trying. I think that's all God expects."

"What do you mean by God wanting to be active in everyone's lives?" asked my papa from the doorway.

Rob thought about it a minute. "Maybe I said that backwards," he answered. "God wants us to actively seek His life."

"How do you do that?"

"Like I said, He wants us to live the way He intended people—all people—to live. He wants us to actively live that way instead of just taking things as they come. He wants us to be involved with Him, so

that He can be involved with us."

"How does He intend people to live?" I asked. "Do you mean being nice . . . being good?"

"Sure, in its simplest form, I suppose that's about it." Rob nodded. "To be kind, gracious, unselfish, slow to speak, slow to anger, giving, considerate, compassionate—to do what Jesus said."

"But what do you mean . . . involved with Him?" asked Katie.

Rob thought a few seconds.

"To bring Him actively into your life," he said, "—into your thoughts and your attitudes, into how you treat people and how you make decisions, how you think about things, how you approach everything in life. It means asking God what He wants us to do, when we're uncertain about anything."

"You mean praying?" I asked.

"Yes—praying about how to live and what God wants us to do. It's not really very complicated."

Jeremiah now came around from the side and sat down on the grass. Before much longer Josepha had joined us from the kitchen. Now everyone was listening to what Rob was saying.

"We've tried to do what you're talking about," I said. "Henry has helped us a lot too. He always talks about obeying what Jesus said too, don't you, Henry?"

"Ain't nuthin' more important den dat—prayin' an' axin' God what ter do . . . den doin' it."

"But I've never heard anyone talk like you did in your letter about what was going on inside you," I said, "about your own sin and wrong attitudes, about what God was trying to do inside to change you. You talked about Him making you more like Jesus himself."

"I never heard da likes er dat before," said Josepha.

Rob smiled. "I suppose that is a pretty bold thing to

say you want to make of your life."

"Who can possibly do dat?" Josepha asked.

"I believe we all can, if we make that our daily prayer," replied Rob. "At least that's my opinion. I believe that is what God is trying to do in all of us. I believe that is the one prayer He wants us all to pray, and to keep praying all our lives. I don't mean we can totally be like Jesus himself, but we can ask God to work toward it in us."

It was silent as we all thought about what a huge idea Rob was talking about.

"It's a growing process that everyone has to learn for themselves," Rob went on. "There's no right or wrong way to learn to do what Jesus said and live out what God wants us to do. I happened to have an experience early in my life that forced me to confront who I was at a young age. From what you've told me about your friend Micah, he had an experience with the man Hawk he talked about in his letter when he was young—again, an experience that forced him to confront who he was and what he was becoming as a person. The two of you," he said, looking at Katie and me, "had an experience together that forced you to confront different aspects of your lives and your character in different ways and ask questions about what God wanted of you. It's a growing process that comes to us all, but in different ways. We all face different circumstances, but I think they are all intended to point us in that general direction—to teach us to ask, 'God, what do you want me to do, what kind of person do you want me to be?' I think that is why Jesus said the kingdom of God is like seeds that grow in people differently."

The conversation continued for another hour. I think we were all really changed by it, but, like Rob *said, each of us in our own individual ways.*

Later that afternoon I went out by myself. I walked through the field we had finished the day before. There were a lot of stalks lying on the ground, a few weeds along with them, and bits of cotton we had missed. A few birds were about, pecking in the dirt to find the seeds we had left behind. And over in the distance sat the wagon piled high with the white fruit of our labor.

So much of the conversation was still going through my mind, and all I could do was say, "God, I want to be the person you want me to be. Show me what you want me to do."

❧ ✵ ☙

As the conversation on the front porch broke up and everyone went back to what they had been doing and Mayme walked out into the fields alone, the two brothers rose and wandered away from the house together.

"What do you think, brother Ward, shall we go check on that field we're going to start tomorrow?"

"Sure," said Ward, following his brother down the steps of the porch.

As Ward and Templeton continued toward the fields, neither spoke for several minutes. Both were absorbed in new and unexpected reflections.

"That Paxton's quite a kid," said Ward at length.

"He'll be a good husband for Kathleen."

Ward nodded, still thinking.

"A mite religious," he said.

"He's a preacher's kid," Templeton said, nodding.

"Yeah, but I've got the feeling there's more to it than that. I agree with what Mayme said—I never heard a preacher say those kinds of things."

"How many preachers have you heard in your life, brother

Ward?" chided Templeton with a good-natured grin.

"Maybe not as many as I should have! But I've heard my share."

Templeton chuckled but quickly grew serious.

"I think I know what you mean—I've never heard the kinds of things young Paxton said either. Pretty remarkable when you stop to think about it."

"Even Mama, as religious as she was, never said those kinds of things. I mean, she was a good woman and all. She taught us to treat folks with respect. But I never heard her talk about asking God what He wanted you to do."

He paused.

"Tell me, Templeton," said Ward, "you ever ask God what He wanted you to do?"

"Can't say that I have, at least not in so many words."

"Me neither. I always did what I wanted to do. I think I usually tried to do what I thought was right. But I never thought about what God might have to say about it. That's a different way of looking at things."

"A lot different than I been used to looking at things too."

Ward began to chuckle.

"What are you thinking?" asked Templeton.

"I was just thinking about Mama," replied Ward. "She'd be shocked to hear us talking like this."

Templeton smiled. "She'd be pleased, though," he said. "She was a good lady, like you say. I wish I'd paid more attention sooner."

They continued on in the direction of the river. Both were thoughtful for the rest of the day.

And all over Rosewood, spiritual seeds were sprouting and sending down roots in different directions, which would, in their own time, produce their manifold and varied fruit.

The harvest continued, though without Rob for the next several days. He accompanied us to the fields but couldn't lift his hurt shoulder enough to grasp the cotton with both hands. He remained sore for some time, but was back picking with the rest of us by week's end.

Tedious though picking cotton was, there was something special about all of us working hard together. There was laughter and talk and it felt good to be working hard for something so important. Occasionally, Josepha and Henry would lead out in singing a spiritual and the rest of us would join in, reminding us of the long history of what we were doing.

Strange as it is to say it, I think Rob enjoyed it most of all, being such a part of what had held Rosewood together for so long, and part of what had been such a part of the life of those of us who were black. Though Maryland had been a slave state, people that far north really didn't have much of an idea what Southern plantation life was like.

When he and Katie walked off hand in hand at day's end, sweating and hot and tired, I know they felt closer because of the bond of shared work. In the same way that Rob's words about being actively involved with God had gotten into the rest of us and were, I suppose you'd say, growing in our hearts and minds, Rosewood and its hard work were getting into Rob and growing new things inside him too.

A couple weeks later, Henry secretly told Katie and me that Josepha's birthday was coming up and that he had something special for her.

"She'll be suspicious," he said, "ef we tell her somebody else is fixin' supper, so we's jes' let her go on as usual. But it'd be right fine ef you two could bake a *cake or sumfin'. I's try ter keep her out ob da kitchen fo da mornin'."*

"We'll be happy to, Henry," said Katie. "That will be fun!"

Josepha did get suspicious when Henry wouldn't let her come up to the big house for lunch. When she did come about three o'clock, she sniffed around and I know she smelled something, even though the cake had been out of the oven and hiding as it cooled in Jeremiah's cabin for three hours.

But I think she was still surprised when out came the cake with candles on it, followed by gifts from all of us. We'd never known her birthday before and she was surprised that Henry told us.

Henry saved his two gifts for last. They were two packages about the same size, wrapped in colorful fancy paper and tied with ribbon. When Josepha picked up the first of the two, she almost dropped it because it was so heavy.

"What dis be!" she exclaimed, holding it tightly as she carefully tried to peel off the paper without tearing it. Then she pulled out the most beautiful book I had ever seen, bound in leather and engraved on the side.

"Why it's da Pilgrim's Progress*!" said Josepha. "Dat's da handsomest book I eber seen. I been wantin' dis book my whole life."*

"I had Miz Hammond order da nicest one she cud," said Henry. "Dat's what I wuz speakin' wiff her about dat day she wuz here an' you got a little riled at me."

"I wuz jes' curious, dat's all!"

Henry chuckled.

"Open the other one, Josepha," I said.

Josepha set the book down on the table as tenderly as if it were a baby, then picked up the second package.

"It be jes' as heavy—it be anuder book?"

"Jes' open it an' fin' out," said Henry.

Again Josepha carefully peeled the paper back. She gasped in surprise. "It's a Bible! Oh, Henry . . . da mos' beautiful Bible I eber seen!"

She leaned over and gave him a kiss.

"I ain't neber had anythin' so nice as dese!"

Josepha asked if we could read The Pilgrim's Progress *together in the evenings after supper, out of her very own book. Of course we all agreed. We started that same night.*

⁂

Sam Jenkins
48

Sheriff Sam Jenkins was the last person anyone at Rosewood expected to see riding toward them. The only thing they could be certain of was that it wasn't a social call.

He rode straight into the field, knocking over cotton stalks and trampling good cotton to the ground. He rode straight to where Papa and Uncle Ward were working with Aunt Nelda.

"Well, this is a touching sight," he said, looking around. "Futile but touching. Why don't you boys just give up on all this? You'll never win in the end."

"Don't bet against us, Sam," said Papa.

"Suit yourself. But you're wasting your time."

"What can we help you with, Sam? You didn't come out to inspect our harvest."

"You're right. I didn't. I'm looking for someone. I got a feeling he's here with you."

He glanced around the field again where the rest of us were spread out over about a hundred yards.

"Tall, white kid . . . friend of Henry's nigger boy . . . caused some trouble in town. Ah—I think I see him over there."

"Rob!" called Papa. "You want to come over here a minute?"

As Rob walked across the field toward them everyone else followed till we were all standing around the sheriff, who was still sitting on his horse.

"Rob, this is Sheriff Jenkins. He's here about that trouble you and Jeremiah had in town yesterday.—Sam, this is Rob Paxton."

The sheriff looked him over, and slowly a smile spread over his lips.

"Judging from that shiner on your forehead and that bruise under your ear, not to mention the way your left arm is hanging like it might hurt a little, I take it you were involved."

"I was there," said Rob.

"I've had a complaint filed against you, son," said the sheriff, "for assault."

I heard a gasp of shock and glanced over at Katie. Her eyes were on fire!

"The report was filed by Deke Steeves," said Mr. Jenkins. "Do you know anything about it?"

"Yes, I was involved in a little fracas with him."

"So you admit that the charge is true?"

"I did not say that, sir," said Rob calmly. "Actually, the charge is a lie."

"Are you accusing Deke Steeves of filing a false report? That is against the law."

"I am well aware of that, Mr. Jenkins. To answer your question—I accuse no one of anything. Without knowing how you came by your information, I am simply telling you that it is untrue."

"Says you." Jenkins smiled.

"Yes, sir," said Rob, if anything, even more calmly than before.

"And who is to say you aren't lying?"

"I make it my practice never to lie, sir. If I had assaulted Mr. Steeves, I would be the first to admit it."

"You seem to be very sure of yourself, Mr.—what is it . . . Paxton."

"Yes, sir."

"So what do you suggest I do, Paxton? I've got a warrant in my pocket for your arrest, and yet you say that Deke Steeves is a liar?"

"You've heard everything I said, and at no time did I call anyone a liar. I have only asserted that the report, as you have it, is not true."

"Have it your way," said Jenkins.

"But to answer your question about what I would suggest, I would say that you should be very sure of your facts before making an arrest, sir," answered Rob. "It is the essential first rule for an officer of the law. You might also consider secondary witnesses."

"I suppose you mean this nigger here," said the sheriff, nodding in Jeremiah's direction.

I knew my eyes were flashing then!

Rob winced at the deprecation.

"His race is hardly a factor, Mr. Jenkins," he said. "He did hear and see everything that passed between Mr. Steeves and myself. I would think some kind of corroboration would be useful in helping you avoid the charge of false arrest that could be put forward in such a case if you were to act prematurely and hastily."

Uncle Ward nodded in Rob's direction. "Paxton here knows something of the law, Jenkins. He is a sheriff's deputy up north."

"It is only a suggestion, sir," Rob continued. "I have no authority here, I realize. But if you do indeed have a warrant for my arrest and are determined to enforce it here and now, I will go peaceably."

Jenkins glanced about, slowly beginning to realize

that he was being made to look like a fool in front of all these idiots he hated . . . and by someone he didn't even know!

"You haven't heard the last of this, Paxton!" he said, spitting out Rob's name like venom.

Then he turned his horse around and galloped off across an unpicked portion of the field.

"Rob!" exclaimed Katie. "What would you have done if he'd arrested you!"

Rob laughed. "I would have told you to wire John Heyes in Hanover, Pennsylvania. Once John heard I was locked up, I have the feeling your Sheriff Jenkins would quickly realize he had started far more trouble for himself than he had bargained for. John would be here within forty-eight hours, and it would not go well for the good Mr. Jenkins when they met."

Of all of us, Rob was the least shaken by the event as we returned to work. But he didn't know these people like we did.

HERB WATSON
49

THREE DAYS LATER MR. WATSON APPEARED AT Rosewood to talk to Ward and Templeton Daniels. He looked serious. They went into the house together and sat down.

It was silent for several minutes.

"What is it, Herb?" asked Ward at length. "How bad can it be?"

"It's bad, boys. I can hardly bring myself to say it."

"Come on, out with it."

"The pressure I've been telling you about. . . ." Watson finally began, "it's grown worse. When I came to see you before, I hoped things would settle down. But they haven't. It's more than just my selling supplies to you now. Spoiling their attempt to kill Henry last year, along with the livery fire, made them plenty mad. But now they plan to get rid of you for good. The threats are getting dangerous."

"What kind of threats?"

"I just had a visit from Sam. He sounds like he's on a vendetta. If I don't go along, they will burn my warehouse down."

"What!"

"That's what he said."

"But that wouldn't just get even with you, it would hurt the whole community."

"And put half the plantation owners of the county out of business," added Watson. "I know that. They've got to have someplace to sell their crops too, but when people get filled with hate, they don't think straight."

"You said if you don't go along," said Templeton. "What exactly did they mean?"

"Sam laid it down in black and white—I can't buy your cotton crop at all, not at any price."

"What! Herb, that will ruin us. We have to sell that cotton!"

"I know . . . I know. I've wracked my brain trying to think of something. But as things stand now, I don't know what to do."

"We'll sell it somewhere else!" said Ward angrily.

"That's fine," said Watson. "I hope you can do that. That's obviously the best solution all the way around. But . . ."

"But what, Herb?" asked Templeton.

"All I'm saying is that you might not get your cotton to Charlotte . . . or *anywhere*. There are forces at work here that are *determined* to see you fail . . . no matter what it takes."

"Are you saying that they would be watching us that close, that if we tried to transport it, they would prevent us?"

"Yes, that's what I'm saying. Your crop could be stolen, your fields set on fire—who knows. They are absolutely determined that you are *not* going to sell this crop."

❊

We all knew something terrible had happened as a result of Mr. Watson's visit. Papa and Uncle Ward were sober the rest of the day. But we kept picking.

"What do you think it is?" I said to Katie when we

passed each other on one of the rows.

"I don't know," she said. "Maybe the price is going to be even lower than they expected."

"Then we have to get every bit of cotton off these stalks," I said.

We went on picking.

Mr. Watson's Offer

50

Two days later Mr. Watson called again. He and Ward and Templeton went inside the house and sat down together in private.

"I've been thinking a lot about our conversation the other day," he said, "and about your situation. I've come up with an idea that might solve it."

"We're open to any suggestions, Herb. You know someplace else we might be able to sell our cotton and where we could safely transport it?"

"No, it's nothing like that," replied Watson. "It's a completely different kind of solution."

"We're listening," said Ward.

Mr. Watson stared down at the table a few seconds. It grew quiet as they waited.

"Tell me—" He paused again, then eyed the two brothers seriously. "—have you ever thought of selling your place?"

"Selling . . . selling *Rosewood*!"

Watson nodded.

"No . . . never," replied Templeton.

"For one thing, it's not ours to sell," said Ward.

"That's not the way I hear it."

"It's Kathleen's . . . it's all of ours."

"Technically, perhaps, but you two make the decisions," said Mr. Watson.

"Don't be too sure." Ward smiled.

"It's out of the question, Herb," said Templeton. "We could never sell Rosewood."

"What if you can't pay your taxes? It'll be sold for auction and you'll get nothing."

"We'll pay them."

"But what if?"

"If it comes to that, then maybe we'd be forced to consider it . . . are you saying that you'd be interested?"

"I might be. I've thought of getting a small place outside town. This is considerably larger than I'd envisioned, but . . . well, I'd just hate to see you lose everything. Consider my offer. It might be your only option."

"What would you do, Herb?"

"I'd move out and manage the place. I've got men who can run the mill. So I'd hire some hands and grow crops and raise some cattle and horses along with them . . . just like you're doing."

"In other words, expanding your holdings at our expense?"

"Come on, boys, that's not what I mean and you know it. I'll give you a fair market price, plenty to set yourselves up somewhere else. This house, your animals, outbuildings, all the land—this place is worth a lot of money. You know, one of the things that might be driving this thing is exactly that."

"What?"

"That this is such a prime piece of property, right on the river, some of the best growing land in the county. Someone else may be trying to get their hands on it."

"You heard something?"

"No, I've heard nothing and I'm suggesting no one. All I'm saying is that if you sold to me, you'd get what it's worth and it'd set you and your people up right handsomely. The house is probably worth five thousand, the land another ten, this year's crop a thousand or two thousand. Then there's the stock, the other buildings, that new place Henry fixed up. You've got a small fortune here. I just don't want you to lose it all and get nothing."

Ward and Templeton sat silent, still stunned.

Several seconds later they rose and walked their visitor outside.

"I know we've sounded a little irritable, Herb," said Templeton. "You've got to understand how hard this is for all of us."

"I do. It's a tough situation."

"But we appreciate your trying to help."

They shook hands. Watson mounted his horse and rode off. They watched him go.

When they were alone, Ward voiced a question that had been nagging at him.

"You think there's any chance that he's in on it with them," he said, "that it's a ploy to get Rosewood himself?"

"I would stake my life against it," said Templeton. "Herb's a fair and honorable man. It sounds like he's willing to make us an offer that's more than reasonable under the circumstances. If what you say was true, he could wait till we're foreclosed on and buy the place for taxes like anyone else. No, I think his offer's legitimate."

"We should talk to the girls," said Ward, looking toward the fields.

"You know what they'll say."

"We still have to talk to them."

"There's one other thing," added Templeton.

"What's that?"

"Maybe it's time we're supposed to do what young Paxton was talking about—ask God what *He* wants us to do."

Rosewood's Owners Talk It Over

51

We saw Mr. Watson riding away in the distance from where we were working.

We still suspected nothing of what his visits were about. We assumed it was about the price of cotton or something like that.

Ten minutes later Papa and Uncle Ward wandered slowly back out toward us, talking between themselves. Again they were somber. Their hearts didn't seem to be in the picking like before. We could tell something was wrong and it dampened everyone's spirits. Papa and Uncle Ward kept to themselves all afternoon, talking quietly away from everyone else.

That evening we finally found out what Mr. Watson's two visits had been about.

About four-thirty they called us together. They had already sent Josepha and Aunt Nelda in a couple hours before.

"We're going to knock off early today," said Papa. "Go back and clean up, take a bath, put on some clean clothes. Josepha and Nelda are fixing us a nice supper.

Then we have to have a serious talk."

Katie and I looked at each other with expressions of question. I could tell Katie was worried. So was I.

After a quiet supper, the men got up and asked us all to join them in the parlor.

"You too, Nelda," said Uncle Ward.

"But I'm not . . . you know, involved with Rosewood in the way the rest of you are."

"Look, Nelda," said Uncle Ward. "I was the black sheep of the family, remember. I was the one who left. But these folks all welcomed me back and made me feel like part of the family again. If I can be, so can you. You're in this family now too, right along with the rest of us."

Poor Aunt Nelda! Her chin and lower lip started to quiver and her eyes filled with tears. Then she rushed over and gave Uncle Ward the biggest hug of his life!

"You're a good brother, Ward," she said. "You were never really a black sheep in my eyes. Thank you!"

"You too, Rob—whatever concerns Katie concerns you now. And you too, Jeremiah—you and Mayme have to make your decisions together."

When we were all seated, Papa began.

"We wanted to talk to you two girls—and you, Nelda . . . Rob, and the rest of you," he said. "We are Rosewood's family now. We have some major decisions to face, and we have to make them together."

"What kind of decisions, Uncle Templeton?" asked Katie, her voice trembling.

He drew in a long breath.

"About the future of Rosewood," he said.

He glanced at Uncle Ward.

"Go on, brother Templeton," said Uncle Ward. "You've been here longer than me. You've got a right to speak for us both."

Papa sighed and scratched the back of his head. "The late taxes are no secret," he said. "We've got some financial problems, but they're not as serious as the two of you faced—"

He glanced first at Katie, then at me.

"—back when you were alone. Of course, Ward's gold helped you out some then. But I think if we keep working hard, we can get out of this fix we're in. Nelda's offered to help too, which we appreciate, Nelda—"

He looked over at his sister and smiled.

"—but I'm afraid the problems are bigger than just money. If it were only money, we could figure something out. But it's not just financial. It's . . . it's the problems we've got in the whole community. It's everything . . . Sam Jenkins, Dwight Steeves, the Klan. People are against us, and they're going to keep being against us."

"But the cotton—" began Katie.

"The cotton won't be enough, Kathleen," said Papa.

"Why not?"

"Because, like I said, the problems we've got are bigger than just money . . ."

Again the two men looked at each other.

"—because Mr. Watson can't buy our crop," Papa added.

"What . . . why not?" said Katie. The full force of what Papa had said hadn't sunk in all the way yet.

"He's received threats. He can't do any more business with us at all. If he does, he could be ruined. Don't forget what happened to the livery. We can't put him in that kind of danger. He's been too good a friend to Rosewood."

"Can't we sell the cotton to somebody else?" I said.

"There is no one else," said Papa, looking toward me. "What I'm trying to get you both to see, Mary Ann, is that it's not just about selling the cotton. Even if we

try to take it elsewhere, they will destroy our crop, or steal it, or burn our fields."

At last we began to realize how serious a thing it was.

"Then . . . what are we going to do, Uncle Templeton?" said Katie. "We have to sell the cotton!"

"But I'm telling you, Kathleen . . . we may not be able to."

There was a long silence. Again Papa drew in a deep breath.

"Mr. Watson came yesterday with a potential solution," he said after a few seconds. "I don't like it. Ward doesn't like it. You're not going to like it. But it might be the only way out of this mess we are in. The long and the short of it is . . . Mr. Watson has offered to buy Rosewood."

The words fell like a silent bomb in the room. Katie and I sat there with our mouths hanging open. We couldn't believe what we'd heard.

"You mean . . . sell Rosewood?" said Katie in disbelief. Tears were filling her eyes.

"I'm afraid that's what we mean," replied Papa. "But all four of our names are on the deed. Ward and I have decided that we won't do it unless all four of us agree. Even if all three of the rest of us say yes, and you say no, Kathleen—we won't sell. We're in this together."

"But, Uncle Templeton, we can find a way out of this!" insisted Katie, tears flowing down her cheeks. "We always have. We have always found a way before, even when it was just Mayme and me."

"Times have changed, Kathleen. We may not be able to work our way out of this. What good will it do if we have a great harvest and they burn us out?"

"I don't know, Uncle Templeton," she said, wiping

at her eyes, "but there has to be a way. There just has to be!"

Rob put his hand on Katie's shoulder, but even he was quiet.

We all stared at the floor. No one said anything. My insides felt like I'd swallowed a stone and it was sitting in the pit of my stomach. It was the worst blow I'd ever felt in my life since losing my family.

What made it so unbearable was that from Papa's voice I think both Katie and I somehow knew that this was a more serious crisis than anything we had yet faced. Papa was such an optimist—his cheerful expressions, his winks and grins. He could always see the good in anything.

But now he sounded defeated. We sensed not just the desperation in his voice . . . but also the fear.

And if he was afraid, what else could we possibly be than afraid? If he was worried, then it really must be serious.

Maybe this was the end after all. As I sat there, I realized I was crying too.

"I'll never leave Rosewood!" said Katie after a minute. "This is our home forever. I don't want to think of such a thing as selling. We'll never leave . . . and—"

Katie burst into tears. Rob tried to comfort her by reaching for her hand. But she jumped up and ran upstairs.

Rob and I glanced at each other. We were both thinking of Katie. Always before I would have been the one to go and talk to Katie and comfort her, as she would have done for me. But now things had changed. I wondered if it was now Rob's place to go talk to her.

Rob must have known what I was thinking. As he looked at me, he nodded toward the stairs. I knew he was telling me to go to Katie.

I rose, left the room, and followed Katie upstairs.

When I walked into her room, she looked at me with that same look on her face as the first time I saw her. She looked scared and hopeless.

I walked to the bed and opened my arms and we both cried as we held each other.

Everyone was quiet after Katie and Mayme left the parlor.

After a bit, Rob said, "You know, for what it's worth, I remember something my father always used to teach us when we were young when trying to figure out what to do. He said that there were four things to do. You talk about it with the others who are involved. You pray and ask God what He wants you to do. You look to see if something in the Bible offers any direction. Then you wait for circumstances to indicate what step you should make. He said that God will always speak eventually through your mind, heart, or circumstances to show what He wants you to do."

"That's good advice, Paxton," said Ward.

"It seems to me," Rob went on, "that you're doing all you can and now you just have to pray and wait to see what He will do through the circumstances that develop."

"Well, young Paxton," Templeton said, "it looks like we need to do just what you were talking about—ask God what He wants us to do and try to figure out what that is."

"Then why don't we ask Him right now?" said Rob.

Templeton and Ward glanced at each other, but Rob had already bowed his head and begun to pray.

"Our Father," he said, "these dear people are stuck in a difficult situation and they need your help. They need to know what you want them to do. I pray that you will speak to them through the circumstances that come in the next days and weeks. Whatever those circumstances are, I pray that you will make your way for them plain."

The room was quiet a moment. Then Henry's voice broke through the silence.

"Amen, Lord," he said. "We's be needin' a word from you an' we's needin' it right quick, Lord."

Then Templeton prayed, and he told Mayme later that it was the first time he had ever prayed out loud in front of other people.

"It's like they say, Lord," he said. "We don't know what we're supposed to do. So if you don't mind, we're asking you to show us. If you tell us what to do, we'll do our best to do it."

A few quiet *Amens* came from around the rest of the room.

Final Determination

52

Katie was more determined now than ever to see the harvest in and sell it somewhere.

I woke up early the next morning and went to the window. I had a feeling I knew what I would see.

I was right. There was Katie in the distance already in the field we had started three days before, working her way down a long solitary row of cotton all by herself. I had seen it before when Rosewood was threatened. Katie would do everything she was physically capable of to save her beloved home, single-handedly if she had to.

Then I saw Rob walk out of Jeremiah's cabin. He walked slowly toward her.

They embraced and stood a moment in each other's arms. Then they stepped back, Katie handed Rob a second satchel, and he took up on the row beside her.

I wondered if even Katie's determination would be enough this time. Whatever happened, it would happen to all of us together.

I got dressed, pulled on my boots, and went downstairs and outside to join them. Jeremiah had already followed Rob out. He came toward me and gave me a hug and smiled sadly. There wasn't much to say. Then we picked up our satchels from where we had left them the night before, and got to work too.

One by one the others came out too, until everyone was working but Josepha, who was in the big house making coffee and breakfast.

But nobody was talking. Here Katie and I were with Rob and Jeremiah with us, and both of us were engaged to be married to men we loved, but we were all miserable! This wasn't how it was supposed to be.

The rest of the week was much the same. The cotton was piling up in the barn, we had about a third of the fields picked and packed and ready to sell. We knew the other plantation owners were starting to sell their crops. Mr. Thurston had stopped by once and said that the price wasn't as bad as he'd thought and that Mr. Watson was giving the growers a good return. I knew we had enough packed in the barn already to probably pay the back taxes. But Papa and Uncle Ward said nothing about trying to sell. We knew they didn't know what to do.

We just kept picking . . . and hoping.

A couple times men rode by in the distance, pausing and watching us briefly.

"Who was that?" I asked Papa once.

"I can't be sure, Mary Ann," he said. "I think it might have been Dwight Steeves."

One other time I thought I saw Sheriff Jenkins. We all pretended not to notice. But one time we knew for sure that the man watching was William McSimmons. None of us had heard much about him since Micah and Uncle Ward and Papa had confronted him.

But we knew he and the others were watching us and waiting to see what we were going to do.

One night I woke up in the dead of night. I thought

I'd heard a noise. I got out of bed and crept to the window. I saw the light of a lantern down in the yard below. It had been a hot day and my window was open.

Uncle Ward was walking back from the barn with a lantern in one hand and a rifle in the other. Papa had just left the house and was going out to meet him.

Uncle Ward handed him the lantern and the rifle.

"Any trouble?" said Papa.

"No . . . everything's quiet."

"All right," said Papa. "Get some sleep and I'll take it from here."

I stole back to my bed and lay down. They were keeping watch all night! Did they really think someone was going to come steal our cotton?

Or worse!

The Warning

53

A RIDER GALLOPED THROUGH THE NIGHT.

Luckily there was enough of a moon for his horse to see its way along the deserted dirt road. He could not slow down or it would be too late. Many lives, and his own future too, could depend on his getting there in time.

Something had awakened him shortly after midnight. Suddenly he was awake in his bed, with blackness and silence around him.

This was no time for sane men to be awake. Yet some inner sense told him that he ought to get up and have a look around. He crawled out of bed, pulled on his trousers and boots, picked up the candle holder, and went downstairs.

The warnings that had been given him were threatening enough. But had he misjudged their intentions?

A hurried walk throughout the premises, however, revealed nothing. The whole town was quiet except for the occasional bark of a dog. He tried to tell himself that he was letting his imagination run away with him.

He turned and made his way back toward his house.

Suddenly a noise disturbed the quiet . . . booted feet clumped along the street half a block away.

Quickly he blew out the candle and crept back against the wall of his warehouse.

". . . said they'd meet us at one . . ." whispered one of the men as they drew closer.

Cautiously he slipped out to follow them, straining to listen to the subdued conversation ahead of him.

". . . why tonight?"

". . . been given enough warnings . . . time for action . . ."

From somewhere a third man joined them. Under his arm he carried something white.

". . . the horses?"

"McSimmons is bringing enough from his place. Didn't want to wake up the whole town."

". . . meet on the north end of town."

". . . Sam said . . ."

". . . same thing I heard . . . through fooling around . . ."

". . . blood spilled tonight . . . before morning . . ."

". . . that plantation house . . . smoldering cinders . . ."

The listener had heard enough. He hurriedly retraced his steps to his own place. He knew well enough what plantation house they were talking about. Whether he could get there in time to save it and prevent bloodshed, he didn't know.

Five minutes later he was saddling his own horse in the darkness. He would leave town by the southern road, then circle back around, hoping the others wouldn't hear him. He would probably have a forty-minute lead on them, maybe an hour at best.

How to wake his friends without getting his head blown off was a question he had not considered until he neared his destination.

He rode into the yard between the house and barn, then pulled out his rifle and fired two quick shots into the air.

Amid the howls of a couple dogs and a few whinnies and bellows from the barn, lanterns were lit and yells of alarm sounded throughout the house.

"Inside there," he called up toward the second-floor windows, where the reflection of a few lights had appeared. "Hey, wake up . . . it's Herb Watson! Templeton . . . Ward . . . I've got to talk to you!"

A window slid open. Ward Daniels' face appeared along with the barrel of a rifle.

"Who's there?" he called down.

"Daniels . . . it's Herb Watson!" shouted their visitor. "Get down here! They're coming . . . they're coming tonight!"

Ward pulled his head back inside and shut the window. Already Templeton was walking out of the barn, where he had fallen asleep on his watch. A minute later both brothers appeared on the front porch, Templeton carrying a lantern, Ward with his rifle still in hand.

"What's it all about, Herb?" asked Templeton.

"I had to get you out of your beds—there's no time to lose . . . they're coming. They're on the way. We've got to act fast. You've got to get out of here, all of you."

"You think it's that serious?" asked Ward.

"I overheard them. They're determined to kill someone tonight, and burn this place to the ground. They said that blood would be spilled and your house in cinders before morning."

The two brothers glanced at each other. They realized that their friend had never been more serious in his life.

"What about the talk we had . . . about your buying the place?" asked Templeton. "Now there's no time."

"I've been thinking about it riding out here," said Watson. "If you're willing to sell, we could arrange it now . . . right now. As long as we all sign, it will be legal. I had been working on some preliminary sales documents before tonight. I brought them along. They're not perfect, but they'll be legal. You'll have to trust me that you'll get what's coming to you. We'll have to arrange for payment later, after I've got your harvest in. I'll pay you full price for all the cotton that comes in as well as for the house, land, and everything else. Just like I told you."

Templeton thought a minute, then sighed deeply.

"We trust you, Herb," he said. "I don't suppose we have much choice. But even if we did, we'd trust you. You've proved yourself a good friend and a man of honor. Besides that, you may just have saved our lives coming here like this. So maybe you're right . . . maybe the time has finally come. But . . . suppose you do buy it and they get angry and burn you out?

"I don't think they will—it's you they want to get rid of, not me."

"I don't like the idea of leaving you to face them alone. We'd have a better chance if we all—"

"Look, Templeton—if they see any of you, *none* of us will have a chance. The only way there will be any chance of saving Rosewood is if you are all gone when they get here. Don't even think of trying to fight. There are too many of them. They would surround us and have the barn and house in flames in five minutes."

"We could hide out in the woods."

"They'll search the entire area before they're going to believe me. Come on, make up your minds—they're on the way, I tell you!"

Templeton looked again at his brother. As he did, now two young men walked quickly toward them from the direction of what had once been the slave cabins. One was black, the other white. The latter had a Colt 45 in his hand. They had heard the shots, assumed danger, and had come running.

"It's all right, boys, it's Mr. Watson."

"Jeremiah—good to see you," said Watson, extending his hand to the young black man.

"Mister Watson," said Jeremiah as they shook hands.

"This is Rob Paxton, Herb," said Templeton. "He's got himself engaged to our niece."

The two shook hands.

"That's quite a gun you've got there, son," said Watson.

"My grandfather's. I heard the shot, sir. I thought there might be danger."

"There is, Rob," said Ward. "But hopefully you won't have to use that."

"Trouble is on the way, boys," said Templeton. "We've got to get everybody up and dressed. I'll go upstairs and get the women. Jeremiah, you get your father and Josepha up here. Rob, you get started hitching our fastest horses to the two large wagons and the big buggy. Saddle a couple of single horses too. Jeremiah, you get back and help Rob with the wagons and horses. There's nine of us. We won't be able to take much, and we'll have to move fast."

"I'll give you a hand, boys," said Mr. Watson. "Let's go!"

The Decision
54

When Katie and I had sleepily stumbled downstairs to the kitchen, Papa began. His words woke us the rest of the way up in a hurry.

"Okay," he said. "You all heard the gunshots waking us up. That was Herb Watson come from town to warn us that trouble is afoot tonight. Sam Jenkins, Bill McSimmons, Dwight Steeves, and the rest of their crowd are on their way riding out here right now with guns and torches. Herb overheard them. They're going to burn us out this time. It's not just a threat. Herb has reiterated his offer to buy Rosewood here and now—lock, stock, and barrel, and take care of our harvest and give us enough to set ourselves up somewhere else. So we've got a decision to make, and we have to make it fast."

He looked seriously at both of us. Our eyes were wide as we listened, both scared and at the same time stunned with grief.

"We talked about Herb's offer before," he went on. "None of us have wanted to think of selling Rosewood. The time has come when we may have no choice. If we're still here when they get here, they will burn

Rosewood to the ground. And if they get wild enough to start shooting, I have the feeling they will be trying to kill either Ward or me or Henry or Jeremiah. I don't know how to be any more clear than that—if we don't act immediately, you girls may be burying one of us by tomorrow. We have to leave, and leave now. Selling Rosewood to Mr. Watson, now . . . tonight, may be the only way to save it."

Again he paused and looked at us. Nelda had joined us and was holding one of my hands and one of Katie's.

"So . . . there it is. We either stay and fight—and if we do, it will mean with guns, and it'll mean having to shoot to kill or be killed because these men are evil men and they've finally had enough of us. Or it means we sign Rosewood over and sell it to Herb. We lose Rosewood either way."

He looked around. Katie and I were both crying.

The room grew deathly quiet. Even though the danger to us all was imminent, Papa sat patiently. He knew what a momentous decision this was. Our past together, and Katie's whole life, was suddenly on the line. Our whole future was at stake.

It was a decision we had to make together. But everyone in the room knew that it was really Katie's decision, and hers alone to make. It was only because of her that any of our names were on the deed at all.

I looked at her. I knew she was remembering the terrible night her family had been murdered.

"Couldn't we . . . hide in the cellar, Uncle Templeton?" she said, almost in a little girl's voice.

"Kathleen," said Papa in the most tender voice I'd ever heard from him. "If they come and find the house empty, they will either search for us until they find us, or burn the house to the ground as sure as we are

sitting here. We have no choice. It's leave or lose everything."

"He is right, Kathleen," said Uncle Ward. "Herb heard them with his own ears. They are deadly serious this time."

"Kathleen," said Papa, "the only way for us to save this house is for us to be gone and to sell it to Mr. Watson. Even that may not save it. But it's our only chance. We have to love Rosewood enough to let it go."

Again it was silent. It was hard to absorb Papa's words. We all sat down for a minute or two thinking about what he had said. The words had gotten inside Katie and she knew they were true.

She began to weep, then slowly nodded.

"We'll sell," she whispered so quietly we could hardly hear her. But this time, soft as it was, it was a grown-up woman's voice. Then she broke briefly into sobs. My heart was breaking for her.

Papa glanced at me.

"Sell," I said, blinking back my tears.

"Ward?" said Papa.

"Sell," said Uncle Ward.

"All right, then," said Papa. "—Ward, you want to go out and tell Herb to come in? We'll sign the papers and get out of here."

Uncle Ward was leaving just as Josepha and Henry hurried into the kitchen.

Papa rose and walked around the table to Katie. She stood up and fell into his arms. He held her tight for several long seconds as she wept on his chest.

"You're a brave lady, Kathleen," he said. "This may be one of the most courageous things you've ever done. It takes as much courage to know when to let go as when to fight."

Katie nodded, shaking in his arms as she cried.

Slowly he let her go and turned to the others.

"Josepha," he said, "—coffee . . . lots of it . . . and strong. And start packing up as much food as we can carry. Nelda, help her, will you? Henry, the boys are out in the barn. They'll need some help."

"What's it all about, Mister Templeton?"

"We're leaving Rosewood, Henry. We have to leave tonight, right now. The Klan is after us . . . to destroy us."

Uncle Ward and Mr. Watson ran back in.

"All right, then," said Papa. "Let's get these papers signed."

"I'm offering to buy everything," said Mr. Watson, taking some papers out of his pocket and spreading them on the table, "—the furniture, the land, the equipment, all the houses, the animals, and the full cotton crop. I'll pay off your back taxes. It's all spelled out in here. I'm pretty sure they won't do anything to me once they realize you're gone and it's in my name. You're going to have to trust me for the money."

They looked each other in the eyes.

"We do trust you, Herb."

"I brought what little cash I had on hand for you as a down payment and to get you safely away."

He pulled out a stack of bills and set them on the table.

"It's only about two hundred. But it will get you where you're going. Don't even tell me right now where you're headed. I don't want to know. Wire me or write me in care of Mrs. Hammond . . . that is—"

"Yes, we trust her," said Papa. "She will agree to be our go-between and say nothing."

"I'll get you the rest of the money when you're settled and after the crops are in."

Mr. Watson glanced down at the papers in the light

of the lantern sitting on the middle of the table.

"I'll date them yesterday," he said, then drew out a pen from his pocket, wrote on the top sheet, and set down the pen. "You want to read them over?"

"No time, Herb," said Papa, picking up the pen that lay there.

He dipped it in the inkwell that sat in the center of the kitchen table and signed his name on the bottom of the second sheet.

He handed the pen to Uncle Ward.

He signed below Papa's name.

Even Josepha stopped her bustling on the other side of the kitchen and watched. Every eye in the room was on those papers sitting on the table.

Uncle Ward handed the pen to me.

I signed my name.

By this time Katie had recovered herself. She wiped her eyes, then drew in a stoic breath, and took the pen from me. Our eyes met and we smiled. What worlds of aching love those smiles said to each other!

"Well, Mayme . . ." she said.

"Oh, Katie!"

Katie hesitated but a moment more, then signed her name below mine:

Kathleen O'Bannon Clairborne.

And that was it. Rosewood now belonged to Herb Watson.

"Well, Herb," said Papa, "you just bought yourself a plantation. But—and I know I speak for all of us here—if they burn you out in revenge, you don't owe us anything."

The rest of us nodded.

They shook hands. Uncle Ward and Mr. Watson also shook hands. Then Katie turned and faced Mr. Watson.

"Please take good care of it, Mr. Watson," she said, beginning to cry again but doing her best to smile through her tears, then embraced him.

"You can be sure I will, Kathleen," he said. "When all this blows over, I hope you'll come back to visit. I won't get rid of any of your things. I'll pack everything away. Anything you want and aren't able to take now, you can return for anytime."

Katie stepped back. Rob put his arm around her shoulders. Now I shook Mr. Watson's hand.

"All right," said Papa. "We have to pack as much as we can take, and quickly. Herb, how much time do you think we have?"

"Twenty . . . thirty minutes at the most. But you've got to be far enough away when they come that they can't hear you, or they'll come after you."

"I understand.—All right, everyone, listen to me," said Papa. "Essentials only—we need food, clothes, blankets—special things, books, mementos. Josepha, you go down to your place and get what you and Henry need. Nelda, run upstairs and get your things and your two carpetbags, then come down and finish with the food. Girls—you get your things upstairs. But you heard Herb, if there's something you need you can't take now, he can send it to us, or we'll come back for it. Get going . . . hurry! We pull out in fifteen minutes."

Everyone started to run from the room.

Katie paused and looked back one last time at the papers still sitting in the center of the table, then followed me upstairs.

GOOD-BYE

55

Outside Rob and Jeremiah had two wagons, each hitched to two horses, ready beside the house.

Within minutes, things starting piling in—carpetbags, tools, boxes, loose clothes and blankets, boxes and bags of silverware and cookery and jars and plates, food, pans, bags of beans and sugar and dried meat and cheese and what bread we had, rope, pillows, water containers, soap, hats, boots, gloves, spare wagon and leather parts for repairs, saddles, feed for the horses, and the supplies we thought we would need for a long trip. My, but what a mess it was—ten people grabbing and throwing in things faster than they could think about it.

Then came two saddled single horses, and last the smaller carriage. Henry ran up from their house with an armload of clothes and quilts, Josepha's two prized books wrapped in them. As for Josepha herself, she was bustling back and forth from the kitchen with food and pots and what supplies she could carry. Rob now ran to collect his few things. The place was a pandemonium of frantic activity. It was amazing how quickly the wagons filled.

Papa and Mr. Watson walked out of the house into the night. All about them everyone was running back and forth from the house to the wagons.

"I don't know where you'll go to first," said Watson. "The main thing is to get as far away from here tonight as you can. If I know Bill and Sam, they'll send out a search party in the morning. But once it settles down, I meant what I said about coming back for anything you want . . . tools, furniture, family heirlooms, even that piano in there of Kathleen's mama's."

"Thanks, Herb," said Templeton, nodding. "That means a great deal to Kathleen. This has been her home more than any of the rest of ours. She spent her whole life here."

As if knowing they were talking about her, Katie now walked toward the two men.

"This is the second saddest day of my life," she said. "But I want to thank you, Mr. Watson, for saving Rosewood . . . even if I may never see it again."

"You will see it again, Kathleen. I was just telling your uncle that you are all welcome anytime. This will always be your home."

Katie stepped forward and kissed him on the cheek and tried to force a smile.

"Thank you, Mr. Watson," she said in a soft voice.

In another ten minutes things began to slow down and gradually we all began to cluster around the wagons. Then Aunt Nelda came rushing toward Mr. Watson.

"Mr. Watson, I almost forgot," she said. "The horse and buggy that I rented in Charlotte—"

"Don't worry about them, Mrs. Fairchild," he said. "I will take care of them."

"Let me know how much it is and I will send you payment."

Mr. Watson smiled. "I will take care of it," he repeated.

He turned to the rest of us where we stood waiting.

"Get going!" he said, glancing toward town. "I can already imagine that I see faint lights in the distance. Get to the woods as quickly as you can, far enough so that they can't hear you."

We all jumped into the wagons. Katie and I climbed up and sat beside Uncle Templeton in one of the two big ones. Aunt Nelda climbed up beside Uncle Ward in the other. Jeremiah and Rob mounted the two single horses. Henry helped Josepha up onto the seat of the smaller buggy, then jumped up beside her.

"We've got no time for long good-byes," said Papa, glancing about one last time. I saw him blinking hard.

"Thanks, Herb!" he said, then turned and flapped the reins in his hands and yelled and the horses jumped into motion and off we went into the night and toward whatever was our new destiny. If there was anyone who wasn't crying, I don't know who it was.

Whether Katie was sadder to leave her lifelong home, or Josepha to leave her brand-new house that she never thought she would have and that she loved so much, I don't know. Tears were pouring down both their faces. I think I felt more anguish for the two of them than for myself.

We bounced and rumbled past the barn and out of the yard on the road toward Mr. Thurston's.

Josepha and I had once before left Rosewood, thinking we would never see it again. But this was Katie's time to grieve. She and I turned around and looked back as the house and barn began to fade into the blackness of night. We started around a bend in the road. I glanced over at Katie. Her eyes glistened with *tears in the light of the thin moon. She looked over at me.*

"We've been happy here, haven't we, Mayme?"

"Happier than I've ever been anywhere in my life," I said.

"Just as long as I never lose you, I will be happy anywhere. Oh, but I will miss this dear place! I just hope Mama and Papa won't mind too much what I've done."

"They won't mind," I said. "It would have happened a long time ago without your hard work and courage. I think they would be very proud of you."

We both looked back toward the house.

"Good-bye, Rosewood," I said.

For a moment more Katie stared back.

"Good-bye, Rosewood . . ." she whispered.

A few seconds later the buildings disappeared from sight.

STANDOFF

56

BEFORE THE WAGONS HAD EVEN CLEARED THE YARD, Herb Watson hurried his horse into the barn, unsaddled it, and hoped it would not be found in a sweat. Then he ran back upstairs, took off his clothes, and rummaged around until he found an old pair of nightclothes that had likely belonged to Kathleen's father. As soon as he heard the sounds of the wagons fading in the distance, he blew out all the lanterns in the house . . . and waited.

When the angry mob of white riders carrying their torches reached Rosewood, they found it quiet and dark, just as they had expected. Their shouts and yells and taunts brought a light to one of the upper windows soon enough.

But the sleepy head that peeped out of the open window a few seconds later was the last face any of them had expected to see here.

"Watson," shouted William McSimmons, pulling off his hood, "what in blazes are you doing here!"

"Didn't you hear?" said Watson. "I bought this place from the Daniels brothers."

Stunned murmurs and questions of disbelief spread through the group of riders.

"We came on business, Watson," shouted Sam Jenkins.

"Now get down here and tell us what this is all about."

A minute later Watson appeared, rubbing his eyes and holding a lantern and to all appearances recently aroused from bed.

"Where are they?" demanded Jenkins.

"Who?"

"The Daniels and their niggers—the whole brood!"

"I don't know. They're not here anymore. They're gone . . . left. I'm alone."

"You don't mind if we search the place?"

Watson hesitated a moment before answering.

"Let me get this straight, Sam . . . you think I'm lying to you?"

"I didn't say that. I just want to know if we can search the place."

"Why else would you want to unless you think I'm lying? I don't know that I take that kindly, Sam."

The first syllable of a terrible curse burst from Jenkins' lips, but he stopped himself. Herb Watson was one of the most respected men in Greens Crossing.

"If you want to search . . . go right ahead," said Watson.

He glanced up and down the line of riders. "You know," he added, "I'm pretty trusting when it comes to all you boys' cotton and other crops. If I wasn't so trusting, I could tear apart your bales and do some searching of my own. I'd likely find weeds and stones and thistles and probably I wouldn't be able to give you as much for it as you might want. You know what I mean, boys? I'm a trusting man myself. If you can't trust me, then go have a look around. But I'll remember that next time you boys bring your cotton in to me. And I know who you all are. Those sheets don't hide a thing. So go on, Sam, have a look around if you don't believe that this place is mine and that the two Daniels and the rest of them are gone."

Behind him, some of the riders shifted uneasily in their saddles.

"I don't know if I believe any of this, Herb," said Jenkins. "We told you not to do any business with them. Now you tell us you've gone and bought their place."

"Seemed like the best solution. Folks know that I've been talking for a while about getting me a place out of town."

"You let them get away, Herb. Might be that we'll have to burn you out for that."

"You could. But you've got no reason to. You've got me outnumbered by plenty. What good does it do you? I've always treated you all fairly. Are you going to punish me for taking advantage of an opportunity? You can start something here if you're determined. You can burn me out here and now. You can burn my mill in town too if your hate's gone that far.

"But do you really want that? There are no coloreds here. They're all gone and won't be back. I bought this place and have the papers to prove it. The blacks are gone. All that's left are me and you all. I know who most of you are, and your livelihood depends on me and my mill. You need me, or your crops won't be worth anything. I'm the man who decides what to pay you for your crops. So you have to ask yourselves if it's worth it."

Whether Sam Jenkins liked it or not, Watson's words were getting through to the rest of them, even William McSimmons, whose cotton crop was huge. Sam didn't have a crop to lose, but the others depended on their cotton.

"You've won," said Watson. "The Daniels are gone. You forced them out. You got what you wanted."

"Where'd they go, Herb?"

"I don't know. Far as I know, they planned to take the back roads to Charlotte, sell their horses and wagons, and then take the train north. They've got kin in Pennsylvania somewhere."

"When did all this happen?"

"Yesterday," lied Watson.

Finally Sam Jenkins was silenced.

Slowly a few of the men backed away and began turning their horses around. It didn't take long for the others to join them. Within another minute they were all riding off through the night back toward town.

Herb Watson walked back into the empty house that was now his.

"I hope there's some of that coffee left," he said to himself. "That was close!"

Campfire Reflections

57

We'd only gone probably a mile, though by then we were off the main road and on a narrow wagon track through the woods barely wide enough for the wagons, when Papa reined in and told everyone to be as quiet as they could be.

The crickets and other animals had finally gone to sleep and we could hear faint sounds of horses and shouts and saw just the hint of flickering torches through the trees in the direction of the house.

We sat and watched nervously and listened. If they set either the house or the barn on fire, there would be no mistaking it!

Behind us Jeremiah brought his horse alongside our wagon.

"Mister Templeton," he whispered, "I been thinkin' . . . why don't I ride a little way back, real careful an' quiet, an' see what's goin' on? Ef dey does come lookin' fo us, I'll lead 'em on a wild-goose chase. But effen dey don't, leastways we'll know."

"I don't know, Jeremiah . . . I hate to risk it."

Papa thought a minute more, then slowly nodded.

"You're right. Knowing would help us a lot. But you

mustn't let them hear you."

"I's keep the horse quiet, you kin count on it."

Jeremiah turned his horse around and rode slowly back the way we had come.

It became deathly quiet. If we hadn't all been so keyed up and frightened and been through such emotions, we would have been sleepy. But no one was!

We waited . . . kept watching . . . and kept waiting.

If they found us like this, trying to run away, they would probably kill us all and dump us in a gulch. In a way we were in as much danger here, or more, than we would have been back at Rosewood.

At last we heard the sounds of a single horse. It grew louder, then through the blackness we heard a voice.

"It's me . . . it's Jeremiah."

A few quiet exclamations of relief spread through the group.

"Dey's gone," he said when he reached us. "Dey's headin' back ter town an' Rosewood's safe. Dey didn't do nuthin'."

We didn't exactly shout for joy, because we knew we had to keep quiet just in case. But we almost did!

Right then I think the thought crossed every one of our minds that the easiest thing to do would be to go right back home and get into our own beds.

But it wasn't our home anymore.

And going back wouldn't solve anything anyway.

Our future lay ahead of us, not behind. We had made our decision and there was no turning back.

As we settled down, Papa flicked the reins and clicked his tongue to the horses and we jostled into motion.

"You girls might want to crawl back there and get

some sleep," he said. "We've got a long night ahead of us."

When I woke up, the sun was shining, though it was still fairly early. It was chilly and dew was on the ground everywhere. I smelled coffee.

I sat up. There sat Papa and Uncle Ward and Henry and Josepha around a small campfire talking quietly. Josepha's eyes were red like she'd been crying. The three men were somber.

It was a serious time. What we had done would take some getting used to. The sadness was going to last awhile.

I got up and went into the woods and then came and sat down by the fire.

"Get some sleep?" asked Papa.

"I reckon I did," I smiled. I cuddled up next to him and he put his arm around me. "Where are we?" I asked.

"Who knows!" he chuckled. "Probably eight or ten miles from Greens Crossing . . . hopefully north."

"What are we going to do?"

"Keep moving hard for another day or two until we're out of reach of anyone hearing about us or reporting our whereabouts back home."

Rob now wandered toward us from where he and Jeremiah had been sleeping.

"Morning," he said. "This is quite a family I've gotten myself mixed up with! You always lead such exciting lives?"

Papa and Uncle Ward laughed so loud it woke up Katie and Aunt Nelda. I guess we didn't have to try to be quiet anymore!

Josepha wiped at her eyes and struggled to her feet.

"Well, I reckon it's time we see what we kin rustle

up fo breakfast," she said. "Dis here's gwine be a long trip—we's better git started wiff sumfin' warm in our bellies."

We continued on, so slowly it seemed in those big wagons, all day. As we got further from Greens Crossing, Papa and Uncle Ward led us back on main roads and we began moving a little faster. By the end of the second day we were probably twenty-five miles from home and the men thought we were out of danger.

But exhaustion was finally setting in too, from the weeks of work in the fields, then the escape in the middle of the night.

We stopped and made camp about five o'clock. The men made a fire. Josepha and Aunt Nelda and Katie and I got to work boiling some potatoes and fixing some beans and bacon. I can't remember anything ever tasting so good!

While we were sitting around the fire that evening, Katie finally asked what the rest of us were probably all wondering.

"Uncle Templeton," she said, "where are we going?"

"I don't know exactly, Kathleen," Papa replied. "The first thing we had to do was get far enough away that we were safe. Now I suppose it's time we made some plans. Mr. Watson gave us money to help us get to wherever we want to go. Maybe we better decide where that is."

"Don't forget my money, Templeton," said Aunt Nelda. "I've got it safe and sound."

"I won't, Nelda," he said. "Why, that's over three hundred dollars between us all. We're rich. We can go wherever we want!"

He paused and the smile faded from his lips.

"But it may be that we've all got different ideas as

to where that might be," he said. "Nelda, you'll probably want to be getting home. If you want, we could put you on a train and—"

"I'm not leaving the rest of you now," she said. "I haven't had so much excitement in years! I know you've had to leave your home. But we're safe, and that's the most important thing. And as far as where to go, you are all welcome with me in Philadelphia . . . though it might be a little crowded."

"We appreciate that, Nelda," said Uncle Ward. "We all appreciate it a lot."

"There's you too, Rob," said Papa. "You may be wanting to get home too."

"I'm in no hurry, Mr. Daniels. I came down to North Carolina to help. That still goes."

Papa nodded in appreciation. "I suppose what I'm saying," he went on, "is that maybe now we've all got our own lives to live. Rob, you and Kathleen plan to get married. Maybe you'll get your own place in Hanover. Jeremiah, you had yourself a job—maybe you and Mayme will go back there after you're married. Henry and Josepha, you have had to leave your nice new house, but when we get Mr. Watson's money from Rosewood, we'll all split it up fairly and I promise that you will be able to buy yourself a new place somewhere. As for Ward and me, I suppose we can get by most anyplace. Maybe it's time for us to hit the trail again, maybe go back to California like we've talked about . . . go visit the Hollisters and Micah and Emma, I don't know. All I'm saying is that maybe we ought to split up Mr. Watson's two hundred dollars right now, and you'll all be free to go wherever you want to go."

It was silent. His words sounded like a death sentence to my ears! I didn't want everybody to leave and split up!

The silence continued. Everybody was just staring at the ground.

"But, Uncle Templeton," said Katie at last, "it sounds like you want us all to leave and go our own separate ways."

"I didn't mean that, Kathleen," he said. "I just figured that everyone's got to make up their own minds what they want to do and where they want to go. We're all adults, so I can't be telling everybody else what to do."

"Meanin' no disrespect, Mister Templeton," said Henry, "but me an' Josepha, we'd jes' as soon stay wiff you an' Mister Ward whereber you go, dat is ef you wants us. We's kind er figger dat we's a family, 'specially us old folks. Kind er late ter be splittin' up now, dat's what we's thinkin'. California's a mite far fo da likes er us ter go, but maybe someplace closer by where we kin put down new roots an' settle down agin."

"Me too," said Katie. "I want to stay together too."

"And me," I said.

Papa looked at Rob and Jeremiah.

"What about you two young men?" he asked. "What are your plans?"

"I ain't got none yet, Mister Templeton," said Jeremiah. "Mayme an' me, we ain't had a chance ter talk 'bout it. We figgered we'd be at Rosewood. All dis has happened mighty fast. So wiff all dese changes, I reckon I'm thinkin' we ought ter stick together a spell."

Papa looked at Rob.

"Katie and I have talked about our future," he said. "But we've decided nothing. I know how important all of you are to her. This is Katie's family and I told her that I would never want to take her from her family. And now you are my family too . . . or will be, I hope, before too long. I know you would be welcome at my

parents' home. Like Nelda said, it would be a bit crowded. But in the absence of other possibilities, it is something to consider on a temporary basis."

Gradually all eyes turned toward Katie.

"Ever since Mayme and I went north," she said, "I've been wondering about the future. The way things are," she went on, "I don't know if I want to live in North Carolina anymore, or anywhere even close to it. I don't want to have to worry about what people think about my best friend, or about Jeremiah or Josepha or Henry or anyone else. I want to live somewhere where people are respected for who they are inside."

She looked around at all of us, then smiled at me. Then she looked back to Papa.

"I suppose I am ready to leave," she sighed, "and find a place in the North, or someplace else where we can be a family."

She glanced at Henry and Josepha.

"I guess I agree with Henry," she said. "California seems pretty far. Couldn't we find someplace to live together closer than that!"

A few chuckles went around. Again it was quiet. Nobody was anxious to interrupt with their own thoughts at a time like this. We knew Katie had more to say.

"As I have listened to what everyone's been saying," Katie went on, "I realized something. This—right here, all of us together . . . this is Rosewood. We didn't leave Rosewood . . . Rosewood left Greens Crossing. We are Rosewood. It is the family that made it a home for us all. I will miss that dear house and everything there, my special place in the woods, all the memories. And the graves of our loved ones are here and we will never forget that. I'll even miss dear Mrs. Hammond."

We all laughed, and for the first time realized how

fond of her we had become.

"But I would rather be with you all," Katie went on, "even here like this, around a campfire, sleeping on the ground or in that wagon, with no home at all, than to have ten Rosewoods without you."

I looked into Katie's eyes as she spoke, and I could see she was doing what she always did at a time like this. When things got really hard, Katie always seemed to go down inside herself and think about things and come out stronger in the end, stronger than most people knew she was, maybe even stronger than she knew she was herself.

But I knew. I had known all along. She said that we were all Rosewood. But I knew that more than anybody or anything . . . Katie herself was the strength of Rosewood. She was what held us all together.

We were all quiet and stared into the fire.

There was no more talk after that night of splitting up. Wherever we went, we were going together.

The following day Rob rode up beside our wagon.

"Could I talk to you a minute, Mr. Daniels?" he said.

"Sure," Papa answered. "One of you girls want to take Rob's horse?"

"I will," said Katie as Papa reined in.

"I'll go ride with Jeremiah awhile," I said, jumping to the ground.

I ran back to Jeremiah and he pulled me up behind him. Katie mounted Rob's horse and Rob sat down on the seat beside Papa.

"Something on your mind, son?" said Papa as they continued on.

"Yes, sir," said Rob. "I mentioned this to Katie a while back, but I didn't want to say anything about it to everyone until I saw what you and Mr. Daniels thought."

"Go on," said Papa. "I'm listening."

"I know you don't have definite plans yet . . . but I had hoped that Katie and I would be able to settle reasonably near my family. And you have your sister in Philadelphia, and as I understand it, you were raised not far from there."

"Just outside the city," nodded Papa.

"Well, there is a nice piece of property near where I live for sale, with two houses on it, and fifty prime acres. I don't know, but I wonder if it might be a region where there would be family ties, and also where Henry and Josepha and Jeremiah and Mayme, I am reasonably sure, would find a higher level of acceptance."

Papa nodded with interest as Rob spoke.

"Mr. Evans raises cattle and horses and a few sheep. I'm not sure what crops he grows—not cotton as far as I know, but I think sweet corn, tomatoes, maybe a little wheat, a few potatoes."

"And he's selling, you say?"

"His wife died a few years ago and he wants to move to New York to be with his son's family."

"Hmm . . . sounds interesting, all right. Go back and tell brother Ward about it," he said. "Then talk it over with Kathleen. If they agree that it is something we should look into, we'll talk about it as a group. It might have real possibilities."

North
58

It is amazing how far you get if you just keep steadily going.

We only went maybe ten or twelve miles a day. But within two weeks we were into Virginia and moving closer and closer to Baltimore where Rob's parents lived and to Pennsylvania where Rob lived in Hanover and Aunt Nelda lived in Philadelphia.

After what Katie had said around the campfire that night, and then when we all talked together about the property that Rob knew about, new life and hopefulness began to blossom within us. We began to be excited about the future, and anxious to see what God had for us next. We felt like we were on an adventure, almost like Micah and Emma on their way west, or even like Josepha had been so many years ago on the Underground Railroad. We weren't in covered wagons, and we were going north, not west. And we didn't have to hide out like fugitive slaves. But we were going to a new life together . . . somewhere, though we didn't yet know where.

If anyone had wanted, as Papa said, they could have taken the train, or we could have stayed in hotels.

But nobody wanted to. We wanted to stay together. Even Aunt Nelda, who was the least used to hardship of any of us, was happy and excited to be part of this with the rest of us.

Though we hadn't even seen the place that was for sale, after Rob described it to us, everyone began talking about it and getting excited. Pretty soon Papa and Uncle Ward and Henry were discussing possibilities and Henry was talking about what he'd like to do differently if he had the chance to build a new house for himself and Josepha. When Jeremiah and I were together, Jeremiah talked about what kind of job he'd like to find. Suddenly it seemed that everybody had ideas and plans and hopes and new dreams. If good could come out of bad, then maybe good would come out of our leaving Shenandoah County after all.

Rob wired ahead about the property. Mr. Evans was expecting us. When we arrived in Hanover, Rob led us with our wagons right into town, where we stopped in front of the telegraph office. We must have been a sight, looking like poor homesteaders with our wagons piled high with everything from saddles to kitchen supplies! Rob jumped down and ran inside to tell Mr. Evans we were there, then to the sheriff's office to see Sheriff Heyes. Mr. Evans said we could pitch camp right on his land, or use his barn or even the empty house if we wanted until we made a decision. He told Rob to take us out to his place and he would saddle up and follow us directly.

As we got closer, Aunt Nelda and Katie and I began to recognize the scenery and realized we'd been along this same road before . . . and not so long ago! I noticed Papa getting real quiet too.

"Are you getting a strange feeling, Ward," he said as soon as we pulled up and got down from the wagons,

"that we've been somewhere around here before?"

They were both looking around in every direction. In front of us stood a large white house with a barn and two or three other small buildings behind it. About two hundred yards away, up a small hill at the edge of a grove of trees, sat a smaller house.

"I've never thought of myself as superstitious," said Uncle Ward, "but I was getting goose pimples up the back of my neck as we rode up. I think we're near the old Daniels claim."

"That's just what I was thinking," said Papa.

By then the rest of us were clustered around them listening. I was getting goose bumps too!

"Couldn't swear to it, of course," said Uncle Ward. "I haven't been here in probably fifty years. But I'm getting faint recollections of a day when Mama and Papa brought us out near here somewhere when we were kids. I couldn't have been more than six or eight. You were younger than that. This house wasn't here then, but something about the road coming up, and that hill over there . . . I don't know, it's mighty familiar in a strange sort of way."

By then Mr. Evans was riding up. He dismounted and walked toward us. "Come on inside and I'll show you the house," he said.

We all followed him toward the house, though Papa and Uncle Ward seemed distracted and were still looking around toward the fields and woods and pastures surrounding the house. So was Aunt Nelda.

It was a big house, not as big as Rosewood, but bigger than a lot of the houses we had passed on our way. And almost the moment we walked in, something happened inside us and we realized that we could live there and be happy there, and that this could be our home.

Mr. Evans showed us all the rooms, took us

upstairs, then back down and out the back door. Still Papa and Uncle Ward were looking away from the house more than at what Mr. Evans was showing us. As we walked into the barn, Papa drew in a deep breath. I could tell he had missed those smells. I saw the hint of a smile cross his lips and he gave a slight nod. I knew inside he was thinking, "Yes, this just might be good . . . I think I like it here."

Knowing that he liked it made me like it. And I could tell that Katie liked it too. And that made everybody like it.

Mr. Evans was as nice to Henry and Josepha as he was to Papa and Uncle Ward. It was like he didn't even notice that they were colored. And the same with me and Jeremiah—he treated us and spoke to us just the same as he did Katie.

"Then over yonder," said Mr. Evans, pointing up the hill to the second house, "is the place I built a few years back to move into myself. It's pretty small, but I figured it would be enough for my wife and me when my son and his family took over the main house. But now it's just sitting vacant."

We walked up to see it, and then returned back the way we had come. When we had seen everything, we all wandered about in different directions, thinking our own thoughts. I saw Henry and Josepha walk off together hand in hand, then Henry put his arm around her. I knew she was probably crying again. This had been so hard on her. I knew Henry was reassuring her. Little Seffie had finally made it to the North.

"I hope you don't mind my asking," said Uncle Ward, "—I mean, this is a nice house you've got and all, but . . . did there used to be an old place somewhere near here . . . an old Quaker homestead? Do you know if it's still standing?"

"You know about the old Quaker place?" said Mr. Evans in surprise. "Yes, it's still standing—it's only a couple miles away . . . that dirt wagon track there leads to it," he added, pointing behind the barn. "Or there's a turnoff from the main road, but that's about a mile longer."

"Anyone live there?" asked my papa.

"No . . . no one's lived in the place for years. But it's mine too—it goes with the property. I always intended to fix it up one day. I figured my son and his family would occupy the main house. But now that that's not going to happen, all three houses go together. I've been doing my best to keep the old one from falling apart, but it needs a lot of work. I had a man out there working on it recently, in fact."

"Could we see it?" asked Papa.

"Sure . . . of course," said Mr. Evans, a little puzzled why an old dilapidated house seemed more interesting to these potential buyers than the new ones. "Why don't you leave your wagons here and we'll ride over on horseback. The road's pretty bumpy and uneven."

We all wanted to go, everyone except for Henry and Josepha, that is. They stayed at Mr. Evans' main house. Twenty minutes later we were on our way, Jeremiah and I together on one horse, Rob and Katie on another.

The moment the old house came into view, we knew why we had all been getting goose bumps. It was the very place Katie and I and Aunt Nelda had visited! It was the old Daniels home!

Papa and Uncle Ward got off their horses, shaking their heads in disbelief.

"This is it, isn't it, Ward?" said Papa.

"This is what?" asked Mr. Evans, glancing back and forth between the two men.

"Unless we're mistaken," answered Papa, "this place

used to be in our family."

"You're not mistaken," said Aunt Nelda. "Ward . . . Templeton, come over and look at this."

She led the way to the small plot of gravestones as the rest of us followed. Mr. Evans was obviously surprised that she knew her way around. For several minutes Papa and Uncle Ward and Aunt Nelda stood staring at the graves and their name-markers.

"This is the place the girls and I visited this past summer."

"This is the place you were telling me about!" exclaimed Rob. "I had no idea it was on the Evans property. I can't believe it. To think that you would wind up here after all that has happened."

"Of course," said Mr. Evans after a few seconds. "Daniels! I never put it together with your names before. I've seen these stones before but never thought much about it. I bought the whole place when I came to Hanover years ago. When did it pass out of your family?"

"I don't really know," answered Papa. "Do you, Nelda?"

"No—I think maybe in Grandma and Grandpa's time when most of the family moved nearer Philadelphia."

"Well, maybe it's time that it came back into the Daniels family," said Ward.

"I definitely think so, brother Ward," said Papa.

Sometimes things can happen fast, and sometimes slow. We probably could have thought about it for weeks or months, or looked at other places for sale and taken a year to make up our minds what to do. But somehow I think we all knew that this was the right place for us to start our new life together. The moment Papa and Uncle Ward had seen the "Daniels" names on those gravestones, they knew we had all come home. So it didn't take us long to decide to buy Mr. Evans' place. Rob worked right there in town, his parents were less than fifty miles away, Aunt Nelda's home was only two hours away by train. What Mr. Evans was asking for the whole property and all three houses was only about half what Papa thought we would eventually receive from Mr. Watson. And he was leaving most of the furniture and his farm equipment to go with it, so it wouldn't be like moving into a house with nothing in it. And Mr. Evans was so happy to be able to sell his home and farm to people who would love it and had such a connection to the property. I think he might have been happier about the arrangement than the rest of us!

I think Mr. Evans knew almost immediately that we were going to buy his property too because when Papa started talking about finding us a hotel, he just laughed and said there was no need for that. We'd be welcome to stay on the property. We'd been camping out all the way anyway, so it wasn't a hardship to keep doing so. But he insisted, even on that first night, that all of us women stay in the extra rooms in the house and use the kitchen and anything else we wanted. And within days he was happy to have us there because he enjoyed Josepha's cooking along with the rest of us! The next day Katie and Rob left to visit the Paxtons in Baltimore.

Aunt Nelda stayed three days, then Papa and Uncle Ward took her to catch the train home. I don't think she wanted to leave. But after that we saw a lot more of her and she came to visit at least once a month. The extra room in the house gradually came to be called Aunt Nelda's bedroom. Within a week Jeremiah had a job at a mill near Hanover about four miles away, and Papa and Uncle Ward were settling on the arrangements with Mr. Evans for the purchase of his property.

As soon as we were settled, Papa wired Mr. Watson, then Mr. Taylor at the bank in Greens Crossing. Mr. Watson had already paid off our taxes. Papa made arrangements with Mr. Taylor for closing all our bank accounts. Mr. Taylor sent us all papers to sign. Mr. Watson suggested that Papa and Uncle Ward come down to Greens Crossing in a few weeks, after he had sold all the cotton from the harvest to the company from Charlotte. By then he would have the money to pay them for Rosewood.

When they returned, there was money to pay Mr. Evans for his property and money left over for what we would need and to get started with the following year's crop planting.

It was time to begin our new life.

New Rosewood
59

What are we going to call this place?" asked Uncle Ward once the decision had been made.

"Why don't we call it New Rosewood?" suggested Katie.

We all looked around at each other.

"I think New Rosewood it is!" laughed Papa.

Papa and Uncle Ward rode over to the old Daniels farm every day and immediately began making plans. It was still an area where lots of Quaker people lived. They knew that they would spend the rest of their lives on the Daniels homestead, and I'd never seen them both so content and at peace with their lives.

They began working on it before Katie and Rob were even back from Baltimore.

Mr. Evans and Papa and Uncle Ward hit it off so well that before the final papers were signed, Mr. Evans wanted us to move in so that we would be all settled in before winter. We had arrived about the third week of October and the weather was slowly beginning to turn. So after a few days of getting settled, Katie and I shared a room together, Papa and Uncle Ward shared another room. The house had five bedrooms, a nice sitting room, a kitchen not quite as big as Rosewood's, but adequate for us. It had an inside washroom with both a clothes washtub and a bathing tub with a water pump and separate wood stove to heat the water, with drains to the outside. We all thought that was about the most wonderful thing we had ever seen.

Jeremiah moved in with Rob at the boardinghouse in town where Rob had been living since coming to Hanover with Sheriff Heyes. Since it was just temporary, the lady let Jeremiah stay in Rob's room with him and pay a little extra for meals.

Henry and Josepha stayed up in the small house that Mr. Evans had built, thinking that he and his wife would retire there when his son took over the farm and would raise his family in the main house. It had been empty for a long time.

Most suppers we ate together. It was almost like being at Rosewood again, except that the terrain and weather and sounds and the look and feel of everything was different. That took some getting used to. But it didn't take long before we settled into our old routines and got to work on the new place. Hard work is the best thing in the world to drive out sadness, and we were all hard workers. Even though the Evans place was in wonderful condition, we found plenty to keep us busy and there were so many new things we wanted to do. Papa and Uncle Ward were talking about fields and woods they wanted to clear and roads they wanted to build and areas they wanted to fence, and Mr. Evans was as excited about the proposed changes as they were.

The three men rode over to the old homestead every day and got to cleaning and repairing and furnishing the upstairs to make it livable. Some of the time Josepha and Katie and I went with them to help, some-

times we stayed at Mr. Evans' place because there was a lot to do there too. It was hard to get used to a new house with new things in it—different chairs and beds and wardrobes that had belonged to someone else's family. The house wasn't as spacious as Rosewood, but it was much closer to town, which was a great benefit. People were so welcoming and nice that we began to make new friends almost immediately. Katie and I and Josepha got dressed up and walked through town almost every day looking in the shops and meeting people. Within days we were greeted with, "Oh, you must be the people buying the Evans place!" And not once did Josepha or I feel anyone looking at us resentfully because of the color of our skin.

One day when we were at the old farm, Josepha and Katie and I were out shoveling and hoeing at the old garden to get the soil softened and ready for the next spring. There hadn't been a garden planted there in years. The three men were banging and sawing away in the old house. It was a nice day in mid-November. The leaves on the trees were almost past their color and mostly brown, but it was still warm enough to work outside and enjoy it.

We looked up and saw a young black girl of sixteen or seventeen walking toward us holding what looked like a loaf of bread. It is funny to say it, but she looked young to me. Yet such a short time ago Katie and I had been younger than that, struggling together to keep Rosewood going.

So much had happened in our lives!

"Thou must be our new neighbors," said the girl in an odd speech that mingled old and new. Her voice was black but her speech was white—an old-fashioned white that reminded me of the Quaker Brannons. "We have been wondering who moved into the old place. It

has been empty for as long as I have been alive, and they say much longer than that."

"We're not really moved in," said Katie. "But we're working on it. We are still living in the main house over there."

"Mr. Evans' house?"

"Yes. We are buying it from him. Do you know him?"

"He is our friend."

"How nice. I am Katie Clairborne. And this is Josepha and this is Mayme."

"I am pleased to make your acquaintance," said the girl, shaking each of our hands. "My name is Calebia Eaton. I live with my father and mother over there."

She pointed in the distance.

Josepha squinted in the direction she was pointing.

"Dat be a horse in dat weather vane on da barn?" she asked. Now that she pointed it out, I saw it too. I hadn't noticed it before.

"That is the wind in the horse's head," said the girl. "That is why we are here—my mother followed the wind in the horse's head from the South. Her name is Lucindy. She came here on the Underground Railroad. She and my father used to be slaves. But they escaped and came here. But there are no slaves here. I have never been a slave. You see that man in the field there—"

Again she pointed.

"That's my brother Broan. He shall be over to meet you when he is done with his work too. So will my mother. But she is doing Mrs. Mueller's wash today—they are the people my mother and father work for. She could not come just now. She wanted me to bring you this and welcome you to Hanover."

She handed us the loaf of bread.

"It is still warm," said Katie.

"Yes, ma'am. I just baked it this morning."

"Thank you very much," said Katie. "This is very kind of you. Give our regards to your mother."

"I shall. Good day to you. God be with thee."

New Beginnings
60

All the arrangements were completed by the end of the year. Mr. Evans moved north in time to be with his son's family for Christmas.

By the following spring of 1871, we were pretty much settled. Henry and Josepha were still living in the smaller of Mr. Evans' houses, though they planned to buy a few acres of the property from the rest of us and build a new house on it. The rest of us were still in the larger house, though the old homestead was just about ready, and Papa and Uncle Ward planned to move there.

Rob and Katie and Jeremiah and I were married that May. We were married outside on the old Daniels farm. Several families from Hanover came, including the Muellers and Eatons. I invited the Brannons and Davidsons from Virginia, and they both came too.

Mrs. Hammond, Mr. Thurston, and Mr. Watson took the train north together from Greens Crossing to attend. And Mr. Evans returned from New York.

Rob's father performed the ceremony, and quite a few of Rob's relatives and friends came from in and around Baltimore. And, of course, Sheriff John Heyes, who had become one of Rob's best friends, was there with us as well.

The day was sunny and warm and the country all around us was fragrant and alive and growing.

Katie and I got ready inside the house called New Rosewood, which by then was as nice and modern a house as you could imagine after all the work the men had done on it.

Josepha and Aunt Nelda and Mrs. Hammond and Lucindy Eaton helped us get dressed and fix our hair. Aunt Nelda helped us make our wedding dresses. We had taken several trips to Philadelphia over the winter for fittings with a seamstress friend of hers. Both dresses were white, though of completely different designs. Katie's dress had lots of lace and ruffles. She wanted to wear something frilly like she and her mother had worn before the war. My dress was more practical, I suppose you'd say. I wanted something I could keep wearing later. That's what I thought my mother would have done too, before the war. My, how things had changed! The women fixed up Katie's long blond hair and my black hair with curls and flowers and little braids. Katie was so beautiful! She said I was too, and maybe we both were.

Outside we heard carriages and horses arriving for almost an hour. When we finally walked outside, it was shocking to see how many people had actually come. Here we were in a new place and we already had more friends than we ever did in Greens Crossing! Katie and I had worked so hard in those early years to hide and not be seen and to have people not notice us . . . now here we were the center of attention!

We asked Josepha to sing an old wedding spiritual as we walked forward through the people to where Rob and Jeremiah and the minister, Rob's father, stood waiting for us. You might say that we were each other's maids of honor, and Rob and Jeremiah were each other's best men. As Josepha began to sing in a low quiet tone, a hush descended over the whole place. It was like nothing I'd ever felt in my life. Her voice and the melancholy tune so captured the feel of what it meant to be black at that time in our country's history. Nobody but someone who had been a slave all those years like Josepha had could sing with the feeling she gave that song on that day . . . about dreaming of freedom, and then finally finding the freedom of new life in a new land, and then finding the love that only a man and woman can share. It was a song about dreaming of freedom and dreaming of love . . . and finally finding them. It was as if Josepha was singing about her life as well as setting the perfect tone for our marriages too.

It was almost like listening to a history of slavery itself, and then realizing that slavery really and truly was over and done with.

As Katie walked slowly forward on Uncle Ward's arm, and as Papa and I walked beside them, for those few minutes all the beaming happiness that we felt inside, and all the smiles that we'd seen on everyone's faces as we walked out of the house, all those expressions became thoughtful and serious. As Josepha sang, a feeling of sad yet victorious grandeur filled us with a sense of the majesty of the struggle for freedom and what it meant to so many people. It was as if Katie and I were symbolic of the past our country was leaving behind, and the triumph and hope of the future.

I looked over the people, some sitting, some standing. They were all so dear to me!

Of course, Katie hadn't been a slave like I had. But she had joined the struggle with me and had fought for me in her own way. Our fight to save Rosewood had ended up here, many miles away, where part of our family had started out when they first came to this country. It had been a long journey, just as Josepha was singing about. Katie and I were now walking toward a bright new future that neither of us could yet see . . . where our dreams of freedom and dreams of love maybe would come true after all. We had been sisters, cousins, and friends together.

Now we were about to become wives!

Slowly Josepha's voice came to the end and faded high and soft into the hush of the tiny breeze blowing across the southern Pennsylvanian countryside. Everyone stood another few seconds in almost numbed silence at the power of the old spiritual and all it meant in so many lives.

Then the spell was broken. In front of us stood Rob and Jeremiah, both dressed in their finest. Out came the smiles again!

At last Reverend Paxton's voice broke the silence.

"Dearly beloved," he said, "we are gathered here today to unite not one, but two men and two women. All who know the story of these two remarkable young ladies know why it is only fitting that they be married together in this manner."

He now looked at each of the four of us.

"You can imagine what a happy occasion this is for me," he went on, "as a father to send my own son along on his future. But greater than that is the celebration on this day of many lives, and of Christ's work of renewal in the face of heartache. All four of these young people before me have faced the tragedy of the loss of loved ones, close family members. You two young women, Kathleen and Mary Ann, lost your entire families to the cruelties and inhumanities of a dreadful war and its aftermath. Jeremiah, you lost your mother to

the evil institution of slavery. And Robert, you and all of our family suffered the loss of your dear sister, my own daughter, to a tragic murder in which I was the intended victim.

"So you each stand before me today having suffered. The loved ones you have lost can only share this day with you from heaven, but they cannot be beside you in the flesh. Yet in spite of this, we all rejoice to be here, as we in faith believe that they rejoice with us at God's side. We rejoice because God is a God, not of perfect lives but of new life and restoration. Out of tragedy He is always able to renew life. Each of you is a testimony of that renewal. Your story is a story of goodness emerging out of defeat, of hope flowing out of loss, of joy growing out of sorrow, and love blossoming out of despair. As my son is ever reminding me, there is indeed no limit to the extent of this renewing work that is in God's heart to accomplish in His creation.

"I do not promise that after this day you will be without sorrow or that happiness will follow you every day of your lives. We live in too imperfect a world for that. But I think I can promise you that God's life will continue to grow within you if you will let it, and that your lives together will therefore always be good. We rejoice with you that you have found one another, that you have discovered love together, and that you have all become strong in that process of growth and discovery. What better foundation for marriage can there be than that!"

He paused, then looked up with a smile.

"Who gives these women to be united to these men?"

Papa and Uncle Ward glanced at each other, then at Katie and me.

"We do," they said together. Then they turned and

sat down beside Aunt Nelda.

Reverend Paxton looked at each of the four of us again, his gaze settling on his son.

"Do you, Robert Paxton," he began, "take this woman to be your wedded wife, to have and to hold from this day forward, for better, for worse, for richer, for poorer, in sickness and in health, to love and to cherish, till death do you part, according to God's holy ordinance?"

"Yes, sir—I do," said Rob.

"Do you, Kathleen Clairborne," he said, now turning to Katie, "take this man to be your wedded husband, to have and to hold . . ."

Things can run so quickly through your brain. I was trying so hard to concentrate. But as Reverend Paxton spoke to Katie, so many images suddenly flitted through my memory.

Like the first time Katie and I saw each other after our families had been killed . . .

SLOWLY I WALKED into what I took to be the kitchen. Suddenly I stopped dead in my tracks. In the middle of the doorway stood a girl a year or so younger than me. She was staring straight at me through big eyes that looked even more afraid than mine.

She wore a long pink nightgown and furry slippers that had bloodstains on them. Her face was whiter than was natural even for a white person.

I was too numb to be surprised. I looked at her, and she looked at me. We just stood—two silent statues staring at each other, one white, the other colored.

Then I saw her blink. But we kept standing there staring, neither of us knowing what to think. Still less knowing what to say.

"My . . . my mother is dead," she whimpered.

I stood there another few seconds in a trance. But

somehow the sound of a human voice finally broke me out of it.

Slowly I found myself walking toward her. She stood there as I approached, watching me with those huge blue helpless eyes.

Then suddenly we were in each other's arms.

And the night Katie thought up her daring scheme . . .

IN THE MIDDLE of the night, I woke up suddenly.

Katie was yelling and calling my name.

"Mayme . . . Mayme!"

I jumped out of bed terrified and hurried out into the hallway. Before I could reach her room, Katie nearly knocked me over.

"Mayme . . . Mayme!" she cried, running out of her room. "I've had the most wonderful idea! Come into my room and I'll tell you."

I followed her, not knowing what to make of it.

"You said it yourself, Mayme," she said after a bit. "We're in trouble if anyone finds us alone. So that's what made me realize what we need to do—we've just got to make sure no one finds out we're here alone—we'll pretend we're *not* alone! We'll pretend like my mama and papa are still here! We'll make it so believable that no one will ever find out! Not my uncles or anyone in town . . . or anyone!"

And the day when my papa, before I knew he was my father, discovered that his sister's family was dead . . .

TIRED AND WORN though he looked, the man seemed like a dandy in my eyes. His white shirt had ruffles and bright buttons down the front.

I came and stood in the open door and waited. Katie

just stood there in front of her uncle staring at the floor. He glanced around the place and seemed to think it didn't look right. He looked over at me, and this time held my face in his gaze a few seconds. A puzzled look seemed to flit through his eyes. But then he looked back at Katie and gradually a serious expression came over his face.

"Kathleen," he said, "I think it's time you stop stalling. There's something you're not telling me. I know Rosalind's not on a trip—she wouldn't leave you alone or have left the place like this. I want to know what's going on here."

I could see Katie starting to tremble.

"Oh, Uncle Templeton," Katie suddenly cried, "—she's dead! They're all dead!"

She burst into the most mournful wail and began to sob, like a dam that had been held back all these months was bursting inside her. At the word *dead*, her uncle's face went ashen.

He sat there stunned, his eyes wide, his face white. Katie now walked toward him, put her arms around him, leaned her head down on his neck where he sat, and continued to sob.

A few minutes later Katie and her uncle walked outside. Katie had her hand in his and led him away from the house in the direction of where she and I had buried her family.

Katie took him to the spot, then stopped. They just stood there looking down at the graves, not saying a word. Slowly her uncle stretched one of his arms around Katie's shoulders and pulled her to his side. She leaned her head against his chest and again began to cry.

I heard Reverend Paxton's voice again. He was just finishing what he had been saying to Katie.

I glanced over at her. The Katie of my rapid recol-

lections was now a beautiful grown-up bride!

"—from this day forward, for better, for worse, for richer, for poorer, in sickness and in health, to love and to cherish, till death do you part, according to God's holy ordinance?"

"I do," said Katie softly.

Reverend Paxton turned to Jeremiah.

"Do you, Jeremiah Patterson," he said, "take this woman to be your wedded wife . . ."

I couldn't help my mind straying again, this time to the first moment I set eyes on Jeremiah . . .

"MO'NIN' TO YOU, Miz Kathleen," called out a friendly voice.

I turned to see a tall, lanky black man on the side of the street tipping his hat and smiling broadly.

"Hello, Henry," said Katie, pulling back on the reins, then stopping the horses.

The man approached. I saw his eyes flit toward me for a second. But I still kept looking straight ahead. It was a little hard, though, 'cause sauntering up beside him a couple steps behind was a black boy just about as tall that looked to be Katie's and my own age. I could feel his eyes glancing my way too.

"How's yo mama, Miz Kathleen?" he said.

"Uh . . . everything's just fine, Henry."

A funny expression came over his face. He paused briefly, then looked to his side and then back. "Ah don' believe you two ladies has eber made erquantence wif my son Jeremiah.—Jeremiah," he added, looking at the boy, "say hello ter Miz Kathleen an' Miz Mayme."

The young man took off the ragged hat he was wearing, glancing down at the ground and kind of shuffling like he was embarrassed, then looked up at the wagon.

"How 'do," he said. "Glad t' know yer both."

And the evening Jeremiah asked me to marry him . . .

Emma had left the door ajar. There stood Jeremiah holding a little bouquet. He had a sheepish look on his face, which wasn't like him, and he smelled of lilac water, which was even less like him!

Immediately I felt the back of my neck getting hot!

"Here," he said, handing me the flowers. "I brought dese fer you."

I took them and smiled.

"I thought maybe we cud go fer a walk or somethin'," he said.

As we left the house together, I knew something was different about this visit, and I more than halfway suspected what it might be.

Jeremiah was so nervous. I might have felt a little sorry for him if I hadn't been nervous myself. If Jeremiah was going to say what I expected him to say, I'd been thinking some already about what I would say too.

"I talked ter yo papa da other day," said Jeremiah after we had walked a ways. "I been aroun' here close on three years an' you an' I's gettin' older. An' I figger it's time we wuz thinkin' 'bout some things. So I . . . uh, axed yo papa if he thought I wuz da kind er young man he'd approve ob ter be wiff you. And he said I wuz an' dat he'd be right proud ter call me son. An' den he shook my hand an' tol' me ter talk ter you, an' so here I am an' I reckon I'm axin' if you'd like ter be my wife."

My, oh my! He just blurted it out all at once!

Sometimes you have too many words and they come out so fast you stumble over them. Sometimes you don't have enough words and you can't think of anything to say. But this was a time when I had a mountain of words I *wanted* to say, but couldn't manage to get a single one out!

"Of course I want to be your wife, Jeremiah," I said softly. "I can't imagine being married to anybody but you. I'm so happy when I'm with you. I love you and . . . I reckon my answer's yes."

Again my mind came back to the present. Jeremiah and I had grown up too!

"—to have and to hold from this day forward, for better, for worse, for richer, for poorer, in sickness and in health, to love and to cherish, till death do you part, according to God's holy ordinance?"

"I do," said Jeremiah, then glanced at me with a smile.

And finally he turned to me.

"Do you, Mary Ann Daniels," he said, "take this man to be your wedded husband, to have and to hold from this day forward, for better, for worse, for richer, for poorer, in sickness and in health, to love and to cherish, till death do you part, according to God's holy ordinance?"

"I do," I said.

Reverend Paxton paused briefly, looked at all four of us again, and then went on.

"Inasmuch as you, Robert, and you, Kathleen, and you, Jeremiah, and you, Mary Ann, have declared before God and these witnesses your wish to be united in marriage, and have pledged love and fidelity each to the other, I now pronounce you—you, Robert and Kathleen, and you, Jeremiah and Mary Ann—man and wife."

Jeremiah kissed me as Katie and Rob embraced and kissed.

"Ladies and gentlemen, please come and greet Mr. and Mrs. Jeremiah Patterson, and Mr. and Mrs. Robert Paxton!"

Then from everywhere a crowd swooped upon us with hugs and kisses and congratulations.

Within minutes Mrs. Hammond and Josepha and Aunt Nelda and Mrs. Mueller and Lucindy Eaton were bringing food and drink out of the house to set on several tables and somebody had begun to play lively dance music with a violin. The festive spirit of the day continued.

It wasn't just greeting us that went on for the next several hours. Everybody was visiting everyone else too. It was like a reunion of many friends—a whole community gathering. We'd never been at anything like it in Greens Crossing, especially with so many people of different color!

I was surprised to find out that Mrs. Davidson and Lucindy Eaton were already good friends, and that Lucindy had stayed with the Davidsons during her journey on the Underground Railroad. So too were Mr. Davidson and Mr. Mueller. The only people missing were Micah and Emma, who sent us a telegram. It wasn't as good as their being there, but it was nice to know they were thinking of us.

Midway through the afternoon I saw my papa and Mr. Davidson walking off slowly together with their backs to me. They seemed to be in earnest conversation about something. How I would have loved to hear that talk!

For what seemed an hour I hardly spoke more than a few words to Jeremiah or Katie or Rob because of all the people wanting to talk to us.

Then came a moment when I bumped into someone behind me. I turned. There was Katie! For a second in the midst of the commotion, we were alone in our new white dresses.

"Mayme!"

"Oh, Katie."

The next instant we were in each other's arms and both crying. Again I remembered that first day we'd met and how, not even knowing each other, we had found solace in each other's embrace. I guess those hugs, then and now, were sort of like bookends, with a whole lot of stories in between.

"Are you happy, Mayme?" asked Katie as we stepped back and she looked deeply into my eyes.

"Oh yes!"

"Me too."

"I'm so glad," I said. "What a wonderful day. Thank you for everything."

"We'll always stay friends . . . promise?"

"What else would we be—of course!"

"Marriage won't change it?"

"Never. We will always be sisters, cousins, and friends."

Katie embraced me again.

"Have a happy life, Mayme," she whispered. "I love you."

"You too, Katie. I love you too."

❧ ✵ ❧

The Rest of Our Lives

61

It was the two men, not Katie and me, who suggested that we spend the first part of our honeymoon together. That afternoon we were accompanied by half the wedding party to the late train through Hanover to Philadelphia, where we had made reservations at a hotel. We spent two days there in Philadelphia, then took the train to New York City and spent four days there sightseeing together. Then Katie and Rob took the train west to Pittsburgh, then on to Cleveland, and finally back home, while Jeremiah and I went north to see Boston before we came back home.

By the time we arrived, Papa and Uncle Ward were out of Mr. Evans' main house at New Rosewood and had moved to what was by now known as the Old Farm. Rob and Katie moved into the big house.

Jeremiah and I moved into the small house, though the men had already begun remodeling it to add two rooms so that it would be big enough for a family.

Henry had bought ten acres of the property on the western border with good pastureland. He and the other men had already laid the foundation and put up the first walls for what would be Josepha's new home.

In the meantime Henry and Josepha, though they had plenty of invitations to do otherwise, were camping out right there as the new house went up. At the wedding, when news of the building project spread around, Mr. Mueller from Hanover and Caleb Eaton and many of the men from the area joined together and came to help. It wasn't exactly like a barn raising, but almost. Within two weeks, Henry and Josepha had walls around them and a roof over their heads. There was still a lot to do inside, but they were snug and out of the weather and Josepha was happy as she could be. Henry took a job at the livery in Hanover for a while, but his dream now that he had land to call his own was to raise horses.

Rob continued to be deputy to John Heyes for another four years, though he helped Papa and Uncle Ward with the crops on the land that still belonged to all four of us. When Heyes retired as assistant sheriff, Rob was offered the job by the county sheriff in York. After that he had too many responsibilities to help on the land as much.

Jeremiah continued to work in the mill, though he also helped with the crops and animals and other work about the place whenever he could. Gradually we planted less acreage in crops because we didn't really need to, and besides, we all had our own gardens and livestock to look after.

Two years after the wedding, Jeremiah and I had a baby girl. We named her Kathleen Ann. She was followed by a boy, Henry Micah, then two more girls, Sephira Ruth and Emmaline Abigail. Josepha was the happiest and most attentive grandmother you could imagine. And my papa and Henry were so proud of their little black grandchildren!

Rob and Katie had three children, two boys and a

girl—Richard Daniels Paxton, Rosalind Mayme Paxton, and David Templeton Paxton.

My papa and Uncle Ward spent the rest of their lives as men of the earth at the Old Farm. They kept talking about going to California and wrote to Micah and Emma about it, but they never made it. Increasingly they became involved with Henry and his horses as they got older. Just like in Greens Crossing, everyone called them the Daniels brothers. But unlike in Greens Crossing, everyone loved them.

Henry finally began to raise and sell horses. He sold half interest in a promising young filly to a trainer in Kentucky, who took the horse to the third running of the Kentucky Derby where she placed third. You should have seen Henry all dapper and dressed for the race, and Josepha in a new expensive dress and wide-brimmed hat! They looked like distinguished black aristocrats from some foreign country! Their horses began making money after that, and within a few years their little plot of land, which they called Patterson Acres, became known as a training center. Rich men were always coming and going to get Henry's advice on horses and training methods. He came to be recognized as one of the region's most knowledgeable breeders and trainers.

Jeremiah kept on at the mill. After seven years, when he had worked his way up to assistant foreman, his boss retired and put the mill up for sale. Jeremiah asked if he would have any objection to selling to a black man. The man replied no, saying that Jeremiah was one of his best men. Excitedly, Jeremiah put the matter before his father and Papa and Uncle Ward. Between the three of them, we were able to borrow enough to buy it. Jeremiah didn't want to make a lot of changes right away until folks got used to the idea of his owning the mill when he was only thirty one, but after another two years he added a small sign below the main one that said Patterson's Mill. Jeremiah was so proud of that sign! And gradually that's what folks called it. He had once told me he'd like to own a livery stable. Now he owned a mill that eventually grew to be bigger even than Mr. Watson's. Jeremiah was a successful businessman!

Back in Greens Crossing, Mrs. Hammond finally became a real "Mrs." when she married Mr. Thurston, who had been a widower for several years. She rented out the apartment above the shop to a single man new to Greens Crossing who also ran the store. She came into town from her new home at Mr. Thurston's once a week to place orders and keep in touch with the business.

Sheriff Sam Jenkins was some years later implicated in the hanging of a black man near Charlotte. He and several of his fellow Klansmen were arrested in a temporary wave of anti-violence in Shenandoah County. He did not go to jail, but the scandal cost him the sheriff's job and he was forced to go to work as a laborer at Watson's Mill, working alongside two or three black youths half his age.

With Papa and Uncle Ward gone and not thinking them likely to cause him any trouble, William McSimmons, Jr. eventually ran for Congress to represent North Carolina and won. He and his wife finally realized their dream and spent over twenty years in Washington, where he became a voice in the capital for the new South. Whenever Katie read something about him in the newspaper, she muttered a few angry words and usually threw down the paper in disgust. That's when she tried to talk Rob into running for office. He only smiled and said that God had given him a work to do and he mustn't aim too high. Once Katie's and my story began to become well known, Rob said she ought to run for office instead of him!

Micah and Emma eventually settled in the small lumber town of Roseburg, Oregon on the Umpqua River. They had five children. After working several years in a lumber mill, Micah was asked to pastor a small black church. His practical spirituality soon drew large numbers of whites and blacks alike, and it became one of the largest congregations in the town. Never a more peaceful and compassionate pastor's wife had that congregation seen than Emma Duff, whose loving counsel was sought by the women as greatly as was her husband's wisdom by the men.

It took several years before we were ready to visit Rosewood again. Of all of us, it was hardest for Katie. She knew how sad it would make her to see the old place again. But by that time our young families were growing and we knew Papa and Uncle Ward would soon be too old for a visit, so we planned a trip back to Shenandoah County. By then the danger to us had passed and Mr. Watson was happy to put us up in the house that had been our home for so long.

It is impossible to describe the feelings of going back to a place like that after you've grown up and been away for a long time. Everything looked the same . . . yet different. The trees and shrubs were bigger, but everything else seemed smaller . . . quieter . . . and for some reason sad. So many memories surfaced. Good and happy memories. Yet they were all tinged with the nostalgic melancholy of long ago.

Katie and I didn't talk much when we were at Rosewood. We each had to relive the memories in our own way—Katie walking to her secret place in the woods and finding it overgrown and changed, me riding over to the McSimmons place where no one knew me and all the McSimmons were gone.

We both walked the fields and along the river . . . took our turns in front of the gravestones that Mr. Watson had kept so nicely groomed, with tears in our eyes . . . rummaged through the barn . . . climbed down into the cellar where Katie had hid on that terrible night and where we'd discovered Uncle Ward's gold. One day I was standing in one of the upstairs windows and saw Katie in the distance outside, and in my mind's eye it was almost like she had risen early in the morning and gone out for one final cotton harvest.

So many memories . . . yet that time was now gone.

We were now mothers and our own youngsters were scampering about the place without any idea how deep the memories and emotions were inside us. Everywhere those memories were now accompanied by the excited running shouts and laughter of children—our children!

"Mama . . . look at this!" we each must have heard fifty times during those few days during our visit. The innocent young eyes of childhood—how could they ever know what Katie and I had shared together in that place?

Then it was time to leave again.

Rosewood would ever be dear to our hearts. But we had made peace with the past, and now we looked again to the future.

Our aunt Nelda sold her house in Philadelphia and moved to the Old Farm to take care of her brothers in their advancing years.

Ward Daniels died at seventy-one in 1885.

My father, Templeton Daniels, died at seventy-two four years later.

Aunt Nelda lived on at the homestead, visited every day either by Katie or myself or one of our children or our friends Calebia or Lucindy, until 1898, when, in her seventy-ninth year, she joined her brothers and sister, Katie's mother.

Katie cried on and off for days after her aunt's parting. A generation had passed. Katie was now forty-eight and stood in the front rank of the Daniels and Clairborne lines. That is a sobering thing.

The three were buried side by side in the Daniels plot on the homestead. That's when we realized that we wanted something to commemorate our immediate families too. Katie and I had stones made for each of her family who was buried at Rosewood, and each of my family that I had buried at the McSimmons plantation after the massacre in 1865. The bodies would never lie at the Old Farm, but the stones with their names helped us know that they would never be forgotten.

Jeremiah and Henry were closer than any father and son could be. Henry outlived Josepha by three years. She died at eighty-five; he lived to be eighty-nine and was out with his horses the day before he fell asleep, never to wake up again in this life. I hadn't seen Jeremiah cry in years, but he wept for the loss of his father.

Our son Hank and his new wife moved into Henry and Josepha's place, and Hank continued, in the tradition of his grandfather and namesake, to raise horses.

After eight years as sheriff, Rob stepped down and began to reassess his future. His father had recently retired from the pulpit and Rob began to feel a renewal of the call of his youth to the pulpit. After much prayer and talk with Katie, he took the pastorate of a small church in Hanover, where he attempted to open minds to the wider possibilities of God's love—a message readily embraced by many of the Quaker families of the surrounding region.

As more and more people heard about our story and as the events of slavery and what came to be called the Civil War faded more distantly into the past, Katie and I received invitations to speak and share our story. At first invitations came from nearby towns and communities. But then we spoke in Baltimore, and then at Aunt Nelda's church in Philadelphia, and after a while we got invitations from all over, far more than we could accept. It was amazing how many people had heard of us!

Katie and I kept in touch with Emma by mail through the years. When our children were nearly all grown, we decided to have a new adventure. We were both over fifty. Our hair was graying and I already had three grandchildren and Katie one. We decided to take the train west to Oregon to visit Emma and Micah.

Who says old people can't have adventures? We had the time of our lives! Emma was so peaceful and beautiful.

In 1908 Mr. Watson died, never having married. We received the news first from Elfrida Thurston, then again in an official letter from an attorney in Charlotte, informing us that Herbert Watson of Greens Crossing, Shenandoah County, North Carolina, had in his will left the entire estate known as Rosewood to Kathleen O'Bannon Clairborne Paxton and her heirs, and the assets of the mill known as Watson's Mill to Jeremiah Patterson and his heirs.

We were all stunned.

We sat speechless—Katie and Rob and Jeremiah and I—as Rob set aside the letter he had just read.

"What will you do, Katie?" I asked finally. "Do you want to go back?"

Katie smiled and drew in a deep breath.

"You can't go back, Mayme," she said. "Our lives are

here now. And goodness, I am fifty-seven. I wouldn't want to go back. Rob has his ministry here. We have raised our family here. You are here, Jeremiah's—"

She stopped and smiled again.

"I was about to say that Jeremiah's business is here!" she laughed. "But now that is changed too! Now he has two businesses! This news does make me nostalgic for Rosewood all over again . . . but, no . . . life always moves forward."

She looked over at Jeremiah.

"What about you, Jeremiah?" she asked. "You and I seem both to have suddenly become a man and woman of means!"

Jeremiah just shook his head in disbelief.

"God bless the man," he said. "He was always mighty good to my papa an' me. But this . . . I just can't believe it!"

In the end, Katie and Rob's youngest son David and his family moved back to Rosewood. They sold off about half the acreage, as cotton was no longer as profitable a crop as before, and split the proceeds with David's brother Richard and sister Rosalind.

As for the mill, Jeremiah wanted to go back and look at it before making a final decision. He and I took the train down to North Carolina together. By then Greens Crossing had changed so much. The train came through town now too and so we could come straight to Greens Crossing without going to Charlotte. The town was two or three times the size it had been. New homes and businesses were everywhere. Beside the livery stable was a place selling motor cars!

We walked into Watson's Mill, which was one of the buildings that still looked much the same. I can't even imagine the feelings that must have been in Jeremiah's heart to realize that he now owned the very mill where he had been let go because he was black.

A few workers glanced at us as we walked about, at first not knowing who we were—just a sixty-year-old black man and woman looking around. But gradually word spread and we heard whispers and a few comments about "the new owner."

Jeremiah hardly said a word. It was too overwhelming. We went outside to the loading dock in back. A thin, bent old man was pushing a broom about. He must have been nearly eighty, too old to do any more loading and lifting with the younger men. I had no idea if he was still being paid or was one of those old men who just liked to hang around a place he used to work.

Jeremiah walked over to him. The man saw him and laid the broom against a wall. Jeremiah extended his hand.

"Mr. Jenkins," he said, "it's been a long time."

The man stared at him, almost reluctantly taking the offered hand. "You're . . . you're Henry Patterson . . . no, why—you're his boy," said the former sheriff, still looking him over.

"Yes, sir, that's right," Jeremiah said, nodding. "I'm Jeremiah. My father passed away some years ago."

"Haven't seen you in a while. Looks like you turned out okay."

Jeremiah smiled. "I hope so," he said. "Well, the best to you, Mr. Jenkins."

Jeremiah returned to where I stood, if anything more overcome with emotion than ever. If the heart is willing, the passage of time always seems to help forgiveness along. What Sam Jenkins was thinking, I didn't know, but I knew Jeremiah felt compassion for the poor old man who had once tried to kill him.

We had come south thinking to sell the mill. But after his visit, Jeremiah changed his mind, at least temporarily. He saw what an opportunity it presented to give employment to blacks in the community who were struggling more than ever to find decent jobs.

He met with the man who had been Mr. Watson's foreman for the previous ten years.

"I'm going to keep you on as foreman," said Jeremiah. "The only change I want you to make is in the hiring of young black men who need jobs and who can do the work. I don't want you to show favoritism or prejudice one way or the other, but I want coloreds given a fair shake. When I come back, I want to see colored men working here and telling me they are treated fairly. If they aren't, they will tell me and I'll come to you. I have no reason to either trust you or mistrust you. So for now you have my trust. But make no mistake—I will replace you if I have to. I want the profits kept up like they have been and the men who work for me treated well. I once got fired from this place because I was black, and I will fire any white man who treats any colored man with less than the respect he deserves."

While Jeremiah was with his foreman, I took one last walk through Greens Crossing. So much was new, yet so much was still familiar. I went into the bank where I had had my first bank account. Mr. Taylor was long since gone. No one knew me. I walked back outside and continued slowly along.

I didn't see a soul I recognized. I had once been so afraid of these streets. Now there were almost as many blacks as whites walking along the boardwalk.

Behind me I heard the putt-putt-putt of a motor car. I turned and watched as it went by in the street, spewing black smoke out behind it. New times were coming, and old times were fading away before my very eyes. Imagine . . . a motor car in Greens Crossing!

Across the street there still stood the old faded sign that read Hammond's General Store. I crossed the street and walked in. The little bell above the door gave its familiar ring. Immediately I was assaulted with nostalgic sights and smells. Mrs. Hammond had been retired for years, and the store had passed into other hands. A man came out from behind the counter and asked if he could help me. I smiled and said I was just passing the time waiting for my husband.

Then I turned and left.

Back out on the street again I breathed in deeply and slowly sighed. Everything comes full circle eventually, I guess. Here I was back in Greens Crossing. But it wasn't just that. It was who I was . . . who I had become. People come full circle too, that is if they let themselves grow like Katie often talked about. Restoration comes full circle too, if people let it. Some people do, some people don't. I hoped Jeremiah and I were letting the full circle of restoration grow in our lives. I think we were.

Up the street I saw Jeremiah coming out of the mill. I walked toward him. He saw me and came down the boardwalk to meet me.

He saw the melancholy look on my face and put his arm around me.

"Finish your business?" I asked.

He nodded.

"Me too," I said. "I'm ready to go home."

❧ ✲ ❧

Epilogue: Remembering . . .

And that's the story I promised to tell you a good while back when I started by saying that I used to tell my little brother Sammy stories to pass the time when we were slave kids.

That's the story of how Katie and I survived together, how we grew up together up till the time we left Rosewood to start a new life in the North.

It was a long time ago!

Lots of stories . . . lots of memories.

When our children grew up, Katie and I traveled quite a bit. Sometimes Rob and Jeremiah went with us, but mostly they had their own things to attend to at the mill and at the church. Gradually we were getting old, I reckon, but we kept speaking whenever folks wanted to listen to how things used to be. By then slavery and the Civil War were ancient history and folks figured it was interesting to listen to a couple of old ladies talk about it.

Jeremiah retired from the mill in 1919. We sold the mill in Greens Crossing to a partnership of three of our black employees. Our daughter Sephira and her husband took over the Hanover mill, though they're just about getting ready to retire themselves. Jeremiah was happy puttering around the land with our son Hank who was just as fond of horses as his grandfather had been. Jeremiah went home to be with the Lord in 1932 when he was 83. I cried, and I still miss him, the dear man, but I had a lot of good years with him and I'm so grateful for that. We had a good life together. I still live in our house up the hill from the big house at New Rosewood.

Rob retired from his pulpit in 1914, just as the Great War was breaking out. He was in great demand as a special speaker in churches everywhere, and wherever he and Katie traveled they always drew large crowds. My own personal feeling is that people wanted to see Katie as much as Rob. But that is just one woman's opinion!

Rob lived to be ninety-one and died in 1937. I'm glad he didn't live to see the second great war that was about to engulf the world, for it would have broken his heart.

Rob and Katie's grandson still lives at Rosewood and their granddaughter and her husband live at the Old Farm. Katie's daughter Rosalind lives in the house we still sometimes call Mr. Evans' house with her son and his family.

The hardest part of this whole story is what I have to tell now.

Katie finally left this world where so many loved her just four years ago at the wonderful age of ninety-seven. Her hair was grey, but in my eyes it was the same beautiful, curly blond that it was the day I first set eyes on her. I was at her side at the end as she lay in her bed, surrounded by her sons, daughter, four grandchildren, and two great-grandchildren.

She looked around at her family and loved ones, then took my hand and gave it a gentle squeeze.

"Oh, Mayme," she said softly, "we shared something special together, didn't we?"

"Yes we did, Katie dear," I said.

"I've had a good life," she went on, though her voice was weak. "Thank you, Mayme . . . thank you, all you dears," she said, struggling to lift her head and gaze around at those of her family who had been able to come. "I am so happy . . . I think this is the happiest day of my life . . . good-bye, Mayme . . . I think I will go to sleep now. . . ."

And she did—the sleep that is a waking. We never saw her eyes open again.

Three counties, and those who knew of her all the way across the country to Oregon, mourned the passing of Kathleen O'Bannon Clairborne Paxton. Yes, I have to tell you that I wept for several days. But my tears were for happiness as much as sorrow. For I too am a happy woman.

On that day when I said good-bye to my beloved Katie for the last time, I knew I had to tell her story, and my part in it. I never want anyone to forget her. So that's when I sat down to begin telling our tale.

I'm the last one left from those days. I am over one hundred years old now. That is probably older than anyone ought to be. But I am happy, though weak, and content until the Lord takes me to join my friends of long ago.

Once a week or so, one of my own grandchildren, or Katie's, takes me over to the Old Farm to make sure there are always fresh flowers beneath the granite headstone marking Katie's grave. I miss her. I miss the whole Rosewood family. But I know we will all be together again very soon.

Author Biography

Michael Phillips began his distinguished writing career in the 1970s. He came to widespread public attention in the early 1980s for his efforts to reacquaint the public with Victorian novelist George MacDonald. Phillips is recognized as the man most responsible for the current worldwide renaissance of interest in the once-forgotten Scotsman. After partnering with Bethany House Publishers in redacting and republishing the works of MacDonald, Phillips embarked on his own fiction career, and it is primarily as a novelist that he is now known. His critically acclaimed books have been translated into eight foreign languages, have appeared on numerous bestseller lists, and have sold more than six million copies. Phillips is today considered by many as the heir apparent to the very MacDonald legacy he has worked so hard to promote in our time. Phillips is the author of the widely read biography of George MacDonald, *George MacDonald: Scotland's Beloved Storyteller*. Phillips is also the publisher of the magazine *Leben,* a periodical dedicated to bold-thinking Christianity and the legacy of George MacDonald. Phillips and his wife, Judy, alternate their time between their home in Eureka, California, and Scotland, where they are attempting to increase awareness of MacDonald's work.

More from Michael Phillips

If you enjoyed this book, you will be sure to enjoy the companion series to CAROLINA COUSINS—SHENANDOAH SISTERS, the four books about Katie and Mayme and their scheme at Rosewood. The first book in the series is entitled *Angels Watching Over Me*.

Don't miss *Dream of Freedom, Dream of Life,* and *Dream of Love,* which follow the work of the Underground Railroad, the history of the Davidson family, and also the Quaker roots from which the Daniels line came. As *Carolina Cousins* continues *Shenandoah Sisters,* in a similar way the series *American Dreams* is also connected to them, though beginning prior to the Civil War. In it you will meet some of the same characters you already know, and many new ones.

You will also enjoy the related series, THE JOURNALS OF CORRIE BELLE HOLLISTER, especially *Grayfox*, Zack Hollister and Hawk Trumbull's story.

For contact information and a complete listing of titles by Michael Phillips, write c/o:

P.O. Box 7003
Eureka, CA 95502
USA

Information on the magazine *Leben*—dedicated to the spiritual vision of Michael Phillips and the legacy of George MacDonald—with articles challenging fresh thought in many directions, may also be obtained through the above address.

A Personal Closing Message From Michael Phillips

With the completion in 2007 of the three interconnected series, SHENANDOAH SISTERS, CAROLINA COUSINS, and AMERICAN DREAMS, I will be taking a prayerful look at the future of my writing.

I recently turned sixty. I am grateful and deeply humbled for what God has seen fit to accomplish in the past thirty years since the publication of my first book. Sixty seems a good age to pause to reflect and pray about what He would have me do and write about for the *next* thirty years.

I want to take this opportunity to emphasize what was said in the opening dedication and to thank you who have been such faithful and loyal readers over the years, especially those of you who have written your encouragement to us. You will forever be bound together with Judy and me in this ministry of attempting to make God's work in human life practical and meaningful through the wonderful medium of books.

For those of you who want to continue reading my work, may I suggest some of the following. In my thirty years of writing, these are among the works I consider my most important:

An important look at the future: *Is Jesus Coming Back As Soon As We Think?*

Nonfiction about walking with God: *Make Me Like Jesus, God a Good Father, Jesus an Obedient Son.*

By and about George MacDonald: *George MacDonald, Scotland's Beloved Storyteller, Your Life in Christ* (MacDonald), *The Truth in Jesus* (MacDonald), *Discovering the Character of God* (MacDonald), *Knowing the Heart of God* (MacDonald), as well as Bethany's reprinted editions of MacDonald's novels.

As noted on the previous page, the AMERICAN DREAMS series: *Dream of Freedom, Dream of Life, Dream of Love.*

THE SECRET OF THE ROSE: *The Eleventh Hour, A Rose Remembered, Escape to Freedom, Dawn of Deliverance.*

THE SECRETS OF HEATHERSLEIGH HALL: *Wild Grows the Heather in Devon, Wayward Winds, Heathersleigh Homecoming, A New Dawn Over Devon.*

THE LIVINGSTONE CHRONICLES: *Rift in Time* and *Hidden in Time.*

CALEDONIA: *Legend of the Celtic Stone* and *An Ancient Strife.*

Having been writing for a long time, a number of my books are out of print. This problem is heightened in that every year there are fewer Christian bookstores where the above titles are carried. Copies of most of these books remain available, though some in limited numbers. We encourage you whenever possible to order from your local Christian bookstore. They need your support. If, however, there are MacDonald or Phillips books you are unable to locate, most are available from various sources on the Internet. In addition, you may write to us at the address listed below. *Somewhere* there are probably still copies available of just what you are looking for.

As always, we would be happy and grateful to hear from you.

P.O. Box 7003
Eureka, CA 95502 USA

God be with you each one until we again meet on the printed page.

More From Michael Phillips

Michael Phillips' bestselling Civil War saga traces the efforts of two Southern girls fighting to stay safe during the chaos of a divided country. Born into two different worlds, Katie—the daughter of a plantation owner—and Mayme—a slave freed by the war—must unite their efforts to keep Rosewood Plantation from falling into the wrong hands. But as Rosewood becomes a beacon of hope to those ravaged by the conflict, evil threatens to overtake everything the girls hold dear.

Angels Watching Over Me

A Day to Pick Your Own Cotton

The Color of Your Skin Ain't the Color of Your Heart

Together Is All We Need